She looked up, and ...

Lord Rockleigh wa... ...n her. He might have bee... ...t his expression was not ... , sneering contempt. Mo... ...in, his eyes two needles that pie... ...her to the quick from over his long, elegant nose.

She bent her head again and began writing furiously, speaking the words aloud. "However, the best performance by far was one offered after the play, a heartrending portrayal of outraged innocence given by Lord Rockleigh Conniston." She looked up and cocked her head. "Is that one 'n' or two?"

His face tightened ominously for an instant, and she feared a repeat of the scene in the coffeehouse. She was trying to swallow the dry lump in her throat when his mouth curled into the ghost of a grin.

"Two, Miss Tatlock," he said in a low voice. "Innocence with two 'n's."

Reclaiming
Lord Rockleigh

Nancy Butler

A SIGNET BOOK

SIGNET
Published by New American Library, a division of
Penguin Putnam Inc., 375 Hudson Street,
New York, New York 10014, U.S.A.
Penguin Books Ltd, 27 Wrights Lane,
London W8 5TZ, England
Penguin Books Australia Ltd, Ringwood,
Victoria, Australia
Penguin Books Canada Ltd, 10 Alcorn Avenue,
Toronto, Ontario, Canada M4V 3B2
Penguin Books (N.Z.) Ltd, 182–190 Wairau Road,
Auckland 10, New Zealand

Penguin Books Ltd, Registered Offices:
Harmondsworth, Middlesex, England

First published by Signet, an imprint of New American Library,
a division of Penguin Putnam Inc.

First Printing, September 2001
10 9 8 7 6 5 4 3 2 1

Copyright © Nancy J. Hajeski, 2001

All rights reserved

 REGISTERED TRADEMARK—MARCA REGISTRADA

Printed in the United States of America

PUBLISHER'S NOTE
This is a work of fiction. Names, characters, places, and incidents either are the product
of the author's imagination or are used fictitiously, and any resemblance to actual
persons, living or dead, business establishments, events, or locales is entirely
coincidental.

Dedicated to those matchless (and ageless) Ma'ams—
Elaine, Mary Ann, Donna Jo, Sue, Sherri and Diane

The quality of mercy is not strain'd,
It droppeth as the gentle rain from heaven . . .
  —William Shakespeare
     The Merchant of Venice

The quill can kill as surely as the sword,
Thus, reputation's rapidly interred.
Take heed, you scribes, you literary tribes,
Lest lawyers grow sleek with every sland'rous word.
  —Lord Troy

Chapter 1

There was something wrong with the sky.

For starters, the sun was up. Furthermore, it appeared to be rather advanced in its celestial orbit of the earth.

"Th' sun don't orbit the earth, Roc," Stanley Flemish would have told him. Would have, that is, if he hadn't been standing there beside Rockleigh, struck speechless as he goggled up at the blazing yellow orb.

The two of them had just emerged from the portals of White's, expecting to be met by the cool, dark shadows of early dawn, not the brilliantly bright light of day. No wonder the porters had been moving about so briskly as he and Stanley made their way through the nearly deserted club.

"Damn," Rockleigh muttered as he fumbled with his pocket watch. "It's nearly ten-thirty."

Stanley's narrow frame reeled back against the front of the building's elegant facade. "It's a miracle, Roc. Sun shinin' in the middle of the night."

Rockleigh shot his friend a look of impatience. "It isn't night, you sapskull. It's morning. *Late* morning." His brow furrowed. Had they really spent the night passed out in one of White's back rooms? "And the devil of it is, I have a sneaking notion there was something I had to do this morning. But for the life of me, I can't make m'brain get hold of it."

"No wonder," Stanley said. "Considering the amount of wine we drank last night. Er . . . it was last night, wasn't it? Don't tell me we've slept away a whole day and a half."

Rockleigh appeared genuinely concerned by this possibility. He quickly waylaid a newsboy and smiled his relief when he saw the date on the paper's front page. "No, it's still Tuesday." He passed the boy a coin and tucked the paper under his arm. "Now come along," he said motioning toward a coffeehouse that lay a block away down St. James's Street. "We'll have some breakfast at Melville's to restore us, and maybe then I'll be able to recall my morning's engagement."

Stanley puffed along beside him, working hard to keep up with his friend's long-legged stride. "Curricle race?" he offered breathlessly.

He shook his head, then groaned softly as the combined result of imbibing wine and brandy—and Lord knew what else—began playing havoc with the tender membranes inside his skull.

"Cockfight?"

Roc turned to gawk at him. "In the morning?"

"No," Stanley said quickly, "that would never do." His thin face brightened. "Were we supposed to drive out to a mill? Isn't Clobber Reese due to fight the Spaniard?"

Rockleigh gave this suggestion some serious thought. It jogged his memory slightly, but only enough to whisper that his engagement might be vaguely related to something of a pugilistic nature.

"I've never been this befuddled by drink before now," he muttered sourly.

"Wasn't just the drink," Stanley remarked. "We stopped off at Bacchus before we went to White's—I do recall that much—and you took opium with Doncaster. I've warned you, you know. It's a nasty business."

Rockleigh shrugged. "I've taken opium before on occasion. I enjoy the fruit of the poppy . . . it gives a man perspective."

"And the deuce of a bad head," Stanley said under his breath, eyeing his companion's haggard face. "Anyway," he added, "it couldn't have been a mill—I'd never forget a mill. Perhaps you had an assignation."

Roc's scowl deepened. "*I'd* never forget an assignation."

At least, he amended silently, that used to be the case. The allurements of the fair sex had always been a priority with him, but for the past month he'd been completely lacking in female companionship. By his own choice. This was not surprising, considering the unpleasantness that had erupted outside Covent Garden on that balmy April evening four weeks earlier.

It wasn't his fault his former mistress had gotten into a hair-pulling match with his current *chère amie* on the steps of the theater. A man didn't choose his ladybirds for their decorum, but rather for their lack of it. Still, it had given the tattlemongers a rich tidbit. And it had left him with a sudden distaste for women in general and for uncouth, overpainted doxies in particular.

His amused friends had good-naturedly broken up the fight before the constables could be called in. Roc, who had, for all his notoriety in the *ton,* a natural aversion to being the center of a tawdry public spectacle, hid his embarrassment behind a rueful smile. He'd soon sent the two women packing —with enough of his blunt in their respective purses to make them malleable, if not downright docile. It had been enough of an eye-opener, however, to drive him from the arms of Eros for the first time since he'd grown to manhood.

Stanley trailed him into the coffee shop, where they settled in a rear booth—as far away from daylight as was possible—and ordered a breakfast of beef and bread. When their meal arrived, they fell upon it like men who had been adrift at sea for a month.

"I ought to tell you, I don't like that Doncaster one bit," Stanley said as he dabbed at a bit of gravy with his last morsel of bread. "Bacchus used to be a decent place before Bryce sold it. Well, I mean for a house of vice. Now it's full of unsavory characters. And Doncaster's the worst of them."

Rockleigh looked up from his newspaper and raised one brow. "You think he's a bad influence on me?" There was a glimmer of sardonic mirth in his tone.

"I doubt the devil himself could influence you, Roc, unless you wished it. You go your own way, as always. I only worry that—"

"What?"

Stanley tugged his tangled neckcloth into greater disarray. "At times I fear . . . that your way marches too close to the line."

"And what line is that, pray?"

"The line between what is acceptable and what is not."

"Acceptable to society?"

"I'm talking about morality here."

"So speaks the bishop's nephew," Rockleigh drawled and returned his attention to his paper.

"But—"

Roc's eyes flashed up. "I am in no mood for a lecture, Stanley. Doncaster amuses me, and so do his friends. They are just low enough to give me a sense of my own consequence and just clever enough to make me feel that I am not situated among sheep, which, let me tell you, is how I often feel in the *ton*. And, yes, there might be a loose screw or two in the group, but it's not enough to put me off them. Still, if you don't care for Doncaster, I will visit Bacchus by myself in future."

Stanley looked sullen. "And who will get you home then?"

With a tight laugh, Rockleigh said, "Certainly not you, *mon ami*. You failed miserably yesterday evening. I can't remember the last time I spent the night passed out in White's."

His companion tactfully did not point out that the occasion had been less than two weeks ago. "At least we left White's with our purses intact. I doubt that would be the case at Bacchus. Doncaster's cronies would be on us like a pack of jackals if we ever let down our guard."

Rockleigh reached out and patted his sleeve. "But we don't ever let down our guard, my dear Stanley. Haven't I taught you that?"

He made no reply. It was pointless to argue with Roc. His friend had been master of all he surveyed for so long that it never occurred to him that he might sometimes be at risk. But this recently acquired taste for opium made Stanley very nervous. Roc rarely did things in moderation.

This should not have surprised anyone. Lord Rockleigh Conniston was the third son of the Duke of Barrisford, who had in his own youth acquired the reputation of a hell-raiser.

The duke's first two sons were amiable and biddable, and the eldest was even a bit lackluster. They'd assumed their expected roles without a murmur of complaint. Barrisford's heir, Francis, Viscount Torrance, was mad for agriculture and would make a proper duke when his time came. Lord Trent Conniston, the second son, had been of a military inclination since childhood and was at present on Wellesley's staff in Spain.

But the duke's third son refused to follow family tradition

and enter the Church. Stanley nearly laughed at the thought. On most days, you couldn't get his friend near a church, let alone inside one. "Bad air," Roc always complained. "Too much dust and decay."

Last spring, when their friend Beechum Bryce, late proprietor of Bacchus, was married, Rockleigh had foregone the church service, attending only the wedding breakfast, where he'd cut a dashing figure in a coat of azure velvet with diamond buttons. The bride had commented wryly to her new husband that they should be flattered that such a care-for-none as Lord Rockleigh had cared enough to dress up for the occasion. Upon overhearing this, Roc had remarked sanguinely that he'd bought the coat only because it reminded him of the bride's lovely eyes.

Stanley was glad the nuptial couple had hied themselves off to Barbados—Roc thought nothing of dallying with married ladies, and Bryce was not only protective of his wife—he was also one of the few men in London who could have given Rockleigh Conniston a run for his money in the pistols or fisticuffs department.

No, Roc was definitely not cut out to be a cleric.

Five years earlier, the duke, in an effort to engage his youngest son's interest in *something* worthwhile, had sent him off to India to oversee his holdings there. Rockleigh hadn't bankrupted his father, but the reports from Barrisford's man of business in Calcutta had been less than flattering. It seemed Roc preferred chasing after mountain bandits, hunting with maharajahs, and consorting with British officers' wives to the bothersome details of running an export company. He'd returned eighteen months later with a remarkably tanned countenance and a pet monkey in tow. And, Stanley had recently discovered, an unfortunate taste for opium.

Her Grace, the duchess, had then deeded one of her own properties to Rockleigh, hoping it would give him some sense of responsibility and a connection to the land. Stanley himself had accompanied Roc to the small estate outside Dover.

Inhabited by a lone ancient retainer, the property had fallen into serious decay. Roc had taken one look at the neglected manor house and immediately booked rooms in the nearest village, swearing he'd never overnight in such a shambly place for

fear of the ceiling crashing down upon his head. The village of
Crowden had been a quaint affair, though it wasn't surprising it
held little charm for a man of Roc's cosmopolitan tastes.
They'd packed up the next day and come home to London, and
Roc had never mentioned the property again.

Stanley often wondered what his friend had reported back to
his doting mama about the estate. She'd apparently spent part
of her childhood there and had a fondness for the place. It was
a good thing she hadn't seen the toll time and apathy had taken
on it.

When they were done with breakfast, the waiter removed
their plates and brought more coffee. Roc sipped at it with an
expression of bliss. The ache in his head had subsided to a dull
throb, and his wits were clearing nicely. He set the cup down
and swiped at his mouth with his napkin. And then emitted a
soft moan as his knuckles came into contact with his nose.

Stanley leaned closer. "What's wrong?"

Roc gingerly palpated his long, elegant nose between thumb
and forefinger. "Did I get into a fight last night, by any chance?
It feels quite tender. As if someone fetched me a proper blow."

Stanley peered at him in the dim light. "And if I'm not mistaken, there's a spattering of blood on your neckcloth. I noticed
it in the street just now, but I thought it must be claret."

They both sat in silence then, drinking their coffee and
mulling over this latest puzzlement.

Mercy Tatlock stifled a yawn and decided to wait another
five minutes. Her quarry had but fifteen minutes ago gone into
the coffee shop. It would be a kindness to allow the man some
breakfast before she descended on him, especially considering
how he had spent the night. She doubted anything resembling
solid food had gone down his throat in the past twelve hours.

Locating him this morning had posed little problem. A reliable source had informed her that he often took a late breakfast
at this particular coffeehouse. Recognizing him had also been
easy. On her first day in London, three days earlier, she'd made
it her business to discover his direction in Mayfair and had
camped out across the square from his town house. She'd noted
the tall, stylishly attired gentleman who had left the house at
noon, and having marked him, was subsequently able to recog-

nize him from a distance. Over the past two days she'd seen him several times, tooling his carriage in the park and, just yesterday, viewing the current exhibition at the Royal Academy.

She hadn't been tailing him, exactly. Rather, she got a sense of where the *ton* sought their daily amusements and set herself there to await him. He invariably appeared.

Waiting never troubled her—she was one of those fortunate individuals who was comfortable with her own thoughts. She'd simply weigh the merits of a book she'd read, work out a complicated harmony for the parish choir, plan her next story for *The Trumpet*.

Although *The Tiptree Trumpet* was her father's newspaper—he prided himself on being publisher, editor and copywriter—she had, over the past six years, become his good right hand. It had begun as a lark when she left Mrs. Filbert's Academy. She was ripe for some adventuring, as her father called it, and so he'd put her to work in his office, proofing galleys and calling on the local tradesmen who advertised in the paper. It wasn't long before she was writing her own coverage of local events in their small town in Kent.

It had been awkward at first—she was often the lone female at town meetings, magistrate's hearings and political debates. The male denizens of Tiptree had eventually become inured to her alert presence as she sat in the last row, scribbling away in a tiny notebook. County politics and social reform became her chief areas of concern. She left the more mundane matters of hearth and garden to her mother's pen: Mama had a neat way with a recipe or a cure for tomato blight.

Her education in things ladylike had not prepared her for her first confrontation with the landlord of a run-down rooming house on the outskirts of Tiptree. The building had partially collapsed during a storm, leaving its inhabitants with any number of broken limbs. Her meeting with its owner had quickly turned into a shouting match, and the rough fellow had ended up chasing her down the street.

However, she soon learned to control her erratic temper and to maintain her distance emotionally. Before two years had passed, her father had stopped rewriting her pieces and begun printing them straight from her pen. Somehow she had evolved from composing dreadful schoolgirl sonnets to writing crisp, deliberate prose.

This latent talent came as a revelation to someone who had thought herself equipped for little in life. She was neither very pretty nor very clever, at least not in the way women were expected to be clever, which is to say archly coy and manipulative. But she was clear-sighted, grounded in the here-and-now. That was her greatest gift as a writer.

She made a nice complement to her father. He saw the world as it could be in the future, if men of conscience and insight would make it so. He'd seen it as his sacred duty to help move things along, even if many of his readers (and a few of his own relations) were inclined to resist. Some called him a misguided crusader, but Mercy preferred to think of him as a visionary.

Last month, however, the newspaper's sometimes rash editorial tendencies had gotten them into a sticky situation. Which explained how she came to be hiding in a doorway on St. James's Street of a Tuesday morning.

Still, she had high hopes that she could fix things. After all, Lord Rockleigh Conniston, the target of the editorial in question, might have been depraved, but he was still a man with the usual frailties of his class—pride and complacency. She intended to use both of them to her advantage.

Once she'd prevailed upon him to drop the charges against her father, life in Tiptree would return to normal. Her mother could relinquish her hartshorn and vinaigrette and reemerge from her bedroom, where she had recently taken up residence, declaring herself to be in a fatal and permanent decline.

Unfortunately, Mama was not the only Tatlock inclined to melodrama: Toby, Mercy's younger brother, was not far behind their mother in histrionic tendencies. Mercy would never forget her shock when he returned to their lodgings last night and told her what had transpired outside Bacchus.

And that after she'd made him swear he would do nothing more than follow Lord Rockleigh during the early part of the evening. It was vital, she'd explained to him, that they gather firsthand evidence of the man's dissipated habits. Toby was rather more elated than he should have been at the notion of following a man of fashion as he sauntered from club to club.

Mercy had admonished him to keep out of the way of his quarry—he was to be an observer, nothing more.

So much for her stellar advice.

She sighed and looked at the tiny watch that was pinned to the bodice of her rust-colored spencer. The man had had enough time to down a roasted ox by now. With a firm, confident stride she crossed the cobbled street and went into Melville's.

The reckoning was at hand.

Rockleigh was staring into his third cup of coffee, forcing his brain to replay the events of the previous evening. He'd dined out with several friends, then had separated Stanley from the pack and gone off to Bacchus. Since he'd sworn off women, he hadn't bothered to investigate any of the ladybirds that frequented the place. Instead, he'd allowed himself to be waylaid by Doncaster, and they'd both retired to a small private room. Stanley, meanwhile, had gone off to play cards.

Roc wasn't sure how many hours had passed in the soft darkness of that room. The opium haze had made the passage of time immaterial. He felt only streams of pleasure, a blessed respite from the edgy restlessness that plagued most of his waking hours.

Stanley had roused him eventually, tsking like an old biddy as he got him on his feet and wrestled him back into his greatcoat. Doncaster was nowhere in sight. Roc recalled now that the man had been lingering on the front steps of Bacchus when he and Stanley left. That bothered him. He'd assumed Doncaster had taken opium with him, had gone under and been lulled into a euphoric stupor. Rockleigh misliked the idea of Doncaster sober and upright while he was lying semiconscious on a divan. As he'd said to Stanley, he didn't like to let his guard down with men like Doncaster. It wasn't prudent.

"I'm an idiot," he murmured softly down into his coffee cup.

"Lord Rockleigh Conniston?" It was a woman's voice, cultured and a bit husky.

Roc looked up at once. Stanley had pivoted around in the booth, an expression of disbelief on his face. Ladies did not, as a rule, wander alone into coffeehouses.

"Are you lost, ma'am?" Stanley asked.

"I'd like to have a word with Lord Rockleigh," she responded. The throaty timbre of her voice made it sound almost boyish.

Roc noticed their waiter hovering behind the woman, his expression one of dismay, and he waved the man off. The woman was clearly not a lightskirt, not unless they'd taken to dressing in frocks that were easily five years behind the fashion.

His gaze moved from the discomfited waiter to the woman's face. Plain, he thought. Undistinguished. Nondescript hair beneath a travesty of a brown bonnet. She was intriguingly tall, but didn't possess enough curves to tempt a man, even one who'd been celibate for four weeks. Her mouth wasn't bad, although it was currently pinched into a flat line. Smiling, it might have held some merit.

She never lowered her eyes from his open examination of her person. In fact, she appeared to be examining him right back. Now here was a neat trick. Women, in his experience—which was considerable—never looked directly at a man. They were all sideways glances and coy flutterings. It occurred to him that even Stanley rarely met his eyes, preferring, it always seemed, to address some phantom person over Rockleigh's shoulder.

"I am Conniston," he said at last. "And who might you be?" He didn't bother to rise. He'd pegged the woman as a petitioner, one of those London do-gooders who were long on the shelf and who spent their days looking for handouts from well-heeled members of the gentry. Though last he'd heard, that sort of woman didn't canvass St. James's Street.

"My name is Tatlock." She then paused as if expecting some response.

"I appear to be a trifle muzzy-headed this morning. That name means absolutely nothing to me."

Stanley had shifted back to him and was mouthing something urgently. "What?" Rockleigh said impatiently.

"Tatlock," she repeated, clutching her reticule against her midriff.

"I meant him." He motioned to Stanley. "Come on, Flemish, out with it."

"L-last night," he stuttered. "Outside Bacchus . . . that was the name of the cub who struck you. Tatlock." He bit his lip. "I just remembered it."

Rockleigh shut his eyes for an instant as that missing piece of the puzzle fell into place. He recalled the young hothead stumbling into him on the pavement outside the club, again felt the blow and the subsequent startled realization that the sprat had actually taken a swing at him. And drawn his cork.

All his misgivings about the past evening instantly solidified into one salient fact. He, Rockleigh Conniston, had been so incapacitated last night that he'd allowed a mere boy to hit him. He hadn't even raised a hand to ward off the blow.

Although the irritation he felt bubbling up should have been aimed at himself, it now had a more convenient target in this Tatlock female. He tipped his head back and gazed up at her. "I take it, then, that you are here to apologize for your impetuous relation."

"Apologize?" she said softly, in some confusion. "Oh, you mean for my brother. No, not that. It is of another relation I have come to speak. But first I would like to express my gratitude."

"For what, playing victim to that hot-tempered cub?"

She drew a breath. "For refusing to face him over pistols."

"A duel!" Stanley exclaimed, nearly coming off the bench. "That's what you were to do this morning, Roc. You challenged that young fellow to a duel directly he hit you . . . it's all coming back to me now. Doncaster came forward and agreed to be his second."

"He's only a boy," the woman said forcefully. "With an uncertain temper, I'll admit, but I can't believe you would—"

"He hit me," Lord Rockleigh interjected. "And if I challenged him, then I will meet him."

"But I thought . . ." Her eyes were puckered with concern. "You see, we waited in the park this morning till nine, and you never appeared. Mr. Doncaster said you often took breakfast here, and so I came to thank you for staying away. Well, I mean, I have other business with you, but—"

Mercy was losing her composure. It hadn't occurred to her that Lord Rockleigh had merely forgotten his challenge. She had attributed his nonappearance that morning to a bout of remorse. There was, she now saw, nothing remorseful about this man, which probably meant the rest of her mission was going to be strictly an uphill battle.

"I don't believe we have any further business, you and I," he said. "My only business is with your intemperate brother."

"Aren't you even curious about why I am here?"

He arched one dark brow. "My curiosity seems to be at an all-time low." He motioned to the waiter, who came hurrying over. "If you would see this woman out."

Mercy tugged away from the man. She drew a folded bit of newspaper from her reticule and flung it down onto the table. "Maybe this will refresh your memory."

He opened the clipping and perused it. Mercy watched with satisfaction as his jaw tightened. Mr. Flemish reached for it next, but Lord Rockleigh snatched it away. "No, no . . . it's nothing you need see, old fellow."

"Half of Kent has seen it," she said coolly. Her equilibrium was returning, thank goodness. "And nothing my brother and I have learned about you here in London has shaken my conviction that what is written there is the truth."

Lord Rockleigh's eyes narrowed. "If you will excuse us, Stanley."

"Well, I won't." He set his chin.

"Miss Tatlock will not wish our, er, discussion to be made public."

"I ain't the public," he insisted. "I am your friend."

"Let him remain," she said. She had a feeling this Mr. Flemish might serve as an ally. While by no means as dramatic in appearance as his dark-haired companion, he had a pleasant, open countenance and mild brown eyes. Kind eyes.

He slid over on his side of the booth and indicated that she should be seated. Lord Rockleigh's expression soured as she settled onto the bench.

"Now," she said, crossing her arms upon the table, "let us speak of this libel suit you have brought against my father—"

"Roc, you never said a word of this to me." His friend looked pained.

"If you wish to remain here, you'd do best to keep silent," he growled softly. "I'll tell you the whys and wherefores later, once Miss Tatlock has concluded her business with me."

"I will make it simple, Lord Rockleigh," she said. "You have threatened my father with financial ruin over this editorial our paper ran last month. Even now my family's possessions are being gathered together for an auction. There is no justice in that. They have done nothing wrong. I decided the best course was to face you in person, as my father's representative, and ask you to withdraw the charges."

"Impossible," he stated flatly.

"I was hoping you would be reasonable—for his sake, sir, and for your own."

One dark brow lifted. "My own?"

"If your solicitor pursues this matter, my father will see to it that every editor in the country makes your private life his professional business. Papa can do it—he is very well thought of in that community." She offered him a sly smile. "And you can't sue them all, can you? I doubt even the Regent has that much money."

He observed her with some wonder. "Are you threatening me, Miss Tatlock?"

"I am merely alerting you to the possibilities. Unless you want your every movement scrutinized, your every misstep publicized, you'd do well to rethink this lawsuit. Or else from Hadrian's Wall to Land's End, the name Rockleigh Conniston will become a byword for licentiousness and depravity."

He flicked the fingers of one hand in unconcern. "I believe that may already be the case."

"Then why," she entreated him, leaning forward, "why have you threatened my father? If your reputation is of so little concern to you, why bother with a libel suit?"

"I didn't like his grammar," Lord Rockleigh drawled.

Stanley Flemish guffawed into his shirt cuff, and then fell silent again.

"I am glad this amuses you both," she said stiffly. "Meanwhile, a noble and selfless man faces ruin at your hands. Idle hands, I might add, that never did one decent day's work. But in spite of that, I can't believe you'd take the bread from my family's mouth without a second thought."

Lord Rockleigh hitched one shoulder negligently and leaned back in the booth. "Your family are strangers to me. Well, until last night. Though upon reflection, I can say the less I have to do with Tatlocks, the better."

"Then drop the suit, and my brother and I will return home."

He was silent for a time. Mercy watched him cautiously.

"No," he said at last. "Your father did more than revile me—he set me up for ridicule. I find that intolerable. Furthermore, the accusations he made against me are unfounded. I will take my knocks when they are deserved, Miss Tatlock, but I will not let myself become fodder for some misguided provincial paper pusher."

Mercy's eyes flashed. "He is a deal more than that. He corresponds with Hume and other men of insight. His essays on social reform are widely read—several have even been published in America."

"Oh, well then . . ."

She disregarded his sneer. "His editorials have frequently spurred our local politicians into addressing issues they might normally overlook. His newspaper, our newspaper, has been recognized as a voice for change in all the southern counties."

"Not for long, Miss Tatlock. I intend to shut him down. Which should serve to shut him up."

She half rose from her seat. "Then you don't know the first thing about my father."

"And you don't know the first thing about me. Threats and thinly veiled blackmail tactics won't move me from my purpose. You want simple truths, ma'am, so I will give you one. I was maligned by your father, and I intend to seek satisfaction."

His choice of words brought to mind his still-incipient duel with Toby. Her voice shook as she spoke. "If you carry out this wicked notion of dueling with my seventeen-year-old brother, if you harm him in any way, you won't need a lawyer to break my father."

"Two birds with one stone, then," Rockleigh murmured.

He'd never openly assayed the role of villain before and was finding it quite stimulating. Especially since the more vile he became, the more animation his opponent showed in her face and bearing. He'd realized he was wrong to judge her plain. With her eyes blazing in anger and her cheeks flushed by frustration, she was quite striking. Tendrils of fair hair had escaped from her coiffure and now drifted against her throat beside the ribbons of her bonnet. Not a pretty bonnet, but such a pretty throat. He wondered idly if her skin could possibly be as soft as it appeared in the diffused light of the coffee shop.

"You are a monster," she said between her teeth.

He smiled slowly. "No, Miss Tatlock, merely a gentleman of the *ton*. Though I fancy there are those who would find little to choose between the two."

"And this does not trouble you . . . that out of caprice you have decided to squash another human being like an insect?"

"Finding a decent tailor troubles me. I give little thought to the condition of other people."

She shook her head. "I wanted to disbelieve the things that were written about you, Lord Rockleigh. I couldn't imagine a man so lost to human decency. But now I see that the editorial let you off lightly." She rose and reached across the table to retrieve the clipping, which lay beside his coffee cup.

His hand snaked out and took hold of her wrist. He looked up at her, and his pale eyes were glitteringly alive with what she could have sworn was amusement.

"Let me advise you of something, ma'am. Never bargain with threats. It makes a man testy. Now, if you'd come here and been conciliatory, if you'd admitted your father's unfortunate mistake, then I might have considered dropping the case."

"I saw those boys myself," she uttered in a low voice. "Saw the ragged children carted into your house in Crowden, watched others being driven away, no longer dressed in rags. I saw the rough men you set to keep watch over them. Nothing in that editorial is a lie."

He loosened his grip on her wrist, but did not release it. "I wonder the military hasn't some use for you, Miss Tatlock—you're such a clever little spy. Except that the conclusion you and your father reached was off by a mile."

Mercy forced herself not to tug away from his hold. His hand was warm against her skin, but it was not a patch on the heated anger that was rising inside her. "Then tell me what you are doing with a houseful of young boys secreted away in Kent."

"I see no need to explain myself. Least of all to you." His grip tightened again. "As for this matter of your brother, you will hear from Mr. Flemish shortly on the matter."

He doesn't know where we are staying in London, she realized with a flood of relief. Toby would be safe.

But then he added, "I take it Doncaster has your direction."

She nodded once, unable to lie. In the park that morning she'd overheard Toby telling his second that they were staying in Rumson Street above the shop of Cornelius Gribbings, the publisher.

"Sir, I implore you. There must be some way I can persuade you not to seek your vengeance on Toby. Strike out at my father if you must, but I would do anything to prevent harm to my brother."

"Anything? Truly?"

He tugged her closer, so that her thigh was pressed against the edge of the small table. His glance raked over her boldly, up and down, and there was no mistaking the message in his eyes.

Then his mouth formed into an expression of distaste and he said silkily, "No, I think not. Even if you were determined to become the virgin sacrifice, I have no patience with a bitch who's not broken to the leash."

Mercy gasped in outrage. And then twisted her hand away from him, making sure to send his coffee cup flying. The dark liquid splattered down the front of his waistcoat and onto his buff inexpressibles.

Rockleigh was on his feet the next instant and had forced her back against the wall beside the booth. One hand was splayed against her throat, unbridled fury glinting in his eyes. He recovered himself at once—well before Stanley, who was calling out in protest, had time to scramble from the booth—and stepped back from her.

She didn't say anything at first, just stood there trembling and white-faced. He wagered his face was as ghostly. Gad, he'd never once in his life laid hands on a woman except for pleasure. But there was something about her that had goaded him beyond merely playacting the villain.

"I pity you," was all she said, her voice deep and full of contempt.

She snatched her reticule from the table and brushed past the hovering waiter. Roc caught the man's eyes and read overt distaste. Stanley was wearing a similar expression.

"Stop gaping," Rockleigh bit out. "How else is a man to react when his privates have been scalded by a shrew?"

Stanley had the sense not to remind him that the coffee was lukewarm at best, but he couldn't keep from uttering in shocked accents, "What's gotten into you? Acting like the worst sort of blackguard, and then using violence . . . on a lady. Have you taken leave of your senses, Rockleigh?" His voice lowered. "Or is it Doncaster's opium that has relieved you of your wits?"

For an instant Rockleigh's jaw tightened, and his eyes narrowed dangerously. "Devil take you, Flemish," he snarled as he swept his hat off the bench. "If I wanted to hear a cartload of pious preaching, I'd join the damned Methodists."

He clapped his hat on his head and went striding out of the coffeehouse.

Stanley drew in a deep, steadying breath before he called the waiter over to settle their bill. Miss Tatlock's news clipping was still on the table, half lying in a shallow puddle of coffee. He dabbed at it with a napkin, and then placed it in his pocket.

He'd go off to his rooms in Regent Street and have a nice restorative nap. And then, once he was calm and rested, he'd read the clipping. Whatever it said, he was sure he wouldn't like it, not if it had turned Rockleigh into a madman.

Stanley had been feeling guilty for the past few weeks, uneasy over writing to Barrisford and alerting him to his son's increasing appetite for debauchery. It wasn't sporting to go behind a fellow's back, but he'd felt obligated to take some action. He'd sat at Barrisford's table any number of times in the past two decades—his father's property shared a boundary with the Bower, the duke's seat in Devon—and furthermore, Rockleigh was his best friend.

Now it appeared he'd done the right thing after all. No one could actually coerce Rockleigh Conniston—Miss Tatlock had quickly learned that lesson—but the duke had sometimes been able to curb him.

Stanley recalled what he'd said to Roc earlier, the carefully worded warning that he walked perilously near the line of decent behavior. In Stanley's mind, he'd just crossed over it. And there was nothing, no amount of drink or even opium, that could excuse that in his eyes.

Had he been wrong about Roc all these years? Wrong in believing that behind the arrogance and the selfishness there really was someone of value? For all his faults, Roc was a man who would come through for a fellow in a crisis, the sort who shared your pleasures and made you laugh over your failures. He was a dashed good friend, but Stanley had to admit that this didn't mean he was a very good person.

He decided, as he wandered along Piccadilly, that he'd let the duke sort things out. Right now he didn't trust himself to speak to Roc—he was too newly disenchanted and his feelings were bruised beyond all measure.

Chapter Two

It took Mercy the entire walk back to Mr. Gribbings's house to gain control of her emotions. Lord Rockleigh's image, looming like a child's nighttime bogeyman, refused to be banished.

"*Arrogant . . . beastly . . . belittling . . . cold . . . callous . . . derogatory . . . indifferent . . . insufferable . . . loathsome . . . malicious . . . remorseless . . . ruthless . . . sneering . . . snide . . .*"

She recited this litany under her breath, working her way through the alphabet. Oh, and *leering*. How could she forget that? No man had ever leered at her, raking her with his eyes until she was sure her cheeks burned scarlet. He was truly the most abominable man she'd ever met, and in her work for her father she'd encountered more than a few rogues.

Toby met her at the door of their lodgings, a suite of rooms above Mr. Gribbings's print shop. Her brother's angular face was awash with anxious expectation. "Not good," she said as she swept past him and hung her bonnet on the wall rack.

His expression darkened. "Not good how?"

"Not good as in he's determined to destroy Father. And he still intends to meet you over pistols." She gave a dry, mirthless laugh. "He forgot the duel. Can you credit that? There we were in the park fretting ourselves into a state, and he was blithely sleeping in his bed."

Or someone's bed, she amended silently.

She turned to him, gripping the back of a wing chair. "Oh, Toby, how could you have tangled with him last night? And I don't care if he did brush against you on the pavement and not beg pardon. You were not to show yourself to him, let alone punch him in the nose."

"He didn't just brush past me, Merce. I told you, he knocked into me. And then had the gall to curse me to my face. Called me a festering boil on the backside of humanity, as I recall."

Mercy nearly grinned—she had a secret penchant for colorful expletives. But then she shook her head and said reproachfully, "I don't care about all that. You had no idea what sort of man you were dealing with. This isn't some farmer's son who would settle for a bout of fisticuffs to make things square. He is fiendish." She'd have to add that last to her list.

"Naw," Toby said as he sprawled back in the chair, looking up at her through his forelock. "Mr. Doncaster says he's just a bit full of himself, which comes from being the son of a duke."

"Well, I can't say I liked that Mr. Doncaster very much either. I'd never trust a man with such shifty eyes."

"He thought you were pretty," Toby remarked. "Willowy, was what he called you. Willowy and fair."

"And just when did this illuminating conversation take place?"

"He drove me home from the park. Well, you did insist that I come back here and sleep. Lord knows neither of us got much last night. And this morning, instead of coming home with me like a sensible sister, you decided you had to go haring off to find Lord Rockleigh Care-for-None."

In truth, she'd been operating on pure nervous energy since last night. But when Lord Rockleigh didn't appear at the appointed time for the duel, she'd convinced herself it was a propitious time to speak with him, in spite of her exhaustion. Seeing how he'd just spared her brother, he might very well be inclined to spare her father, as well.

What a looby she'd been to believe that. And she'd so hoped to end this matter and get them both safely home to Tiptree.

She gazed down at her brother. His light brown hair was sticking up at the crown, in spite of his attempts to tame it into a sleek, stylish cap. It made him appear impossibly young.

"I'm sending you back to Boxwood," she said. "Conniston can't shoot you if you're not in London."

"That's a coward's way out," he protested hotly. "And I am not such a bad shot. Been practicing, you know, with Jack Skillens in the field behind our school. I can shoot the eye out of the king of hearts at twenty paces."

"Conniston is rather more the knave of spades," she said dampeningly. "And Papa has enough on his plate right now without having to nurse you back to health." She added intently, "*If* you even survive the encounter."

The weight of this dire possibility descended on him, and he gnawed at his lip. "I'm sorry I've added to your worries, Merce. I admit I was rash to hit him. I just couldn't hold back my anger at the fellow, not with all the trouble he's caused our family. Still, I can't leave you here alone. Papa thinks we went off to Aunt Clarissa's together. How will I explain coming home without you? He'll get wind of our deceit soon enough in that case."

There was that problem, she acknowledged. Avery Tatlock had never encountered falsehood from any of his progeny, and she hated to add that new disappointment to his burden right now.

"Then we need to go somewhere else. That shifty Doncaster knows where we are staying, and Conniston will have it off him in no time."

Toby's face lit up. "I can go stay with Jack Skillens. Don't you remember? I told you he was here in London visiting his great-aunt."

Since Toby was always nattering on about this topping chum or that capital fellow, she rarely paid his school reminiscences much mind.

"I went to see him yesterday while you were at the Royal Academy. He's bored to flinders in the old lady's house and would like nothing better than having me come to stay."

Since this sounded like a workable plan—she was much too discomposed to think of another—she agreed to let Toby send a message to his friend. Even if he and Jack fell into scrapes on their own, he'd at least be out of Lord Rockleigh's deadly reach.

*   *   *

The predators of London have descended upon Crowden. Flown from their rookeries to make a foul nest in what was once a showplace in this county. And under the protection, one must assume, of a son of the nobility who lends his home, if not his name, to this nefarious purpose.

The trafficking in human flesh is an abomination, and how much more so when it is children who are the victims. Yet, while it is reviled on principle, we in the countryside

*complacently thrust away all thoughts of this disturbing
practice because it is the particular scourge of large cities.
Unfortunately, distance breeds tolerance. However, it is
impossible to stand by and say nothing when this infamy is
visited upon our own district, and so we must speak out.*

Stanley had to stop reading. He had a fair notion of what this
Tatlock fellow was writing about. Prostitution was rife in London, and he didn't doubt it was flourishing in other cities as
well. But Tatlock's daughter had spoken of young boys being
housed at Rockleigh's estate. He grimaced. It just wasn't possible. Not Roc.

He knew his friend had interests in trade; he'd acquired that
leaning from the duke, who, unlike many peers, had no scruples
about investing in manufacturing. But would he sink so low as
to peddle children for money? Stanley didn't doubt there was a
market for such delicate wares—girls fresh from the country or
young boys orphaned and homeless, it made no difference to
the . . . what had Tatlock called them? The predators.

He would have sworn that Roc was strictly in the petticoat
line when it came to amusements of the flesh, but did that rule
out his furnishing playthings to men who possessed different,
baser appetites?

He really didn't want to deal with this. It was too troubling.
He quickly scanned the rest of the editorial, noting only that
Roc was never actually mentioned by name. But the references
to the estate in Crowden were obvious, and near the end was a
phrase that might end up damning Miss Tatlock's father.

*We mourn to see this scion of a noble family, the youngest
son of a Devonshire duke—who is himself esteemed as a
fair-minded landlord—allied with scoundrels and involved in
this unholy commerce.*

Jupiter! That would give most readers about five seconds'
pause before they figured out the Duke of Barrisford was the
peer in question and that Rockleigh was the power behind the
predators.

He returned to the editorial. It ended with a salvo.

This preening tulip of the ton *is in truth a pathetic specimen.
His public vices have given way to private pandering, his
arrogance blinding him to how effortlessly he has been
manipulated by these parasites who feed off our young.*

Stanley sank back in his chair, his face drawn.
"I won't judge him," he muttered to himself. "I just won't."

Later that afternoon, Mercy decided to confer with Mr.
Gribbings on her problem.

The old man, who held something of favorite-uncle status
with the two elder Tatlock children, had been their father's first
editor. Two years out of Oxford, Avery Tatlock, who'd been recently beggared by his father's gambling, had decided to seek
a career in publishing and had been fortunate enough to ally
himself with one of the canniest men in London. Cornelius
Gribbings had little formal education, but he'd cut his baby
teeth on a letter press, and by the time he was thirty, he had
carved out a tidy publishing business.

Beyond the business end of things, Gribbings had taught
Avery Tatlock to be observant and dispassionate in his stories,
but eventually, as his skill as a writer grew, he gained the courage
to write on matters about which he was very passionate.

Mercy, though equally passionate, had not been given leave
by her father to write her own editorials. At the mere mention
of such a thing, her mama had protested that it was bad enough
having *one* rabble-rouser in the house.

Cornelius Gribbings sat and smoked a pipe in his comfortable parlor while Mercy described her encounter with Lord
Rockleigh. She purposely omitted any mention of his rough
treatment, focusing instead on his refusal to be reasonable. But
the old man was too cagey not to read between the lines.

"Pulled your tail, did he? I'm not surprised. Young gentlemen are not at their best first thing in the morning."

"It was past eleven," she pointed out. "And he is not so very
young."

"Not much past thirty, as I reckon. That's young to a man
who has three-score and more years on him, as I do. But never
mind. He was rude to you, and we can't have that. Although I

never did think this plan of yours would work . . . you trying to talk sense to him. That's lawyer's business."

"Father cannot afford a lawyer—he's still paying off the new presses. Not to mention that Toby's university fees are due."

"You had only to tell me, poppet. I've some money put by—"

She touched his sleeve. "Oh, no, Mr. Gribbings. That is not what I was getting at. Though thank you for the offer. I . . . I only thought that if I could speak to Lord Rockleigh, make him see that these are real people he is hurting, not just names on a writ, then he would drop the suit." She looked down at the patterned carpet. "All I have done is convince him to go forward with a vengeance."

"Your brother had a hand in that," he remarked around his pipe stem.

"Conniston still intends to meet him," she said. "I gather the gentleman was so deep in his cups last night that he simply forgot about the duel. I've decided it's safest to send Toby to stay with a friend here in London."

Gribbings patted her hand. "That was wise. I was getting ready to write to your father on that score . . . have him fetch you both back to Tiptree before that young rascal landed himself in the suds again. It's never a good idea to bloody a gentleman's nose in front of his friends. A proud man doesn't appreciate being made to look a fool in public."

Mercy's head tipped up. "That's exactly what Lord Rockleigh said. That the editorial did more than paint him as a scoundrel—it held him up to ridicule, which he found intolerable."

"There you have it," he said with a grin.

"Have what?"

"Your angle, girl. The means to making Lord Rockleigh give up this case. You must embarrass him into it."

A frown creased her brow. If a mild confrontation in a coffeehouse had resulted in near violence, how would he react if she made him a laughingstock? The South Pole wouldn't be far away enough for her to feel safe.

"You start out slow," Gribbings explained, noting her doubtful expression. "A tweak here, a prod there. Nothing illegal, mind, but galling all the same. You make yourself enough of a nuisance in his life and he'll fold. If there's one thing a gentleman can't swallow, it's dealing with small inconveniences. His carriage breaks down; he weathers it like a stoic. His paper doesn't appear for three days running; then you have one very unhappy fellow."

"But it sounds as if you want me to play pranks on him. My father's whole world is at stake here."

"Call them pranks or whatever you like, the point is to make his life uncomfortable now so that he don't make your life uncomfortable in the future. And," he added, knocking the dottle from his pipe into the fireplace, "if it doesn't work, you're no worse off than before. And you've had the satisfaction of nettling him in the bargain."

"I'd like to do more than nettle him," she said under her breath.

"Just think on it and you'll come up with a few choice ways to accomplish it." He rose from his chair. "You've a fertile brain, and in some ways more pluck than your father. He talks big about changing the world, but he's always refused to return to London where he could really be heard. Now look at you, come here to the big city and already bearding lions in their den. Not bad for an apprentice."

She was nearly at the door when he called out, "I nearly forgot. That manuscript I wanted you to look over is in my office." He added, "Perhaps the subject matter—it's about the Punic Wars—might distract you from your own recent skirmish."

She grinned. "Hannibal would have met his match in Lord Rockleigh, I fear."

Gribbings scratched the side of his balding head. "If I may make an observation, Hannibal's pride got him into trouble. He believed himself invincible." He gave Mercy a swift wink. "Any man who thinks that is just ripe for a fall."

Mercy went next door to the print shop, where two of Gribbings's own apprentices were busy running off handbills. They both looked up and nodded to her as she went into the old man's office. The manuscript—a stack of papers bound with twine and fully a half-foot high—sat on his cluttered desk. She hefted it in her arms and turned back toward the work area, wondering all the while what she could possibly do to rattle Lord Rockleigh.

She lingered for a moment in the doorway of the office, breathing in the essence of the shop. There was something comforting about a pressroom—the acrid, nose-crinkling smell of the ink, the soft vanilla scent of good paper and the woodsy odor of newsprint. And underscoring it all, the metronome thumping of the press plates, like a slow, steady heartbeat.

This was the world she had grown up in, playing with lead type ingots the way other children played with wooden blocks. It still felt like home.

She watched with an assessing eye as the crisply printed sheets emerged from the press. Setting the manuscript on a nearby bench, she moved forward and plucked up one of the handbills, holding the still-damp surface away from her gown. It advertised the extended run of the current play at the Orpheum, a musical presentation called *The Song of Elsinore,* featuring Lovelace Wellesley as Ophelia. By tomorrow night, Gribbings's jobbers would have these posters displayed on every available surface, where all of London would see them.

All of London.

She immediately ran back to the house, calling, "Mr. Gribbings! Mr. Gribbings!" He looked up from his chair by the fire and drew off his reading glasses.

"I've thought of something deliciously wicked to taunt Lord Rockleigh," she said with a wide grin. "And not at all illegal. At least I don't think it is. I only hope you know someone who can draw a decent caricature."

The next night, Mercy prevailed upon Mr. Gribbings to escort her to the theater. The poster for the Orpheum had furnished her with yet another inspiration. She had planned to spend some of her time in London writing about the goings on in Town for *The Trumpet,* and there was nothing, she knew, that her father's readers enjoyed so much as tales of actors and playwrights. It had been a provincial mania since the time of Shakespeare.

Of course, she could only present her stories to her father after he'd learned about her clandestine trip to the city, but they might serve as a peace offering. She was sure it would all sort itself out. Her father had never been angry with her once in her life, and she knew he sometimes had reason to be.

The Song of Elsinore had been a revelation—Miss Wellesley's father, the playwright, had transformed the dour Dane into the model of a romantic singing prince. There hadn't been a foggy graveyard or a human skull in sight. *Alas, poor Yorick.*

Mercy's pleasure with the play turned to delight when Mr. Gribbings announced that he'd used his connections with the management to arrange a backstage visit after the performance.

Unfortunately, there was a crush in the reception room. Miss Wellesley seemed to have a regiment of admirers, all clamoring for her attention. Mercy soon lost her escort in the crowd and so found herself a relatively quiet corner with an empty stool and began writing her impressions of the play in her notebook.

The crowd jostled; someone moved out of it and came to stand before her. She assumed it was Mr. Gribbings.

"I know this is bad form," she said without looking up. "But I need to get this written down before I forget the details. Miss Wellesley was quite good, don't you think, if a little overwrought?"

There was no answer forthcoming. She did look up then, and her cheeks instantly flushed.

Lord Rockleigh was standing there, not two feet from her. He might have been backlit and therefore in shadow, but his expression was not difficult to read. Contempt. Seething, sneering contempt. Mouth twisted, cheeks drawn in, his eyes two needles that pierced her to the quick from over his long, elegant nose.

She bent her head again and began writing furiously, speaking the words aloud. "However, the best performance by far was one offered after the play, a heartrending portrayal of outraged innocence given by Lord Rockleigh Conniston." She looked up and cocked her head. "Is that one 'n' or two?"

His face tightened ominously for an instant, and she feared a repeat of the scene in the coffeehouse. She was trying to swallow the dry lump in her throat when his mouth curled into the ghost of a grin.

"Two, Miss Tatlock," he said in a low voice. "Innocence with two 'n's."

He moved away after that, but only to the edge of the crowd, where he caught the attention of a blond Adonis who was toying with a glass of champagne. They exchanged a few words, and then, to her utter astonishment, the Adonis strolled over and introduced himself.

She recognized him now; she'd seen his boyishly handsome face reproduced in any number of newspapers—Lord Troy, England's premier poet.

"I understand from Lord Rockleigh," he said amiably, "that you and I are in a similar line of work."

It was a good thing there was a wall behind her, or she'd have tumbled right off her stool in shock. Not only because this acclaimed genius was comparing her pen scratchings to his immortal poems, but also at the notion that Conniston, her arch-enemy, had sent Troy over to speak to her.

He held out one hand. "See now, Miss Tatlock, the crowd is thinning. Let me take you over to meet Miss Wellesley. I can assure you, she adores anything to do with the press."

The beautiful Miss Wellesley, who could not have been more than eighteen, was charming, a bit bubbleheaded and absolutely thrilled to tell Mercy her entire life's story, up to and including the time she played Lady Godiva during a windstorm at an outdoor pageant.

Although Lord Rockleigh never reappeared, Troy kept her company once she'd finished speaking with the actress, sharing with her several amusing stories about his adventures during a visit to Greece. They would reduce the readership in Tiptree to worshipful sighs of admiration.

Mercy spent half the night writing up her encounter with Lord Troy and the other half trying to sort out why Lord Rockleigh had done her such a kindness. She finally decided that it amused him to do the opposite of what others expected. In her own work she'd used that maneuver to effect more than once. It kept people off balance and made them infinitely easier to handle. But if he thought he could handle her, he was seriously mistaken.

Regardless of the favor he'd done her, she was still going forward with her campaign to torment him. But with perhaps a trifle less anger. Because she'd actually discovered one thing to appreciate about him—he could banter, even when the joke was at his own expense.

Chapter Three

He wondered when it had started to go downhill. His life, that is. Until now he'd been certain of everything, of what each day would bring, of what each evening would offer. He'd been secure in the knowledge that any pleasure in the city was his for the taking. His wealth allowed him endless diversions, and his breeding guaranteed that they could be enjoyed in the best company. Women flocked to him, men admired the sharp edge of his wit and the stylish cut of his waistcoat.

Now he wandered the night streets of London like a lost soul. Stanley, that steadfast little soldier, had forsaken him. For two nights running, he'd not been in any of their regular haunts. Yesterday he had ignored Rockleigh's casually worded note inviting him to dine. This evening, Roc had been reduced to pounding on his door.

"I know you're in there, Stanley. Your landlady saw you come in not ten minutes ago."

He heard muffled cursing on the other side of the door. "I ain't home to you, old fellow."

"This is childish . . . and idiotic."

"Yes, I expect calling me names will win me over."

Roc had left in a huff, mouthing a few curses of his own. He didn't need Stanley to enjoy a night on the town, he resolved. There were Hereford and Vincent to sit at cards with him, and Clipper Donegan to blow a cloud with in the back room of Watier's. There was Beechum Bryce to . . . no, Beech had gotten himself leg-shackled to Troy's sister and gone off to some tropical paradise, bad cess to him.

He'd run into Troy himself the previous night. The fellow

had insisted Roc accompany him to the Orpheum. The current belle of the London theater was performing there, and each night her admirers lined up to pay their respects. Troy was always first in line. Roc had resisted, and then finally given in. It wasn't as though he had anything pressing to do.

The post-play gathering had been a mob scene, as usual, and when he'd stepped away from the throng for a breath of cool air, whom should he spy in the corner of the room but his own personal nemesis scribbling away in a notebook.

She had improved on the brown bonnet, he noted, but only slightly. The simple wreath of silk flowers she'd worn in her hair made her look like an unfledged schoolgirl. It was hard to reconcile that image with the irritating woman who was the source of his current woes—most critically, his rift with Stanley.

In spite of his annoyance with Miss Tatlock, he had passed a few words with her. Arch, needling words on her part. What else had he come to expect? He did have to admit, however, that she had a keen mind and a quick humor. If she'd been a man, he would have found those attributes entertaining, even admirable. In a woman, they were a blasted waste.

As it was, he'd quickly passed her over to Troy, who had a knack for charming women.

Rockleigh now suffered a startling thought. Had he lost his ability to charm the fair sex? The answer was a resounding yes, if Miss Tatlock's reaction to him was any gauge. There was only one way to put it to the test. Besides, it was past time for him to reenter the world of lightskirts and ladybirds—this long, unaccustomed bout of celibacy might just be the cause of his recent malaise. A man got his humors muddled when he wasn't seeking regular relief. His brain fogged, his energy flagged and his whole outlook dimmed.

He was heading in the direction of Madame Montcalm's select establishment when he realized the route he'd chosen would take him past Bacchus. He tried to ignore the seductive whisper that was stronger than any sexual lure.

He needed the insightful oblivion tonight, the gift of the poppy. Doncaster would be inside; Roc had to seek him out anyway, to discover the location of that pestilential Tatlock boy. So where was the harm in dropping in for a few minutes? It didn't mean he'd avail himself of Doncaster's opium. Just a friendly glass of claret and then he'd be on his way.

It was nearing dawn when he finally found his way home. It was ridiculous, really. He'd spent most of his adult life in London. How could a man misplace an entire borough like Mayfair? A bemused coachman had finally taken him up and driven him to the door of his town house—once Roc was able to recall the address.

"It's not safe, guv," the man had admonished as he watched Rockleigh climb out of the carriage and carefully negotiate his way up the curbstone. "A gentry cove like your good self wanderin' about in the streets. You need lookin' after, you do."

Rockleigh waved off this running commentary and focused on getting up the steps of his town house. The front door opened and James, the footman, moved forward to help him into the hall. "Shall I see you to your room, sir?"

"Go to bed," he muttered. "M'valet will see to me."

The footman bit his lip. "I'm afraid your valet gave notice this evening. Something to do with being hit in the head with a bottle of hair tonic."

Rockleigh started back. "I merely winged him on the shoulder."

James shrugged, and then continued to assist his master to the second-floor bedroom. Since it was his dream divine to become a valet one day, he took this opportunity to practice on his employer. He'd have had done better to practice undressing a rag doll, however, since Lord Rockleigh seemed to have lost all his bones and could do nothing more than sag back on the mattress.

"I believe you must be sickening for something, sir."

Rockleigh craned his head up from the bed and looked at him sharply—no small feat in his present state—wondering if the fellow was being sarcastic. But there was only solicitude in the young man's sallow face.

Or maybe it was pity.

Here's a pretty comedown, he reflected as James tugged at his boots. *I'm getting lectures from coach drivers and looks of pity from my footman.*

But that wasn't the worst of it. Just before he left the room,

James turned back to him. "Oh, I nearly forgot, sir. His Grace came by earlier this evening. With the duchess. He said they expect you to call on them tomorrow morning."

With a loud groan, Rockleigh pulled his pillow over his face. He must have done something truly heinous to have such troubles heaped upon him.

Rockleigh's town house was relatively small, but exquisitely modeled. His father's mansion, on the other hand, was enormous and designed by what Rockleigh assumed had been a deranged escapee from a Turkish harem. It sported minarets and miniature domes both inside and out. The arched ceiling of the foyer was tiled in a furious red-and-green mosaic pattern. As children, he and his two brothers would lie on the marble floor and gaze up at it until the vibrating colors made them dizzy. It still gave him a bilious feeling.

Watkins, the butler, who had known him since he was in shirt-tails, took his hat and stick without so much as a word of greeting, and led him to the drawing room. In keeping with the theme of the place, all the rugs and runners were woven in the Persian style, but in unlikely pastel shades. Still, he'd always suspected the carpet in the drawing room was the genuine article with its midnight blues and rich terracottas. How remiss of his mother to have allowed a real antique into her make-believe kingdom.

Both his parents were seated when he came through the door, but his father rose to his feet as Roc approached them across that heavenly carpet.

"Rockleigh," he said in his most clipped tone.

Roc had to admit the man still looked robust, if inclined to some portliness about the chest. His height and the fierce light in his pale eyes were undiminished by age, but his dark hair was showing more gray than black these days. His mother, he noted, had not further augmented her fashionably rounded figure, and her hair was still a bright shade of chestnut. But there were now purple smudges of worry beneath her deep blue eyes.

Rockleigh realized he had not seen either of them for more than a year. He'd run into Trent more recently when he'd been home on leave from the Peninsula. But even Trent, the less irksome of his two brothers, couldn't prevail on him to return home to the Bower.

It appeared now that the Bower had come to him.

"Mother . . . Father . . . I hope I find you both in good health."

"We are tolerable," his mother answered in an uncharacteristically flat voice.

He was in for it now, he thought, if even his doting Mama was out of charity with him.

"As if you ever came home to discover that for yourself," the duke muttered.

Rockleigh shrugged one shoulder. "I find travel wearying."

"And you find the low haunts of London less wearying?"

"A man needs to amuse himself."

"But not at the cost of his family's reputation, sir."

"I assure you, Father, your consequence is far beyond the damaging effects of my misdeeds." He was conscious of his hands, of keeping them still at his sides. He hated fidgeting in front of the old man as though he were an errant schoolboy.

"I am not speaking for myself. It is your brother Torrance who suffers for your lack of discretion here in Town."

"Torry? Why, is he come to London, then? Has the titled farmer left the haystack and the dung heap to visit the capital? I expect I'll be reading about such a newsworthy occurrence in *The Times*."

Her Grace shifted forward. "You haven't earned the right to criticize your brother. He, at least, knows his duty to the family."

"And what, pray, is *my* duty to the family, Mama? I seem to have mislaid the rule book."

The duchess heard something faintly plaintive in her son's voice, but before she could respond, her husband interjected, "Staying out of trouble would be a good start."

"Ah, but to do that a man needs more to occupy him than merely being an ornament to society."

"That's been your choice. I sent you to India so you would get a taste of the industry that puts gold in your pocket. But did you apply yourself?"

"I did," Rockleigh stated. "To the things that were of interest to me."

"Ah, yes, hunting and gambling and whoring."

"Barrisford, really." The duchess fanned herself with one hand.

"I don't see him denying it. No, he'd rather stand here and make light of his brother. Well, sir, let me tell you, Torrance will make a proper duke when his time comes. I thank heaven daily that you were not the firstborn."

"As do I, Father. You have no idea." Rockleigh gave him a closemouthed smile that did nothing to disguise the cautious, edgy anger in his eyes.

"It is imperative that you curb your behavior, Roc," his mother said more gently. "Torrance is shortly to announce his betrothal to Jessica Blythedale. Her family has expressed some concern about your . . . your less savory habits."

"So Torry is to tie the knot, eh? It's about time. He's what . . . nearly fifty?"

The duchess's heart-shaped face narrowed. "He is thirty-four, as you very well know."

"Yes, well, he's always been an old man. And the Blythedale chit will suit him perfectly, since she and her mother are both sanctimonious tabbies."

Lady Blythedale, the baroness in question, had made it her life's work to skewer Rockleigh at every opportunity, starting when he was fourteen and she found him kissing a kitchen maid during a house party at the Bower. His mother, he was sure, received daily reports from the woman of his various misdeeds.

He settled himself in a spindly side chair and stretched out his long legs. His body still bore the effects of last night's overindulgence, and he wasn't sure how long he could have remained standing without trembling visibly.

"I didn't give you leave to sit," His Grace snarled.

Rockleigh rolled his eyes. "Oh, don't come the highhanded duke over me, Father. I'm feeling rather delicate this morning, if you must know."

There, that got his mother's attention. She reached for his hand. "You're not feverish, are you, Rocky?"

"No," he said, trying not to wince at her use of his pet name. "Just a bit out of twig."

His father came to stand before him. "I know what ails him. He's been out on an all-night carouse. I wager he barely had time to change his linen before he came here."

With a sigh, Rockleigh raised his eyes to his meet his father's. They were so alike, it was uncanny. "I find it tiresome that you and I cannot be together for three minutes before you begin lecturing me on my sins. On the very things, I might add, that made you a byword in the *ton* before you were wed."

The duke drew in one cheek. "Since I was wed at twenty-three, the span of my, er, debauchery was limited. Yours appears to have no end in sight."

"Amen to that," he muttered.

His mother pinched him on the arm. "Stop provoking him, Roc." She shot her husband a look of entreaty. "Perhaps it would be best if I spoke to him alone, Barrisford."

"Why? So you can cosset him and soothe his ruffled feathers? I think it is you who should leave, my dear, so that there can be plain speaking between us."

"You nearly parted his skull with a poker the last time I left you alone," she remarked archly. "However, I will amuse myself over there by the window and allow you your masculine tete-a-tete."

With a graceful sweep of satin, she rose from the sofa. She was still one of the most beautiful women Rockleigh had ever seen, even if she did have the decorating sense of a turnip.

The duchess clasped her husband's wrist as she passed. "Remember, we *made* him, Arthur," she whispered against his ear. "In every sense of the word."

The duke pulled up a chair so that he and Rockleigh were nearly knee to knee. "I didn't mean to rip into you the instant you came through the door," he said gruffly. "It's worry that does that to a man, makes him snappish and like to bite."

"Are you saying that you are worried over me? I thought it was your concern for Torrance's upcoming marriage that brought you here."

"It's all entwined, Roc. I . . . I don't even know how to begin. Your other brothers never caused me a moment of concern. Oh, I do worry about Trent off fighting those cursed French, but it's not the sort of worry that eats at a fellow. But you, boy, I worry over you . . . it cuts me to the bone."

"Papa?" It was the voice of a child that had slipped out. Rockleigh quickly covered the lapse with a slight cough. "I thought you only felt that deeply about my mother . . . and your crops, of course."

"I'm not going to let you rattle me, boy. Not this time. There's too much at stake."

"Oh, yes, the blessed heir's marriage."

"Damn it!" his father cried, nearly coming off his chair.

"Barrisford," Her Grace called out lightly, but with a distinct undertone of warning. "Remember what I said."

The duke settled back in his seat and smoothed his waistcoat. "Very well, then, I'll say it right out. You have been seen taking opium. By a number of witnesses."

If there was a hitch in Rockleigh's breathing, it was barely noticeable. "And who might they be?"

"They frequent a house of vice called Bacchus. I believe you are a member."

"So is Trent, if truth be told."

His father sighed deeply. "I am not a prude, sir, though it amuses you to believe that. I was out on the Town at a time when these beaus and dandies you call friends would have been laughed from the streets. Society was less refined then. We fought with swords, and we fought to the death. My brother twice had to flee the country after killing his man in a duel."

"Good old Uncle Rockleigh," he murmured. "Maybe you and Her Grace should have named me after a less rackety relation."

"The point is, I am fully aware of the lures a wealthy young man can succumb to in this city. But I like to think that you are too intelligent to risk your life over a foolish vice."

Rockleigh drew back. "Risk my life? Good grief, I've not taken to the high Toby or joined a band of smugglers. How on earth is my life at risk?"

The duke leaned forward. "You recall that your mother and I lived in India for two years before I came into my title?"

He nodded. "I've heard her speak of it. She didn't care for the flies."

"While we were there, I saw up close what opium can do to a man. It ain't like liquor, Roc. It saps him, drains him, till he's nothing but a husk."

"I can't imagine what this possibly has to do with me."

The duke took hold of his wrist. "We *know*, Rockleigh," he said. "One of your friends wrote to us . . . oh, he didn't come right out and say what you'd been up to. But he was obviously upset about some doings at Bacchus. So I called in a favor at

Bow Street and had one of the Runners fill in for the doorman.
He saw you with his own eyes."

"Damn his eyes," Roc cried, springing up from his chair.
"Am I to be spied upon by everyone? Is no space safe from prying, sneaking, bloody-minded—"

"Rockleigh!" His mother's voice cut into him like a lash.

"Sorry, Mama, but I find it intolerable that my life should be
under such scrutiny. Yes, it's true that I have tried opium. It was
in India that I first sampled it, as a matter of fact. There's little
harm in it that I can see. It offers a pleasant euphoria."

"And each time it takes more and more of the hellish stuff to
reach that pleasant state," his father added darkly.

"I can't say that I've noticed," he drawled as he resumed his
seat.

"He's hopeless," the duke muttered. He rested his forehead
on his palm. "And the pity of it is, I can't even disinherit him."

The duchess left the window seat and came to stand behind
her son. "And what good would that do? Honestly, Barrisford,
I think sometimes you are better with wheat fields and corn-
stalks than you are with people."

She laid her hand on Rockleigh's hair. "Promise me," she said,
leaning to touch her cheek to his. "I am not asking you to live like
a saint—just promise your Mama that you will act wisely. I knew
you'd be angry when you found out about the Runner, but don't
sink yourself in depravity now out of pure pique."

She drew a breath and added softly, "You're not just a Conniston, Roc—you're also a Benning. And we tend to take matters more lightly than your father's family. I've never seen the
Benning side of you, my love. You're all intensity and broody
temperament just like that headstrong man sitting there." She
cast a fond look at her husband. "Be a Benning for a time, can't
you? Enjoy all the good in your life, laugh over something foolish, and leave these dark doings to men of less promise."

Rockleigh sighed. There was no way he could make her understand the demons that drove him. He wasn't sure *he* even
understood them. "I am who I am, Mama. No more, no less."
He rose and placed a kiss on her cheek. "I must leave you now.
Perhaps I will see you again before you return to the Bower."

"Sir," he said curtly as he sketched a bow to his father, who
refused to acknowledge it. He then recrossed the heavenly car-

pet, went through the dizzying foyer and found himself out in the clear air, where he could breathe at last.

The duchess eyed her husband in silence for several long seconds before she spoke. "It's worse than we thought, isn't it?"

He winced at the quavering note of fear in her voice. "He's no better now than when he was fifteen and facing a caning for some scrape. He just gets sullen and uncooperative. And yes, I'm afraid it is very bad, my dear. There is something else that's come to my attention. I am loath to share it with you, but in fairness I must."

She crouched before him and took his hands in her own. "You know how strong I am, Arthur. I managed to survive India and being a duke's wife and bearing three mismatched sons. I even survived the lost wheat crop of '06."

He grinned at her. "You are a blessing, indeed. But this is far worse than our son's predilection for opium. That is the sort of vice a man might outgrow . . . but this new trouble is a taint that will stay with him his whole life long."

"Then end the suspense and tell me."

He drew a news clipping from his pocket and passed it to her. She scanned it quickly and her face blanched.

"Lady Blythedale has a cousin in that part of Kent," he explained. "The woman sent it to her, and she was obliging enough to forward it to me."

"But this is ridiculous," she cried, reeling back on her heels. "There is nothing here but a lot of twaddle. No names are mentioned, only a vague reference to an estate in Crowden and a duke's son."

"There is only one estate in Crowden, my love. The one you deeded to Rockleigh."

She shook the clipping under his nose. "Who is responsible for this slander?"

"A fellow named Tatlock, who owns a paper down in Tiptree."

"Then this man, this Tatlock person, is mistaken. Rockleigh would never, never condone something so wicked as selling children to procurers."

"It's a lucrative business by my understanding. And the cub lives high. Higher than my blunt would allow."

With a martial gleam in her eye, she tossed the clipping into the fire.

He sighed. "You can burn the words, Abigail, but you cannot burn out the stain. If this is true, if even a tenth of it is true, I will cut him dead. I swear it."

"Well, why on earth didn't you tax him with this while he was here just now? Let him speak up and defend himself. And if you were calling in the Runners, why not send them down to Crowdenscroft, so we could discover the truth."

The duke hung his head. "I was afraid. Afraid of what they might find. And petrified that if I asked Rockleigh, he wouldn't be able to defend himself, or worse yet, that he would admit it boldly. That would have killed me, Abby. It still might, just imagining it."

"Oh, bosh," she said, smoothing the hair back from his brow. "These village newspapers are always starting at shadows. Don't you remember when our little *Gazette* began hinting that Squire Welk was a French sympathizer all because his Austrian uncle came to stay? As if German and French sound anything alike."

"That was funny—this ain't. And I don't understand why you always have to take the boy's side of things. You've been spoiling him since he was born."

"It was difficult not to spoil him," she said softly. "He was so like you in every way. And I wasn't the only one who doted on him. When he was a boy, you used to take him about with you through the fields, laughing at every clever thing he said."

"Then what's happened? Have we ruined him, Abby?"

"I hope not. I pray that he's not really turned into a heartless care-for-none."

The duke rubbed at his chin. "I can't even mark when the change in him occurred. While he was at Eton, I suppose. I always thought he'd eventually come up against an older schoolmate who'd thrash a bit of that arrogance right out of him. But then, he was a head taller than the other boys. I daresay he was the one who did the thrashing."

"No, he's not belligerent, thank heaven, just disdainful."

"Maybe you're right," he said, "and this Kent business is all a hum. Lady Blythedale should have known better than to alarm us in such a way."

"You know," she said, "I've just been thinking. I'm not sure I want Torry to marry a girl whose mother is such a prying, sneaking, bloody-minded—"

"Hush, my love," said the duke. "Let's not begin fretting over Torrance. He's the only one who has never given us a shred of worry."

Rockleigh made a beeline for Stanley's rooms the instant he left his father's house. He hammered at the door and threatened to kick it down if Stanley did not open it. Finally the lock grated, and Stanley stood back as the black-haired whirlwind swept into his parlor.

"You!" Rockleigh raged. "You! Who have the gall to act affronted over *my* ungentlemanly behavior. While all the time it was you who had lost any sense of what it means to be a gentleman."

Stanley tipped his head back and studied the ceiling.

"Well?" Rockleigh cried.

"I am not speaking to you, or have you forgotten?"

"No, *I* am not speaking to you. What you did to me was despicable. Lower than despicable."

He headed for the door, but Stanley pushed it shut before he reached it, then turned to face him.

"I take that back," he said in a gravelly voice. "I will speak to you, Roc. But only to say that I am sorry—I assume you have just come from your father's house—but what I did was out of affection for you, with no malice at all. And I never mentioned any of the particulars to him."

"Do you know what they do to snitches in Eton? But you wouldn't know, would you? You never went there."

Stanley's eyes narrowed. "Don't throw your privileged credentials at me, Conniston. I know my own place in society. Still, as far as I can tell, I am a dashed better man than you."

"What's that supposed to mean?" Roc tugged at his neckcloth as if it were strangling him. "I never said I was the better man, only that I went to the better school. I . . . I don't understand any of this. It's as though the world's gone completely mad. You and I have never had words, not in twenty-odd years, and then to see both my parents hovering over me, as though I were at death's door. It scared ten years off my life."

"Good," said Stanley. "Then they did a proper job of it. And now I wish you would go . . . I promised myself I would keep away from you."

"Why on earth would you do that?"

"In case you're tainted," Stanley replied baldly. "I may not have your standing in the *ton,* but my family has a reputation just the same. And I don't want to see it sullied when you become a pa—pa—"

"Pariah? Is that the word your feeble brain is searching for? Confound it, Flemish, if you are going to turn on me, tell me it's for something more than because I manhandled that shrew."

"That *shrew* happens to have impressed me with her manner and her spirit. It took a lot of courage to face up to you as she did."

Rockleigh growled in frustration and cast around for something to throw. He pivoted to the fireplace—Stanley had all sorts of geegaws on the mantel. As he plucked up a glass candlestick, a stained piece of newspaper drifted out from under it. It settled on the hearth by his boots.

"Good God, Stanley," he said in a stricken voice as he knelt down to retrieve it. "Is this what all this dust-up is about? Tatlock's pernicious slander? Didn't you hear me deny everything to his daughter?"

"I heard you, right enough. Only you stopped short of telling her what was really going on down there. If you were innocent, I wager you'd be happy to make a clean breast of it."

"Then you'd wager wrong. I don't explain myself to little nobodies from Kent."

"And what about lifelong friends? Do they get the courtesy of an honest answer?"

Rockleigh shook his head slowly. "What sort of friend are you if you need to hear an explanation? A true friend would not judge me based on newspaper tittle-tattle."

"It's a damning piece, Roc. You have to admit that."

"And the truth behind it is so mundane that I am embarrassed to explain it. So now you know why I am suing that man—he's put me in an untenable position. If I tell the truth, I am made ridiculous. I would rather be thought a trafficker in human flesh, to use Tatlock's inflammatory expression, than become a joke in the *ton.*"

Stanley gazed at him for a time, his brows furled. It gave

him the appearance of a perplexed sparrow. "I never saw before now how much heed you pay to what others think. They believe you a care-for-none, but I suspect you care a great deal."

"I care enough not to be defamed or made light of. Just like any man."

"Don't you think the truth will come out if you have to testify in court?"

"I doubt it will get that far. I've discovered that Tatlock is running close to the wind financially. A few hefty lawyer's fees should put him right over the edge."

"And you would ruin a man with a family, just to keep your pride? It seems willful, even cruel."

Rockleigh nodded. "It does. But then life is harsh, *mon ami.* And harsher still when you make yourself a target for festering lawyers, which Tatlock has done. He took a gamble and lost, and now he will pay up." He retrieved his hat. "And so where will we spend the afternoon? I believe there's an auction at Tattersall's."

Stanley hesitated. "Look, Roc, I'm still not sure I want anything to do with you. It's not that Kent business. I do believe you would never get involved in something so havey-cavey. It's this libel suit that troubles me. Let it blow over. If the *ton* ain't picked up on that editorial by now, they never will. But if there's a trial, the London papers will get wind of it, and it will all get stirred up again. Just let it go, can't you?"

"No, I can't. Crowdenscroft belonged to my mother; it was her childhood home. That Tatlock fellow has sullied it, and unless I can get him to print a retraction, no one will ever believe there wasn't some truth behind his words. I owe it to my mother, if nothing else."

Roc breathed a silent prayer of relief that neither of his parents had learned of the blasted editorial. But then, how would they, sequestered as they were in the wilds of Devon?

"At any rate, since you won't come out with me, at least call on Miss Tatlock's brother. You are still my second, after all." He scribbled the address on the back of a haberdasher's bill.

Stanley traced a finger over the writing on the paper, and then looked up. "I suppose it's pointless to ask you to bow out of the duel."

Rockleigh's mouth twisted. "I don't intend to kill the boy,

Flemish. I am not that much of a monster. But he needs to learn that he can't go about London pummeling his betters on a whim."

Stanley called on the duke and duchess that same afternoon, and after an awkward twenty minutes—wherein Roc's name was never once mentioned—he made his excuses and left. He then found his way to the establishment of one Cornelius Gribbings. It was on a pleasant, tree-lined street in Chelsea, where a smattering of glass-fronted shops mingled with the narrow residences. Miss Tatlock, he discovered, was staying above Gribbings's print shop; there was a private entrance that led up one flight to her door.

She answered his knock on the third rap. When she recognized him, surprise, and then dismay, registered on her face.

"This is not a pleasant business," he said in acknowledgment of her frown. "But I did promise to second Lord Rockleigh. May I come in?"

"No," she said flatly. "My brother is not here any longer. He is visiting a friend. A school chum," she added by way of reminding him of the tender age of Conniston's intended victim.

"A chum, eh?" He added wistfully, "Lord Rockleigh and I were chums back in Devon. But we were rarely at school together, since he is my elder by three years."

"I would never guess that from his behavior. Thirty going on thirteen is more like it."

"He don't care for you overmuch, either," he said candidly. "Which suits me down to the ground. Now is there anything else, Mr. Flemish?"

"It is my responsibility to arrange matters for the duel, and since your brother ain't here, perhaps you could suggest a time for them to meet."

Her eyes snapped. "I would suggest never."

He chuckled. "I know I'm not supposed to tell you this, it being strictly against the rules of *duello,* but he doesn't intend to kill your brother."

"So I should rejoice at the possibility of a mere maiming?"

"Hardly that. Lord Rockleigh will most likely fire into the air."

Her eyes glittered. "In which case my brother might kill *him.* Toby is young, but he's got a good eye and steady hands. He's quite adept at shooting the pips from playing cards."

Stanley gaped at her, and then muttered, "Maybe Roc should shoot to wound."

"Maybe *Roc* should call off this ridiculous farce," she said hotly. "If he kills Toby, he'll gain no honor from pitting himself against a child, and if Toby wounds *him,* he'll look like a buffoon. If Toby kills him," she added with unladylike gusto, "there will no doubt be great rejoicing. So I don't see a positive outcome for your friend in any scenario."

"Has anyone ever told you you have an uncanny knack for twisting words around, Miss Tatlock? It leaves me in the dust. Pity Roc's not here; he likes that sort of thing."

"If Lord Rockleigh were here, I wouldn't even have opened my door. And now good day to you, sir."

"But we haven't set up the—"

The door slammed in his face, and Stanley was left on the landing with his dignity in shreds.

Mercy, meanwhile, leaned back against the oak panel and smiled. How rewarding it had been to see the expression of shock on Mr. Flemish's face when she'd mentioned Toby's prowess with a pistol. She was sure he'd tell his friend and hoped it would put a sizeable chink in Lord Rockleigh's armor of smug arrogance. Not that she had any intention of allowing her brother within two miles of the man. For all she knew, Toby, his own boasts notwithstanding, couldn't hit the wide side of a barn.

She returned to the carton of flyers she was sorting. Five piles, one for each of Mr. Gribbings's hired men. And one small pile for her. She was going to do the honors in Mayfair herself, right across the street from a certain small, but elegant, town house.

Chapter Four

Roc awoke without a pounding headache or a queasy stomach for the first time in months. He wondered what on earth was wrong with him.

Then he remembered.

He'd come home from Stanley's yesterday in such a funk that the notion of going out on the Town had repelled him. After an indifferent dinner—he'd forgotten that his cook had quit a week earlier and wondered, as he dined, exactly who was doing kitchen duty—he'd strolled aimlessly around his parlor. There was a spinet in one corner, but he hadn't played since he was a boy. He then moved on to the small library and perused his collection. Books were sometimes a decent antidote to boredom, but he felt too distracted tonight to read. He mulled over what other people did when forced to stay at home. He hadn't a clue, really.

It occurred to him, after a time, that his mother wrote letters in the evening—to everyone she had ever met, even down to the head gardener's daughter, who had taken a governess post in Ireland. Gargantuan piles of her correspondence would appear each morning at breakfast for his father to frank. She was a gregarious woman, his mother. The Benning side, as she'd said that morning.

We take matters more lightly.

He wondered if he'd been born without the Benning side. Torrance surely had a bounty of it. He rarely got himself in a stew over anything, the great looby. And Trent—well, Trent was in the middle as far as Benning traits went. He was mostly an easygoing fellow. But there were also times when Roc had seen him boil up and lose his composure, usually over a game of cards or sporting event. Trent competed to win, whereas Roc rarely competed at all. He never allowed himself to want anything so much that its loss might upset him.

How neat was it, he mused, that the perfect son for the dukedom was the heir and the perfect son for the army was the second-born? His parents had been fortunate in their first two offspring, each slotting effortlessly into his prescribed life like pegs in a cribbage board. He was the misfit, the peg that wouldn't slot. He wasn't even anywhere near the damned board.

With a hiss of distaste he went to the liquor tray. There were three decanters on it, all of them empty. Nice. He'd have to have a word with his butler. Then he recalled that the man had left his employ two weeks ago. James, the footman, had been doing the honors at the door. He lifted the brandy decanter and observed that there was a shallow layer of golden liquid at the bottom. He tipped it eagerly to his mouth, waiting, but nothing spilled out. The dregs had apparently solidified and glazed the bottom of the cut-glass container.

With a soft curse he set it back on the tray. There was wine in his cellar, he assumed, but he hadn't the energy to find the key and carry a candle down there into the gloom. It wasn't as though he really needed a drink. Instead, he'd sit at his writing desk and compose letters to his friends. Get in touch with his Benning side.

He sharpened the quill point, took a stack of creamy paper from the drawer and opened the lid of the ink pot. He reflected for several minutes. He could write to Bryce, but the man was on a prolonged honeymoon in Barbados and surely had more entertaining things to do than read letters. There was Aunt Bertha, his godmother, who had sent him a dreadful lion's-head stickpin for his birthday. He doubted he'd ever written to thank her. But the gift in question was now the property of his groom, and he didn't know how to convey his thanks without falling into hypocrisy.

It was pointless to write to any of his friends in London; he'd probably run into them in person before his missives arrived. It was clear he was not likely to run into Stanley, but you could hardly write to a man with whom you were no longer on speaking terms.

"You're a sorry old fellow," he muttered. "Torry always said you'd end up alone and miserable. And he said it when you

were seven." It had been one of the only times Torrance had
openly expressed his displeasure with Roc.

In desperation, he began a letter to his eldest brother.

> *Torry,* he wrote in his sloping backhand, *I was just now
> recollecting a time when we were boys . . . I wonder if you
> remember it? You'd just come in from riding and found me
> eating one of Cook's gooseberry tarts out by the spring
> house. You said you were famished and offered me half a
> crown for a piece. When I refused, you told me I could be
> the next duke if I'd share. I still refused and said who
> wants to be a boring old duke anyway? I regret that now.
> Not passing on the offered dukedom, mind, but not sharing
> with you. You called me a selfish wretch and predicted I
> would end up alone and miserable. I wonder if you might
> have been right.*
>
> *Mama and His Grace are in London, as you doubtless
> know, and I understand from them that you are to wed
> Jessica Blythedale. I want to wish you happy, but also to
> point out, as the brother who never does what is expected
> of him, that I am not the only one with that freedom. If you
> are being pressed into this marriage (and I am not sure
> why I should suspect this, but I do), you will find that it is
> quite easy to say no to people, once you have gotten the
> knack of it.*
>
> *Anyway, I wish you well with your crops and irrigation
> and such, and if you decide to act on my brotherly advice,
> consider it repayment for the gooseberry tart.*

He signed it with a flourish and felt an immediate sense of
accomplishment. He'd never written a letter to Torrance in his
life. Trent got the occasional humorous message from him, but
that was because he was living in daily peril and needed bol-
stering. Roc was not quite blind to his fraternal obligations, in
spite of what some prosy people might think.

He sealed the letter, propped it on the inkwell, and then
looked about for something else to occupy him. He wondered
if James played chess. Or even checkers. No, he couldn't intrude on James's free time. The man had enough duties to keep
a regiment busy.

He knew there was a dog-eared pack of playing cards in his desk drawer, but somehow the notion of sitting in his dressing gown playing solitaire was so depressing that he didn't even consider it.

"I am a man of culture and refinement," he said aloud to reassure himself.

Yes, a hollow voice answered from somewhere deep inside him, *a man of culture and refinement with absolutely nothing to do with his life.*

That startled him. It was as though the voice had spoken up right there in the room.

He chose not to pay it any heed. Furthermore, the voice was wrong—he had plenty to do with his life. One night of solitary misery didn't predicate the rest of his existence. Even though he'd written that in Torry's letter, he didn't really believe it.

It was nearly four o'clock when he awoke in his chair by the hearth. It appeared he'd finally found something to pass the time—sleep. What an extraordinary notion.

He was grinning to himself as he made his way upstairs in the dark.

And that explained why he was now wide awake at seven o'clock of a crisp May morning and feeling strangely fit. After James assisted him to dress, Roc sent the footman to order his hack from the mews in the next street.

It was a glorious morning, he thought, as he crossed into Hyde Park, breezy and clear, the sun above him bracketed by pale, wispy clouds, like a glittering topaz set on gauze. His mare was inclined to frisk, swishing her tail like the coquette she was, and champing hard on the bit to let him know she wanted a good run. Since he virtually had the park to himself, he finally gave her her head. They blazed down Rotten Row, heedless of the unwritten rule against galloping. When he pulled up, it was with a shout of pure pleasure. This was a proper way to begin the day. He reined the mare about and did it again, this time causing a few nursemaids to goggle.

His heart was racing now. He could practically feel the blood surging through his veins. When was the last time he'd ridden at anything but a sedate, restrained pace? Not since his last visit to the Bower, he'd wager.

There washed over him then a sudden longing to be back

home in Devon. It was a heart-tugging sensation the likes of which he'd never before experienced. Even as a child, he'd understood that the Bower would not be his permanent home, that he should not let himself grow attached to it. So why was he positively yearning to visit the old pile again?

Writing to Torry last night must have shaken something loose inside him. Or perhaps it was seeing his parents yesterday that had stirred him into homesickness. Whatever the cause, he reminded himself that Devon was not for him, that London was his home now.

He shook off his odd, wistful mood and proceeded through the park at a slow trot. Songbirds caroled in the trees, while honeybees drifted among the spring flowers that grew in profusion along the Serpentine.

Morning, he decided, as he turned the mare back toward Mayfair, was not something to be lightly dismissed. Oh, the night owned him, right enough, but there was a great deal to be said for all this dew-drenched brightness, all these intoxicating scents and intriguing sounds. It was akin to discovering a rich new world, one that had been right there all along.

He trotted down North Audley and turned in toward his square. A few vendors were about on the streets, and when he reached the square, he saw a young woman walking beside the wrought-iron fence that surrounded the garden. He touched the brim of his hat to her as he approached, in charity with all the world, even badly dressed maypoles who were hanging handbills on the fence.

He pulled up his horse the instant he recognized her and leapt down from the saddle, landing practically at her feet.

"Miss Tatlock?" His deep voice was a whisper away from a snarl.

"L-lord Rockleigh?" Mercy stuttered as he stepped even closer.

Her first instinct was flight. She squelched that cowardly notion. But dash it all, he wasn't supposed to be out here—he should still be sleeping. Town beaus never arose before ten. It was practically a law of nature.

"I didn't expect to see you here." She was losing all her color, even as she spoke.

"I *live* here. As if you didn't know." He peered over her shoulder. "And what is that behind you, pray?"

She shifted in front of the fluttering sheet of paper, attempting to block his view with her body. This was pointless, since there were a half dozen of them tied along the railing. He merely moved down the pavement until he came to one that was not obscured.

The drawing was an apt likeness, he had to admit, even in caricature. His windswept hair, his long knife blade of a nose, the wide mouth and the lean cheeks had all been skillfully rendered by the artist's pen. However, the man in the drawing was dressed in the exaggerated clothing of a dandy, a garish ensemble that would have seen the top of the rubbish heap before Roc ever considered wearing it.

"Look to a bumpkin to confuse a man of fashion with a coxcomb," he growled to himself.

The dandy had a wine bottle raised to his lips, while he capered above several diminutive people, among them a man clutching a quill pen in his hand and another holding a newspaper behind his back. Most telling was the fallen figure of Lady Justice lying below the dandy's left boot, her scales askew, her gown agape.

The drawing bore the legend, "Lord Rakeleigh Care-for-None Ravishes Justice."

He turned slowly to Mercy, who was standing stock-still before the iron fence.

"This is *not* a good likeness of me," he said in a clipped, even tone. "For one thing, I never drink directly from the bottle." He conveniently overlooked last night, when he'd tried to guzzle brandy dregs from a decanter.

"I wasn't aiming for verisimilitude," she managed to get out.

"No," he said, moved back to her. "You were aiming for provocation. But you won't have the pleasure of witnessing my anger, Miss Tatlock. I refuse to play."

Then he hooked her by the arm and walked her along the fence, while he calmly ripped down each flyer with a sharp, final snap. When he was finished, he started across the street toward his house, still holding her arm.

"Let go of me!" she cried, dragging her heels on the cobblestones.

"Hush! Do you want to alert the whole neighborhood?" He increased the pressure on her arm.

She twisted in his grip, but she might have been a gnat for all the heed he paid. "What in blazes are you doing?" she growled as they reached his front steps. "I am going to scream for the constable."

He stopped and looked down at her, his mouth twisted assessingly. "No, I don't think you will. I have a mind to do some horse trading with you. It would be in your best interests to hear me out."

"That's as may be. But I have my reputation to think of." She huffed audibly as he thumped her up the first three steps.

"Ha! That's a rare one coming from a woman who pursued me into a gentlemen's coffeehouse. And what of *my* reputation, ma'am?" he added with a grunt as he hauled her up another step. "I entertain a respectable woman, and my name gets crossed right out of the Rogue's Register." She did not acknowledge his attempt at humor, choosing instead to assume a fierce glower. "I think we should both risk our reputations," he added as he deposited her on the landing.

"I don't seem to have much choice." She looked down at his fingers, still encircling her wrist.

"We always have a choice, Miss Tatlock." He released her, pushed the door open and stood waiting.

Mercy weighed her options. He seemed more playful than ominous this morning, in spite of her attempt to rile him with ridicule. There was a curl of incipient laughter lingering around the corners of his mouth. Or perhaps it was merely the beginning of a digestive complaint.

He made a small noise of impatience. She shrugged one shoulder and stepped across the threshold. As he followed her through the door, his footman came hurrying along the hall, fiddling with the buttons of his livery. He looked up at his master sheepishly as he managed the last of them. "Sorry, sir. I took the jacket off while I was polishing the silver."

"James?" Rockleigh said, staring at the man. "You're not James . . . I mean you're the James who's been tending me this past week, but you're not the same James who's worked here for years."

The footman shook his head. "That was my cousin. He left your employ a month ago, and your butler hired me in his place."

Rockleigh assimilated this startling information, then motioned to the street. "Go catch my mare before she demolishes Lady Tewksbury's irises."

James nodded. "Will you and the young lady require tea when I get back?"

Rockleigh looked down at Miss Tatlock, who had finally recovered her color.

She shook her head. "No, I really don't think—"

"Yes," he interjected neatly. "That will do nicely."

As the door closed behind the footman, Mercy turned on Rockleigh, hands fisted at her waist. "Why does it not surprise me that you don't even recognize your own servants? They aren't people to you, are they?"

"People?" he asked absently, as he threw the handful of crumpled flyers down on the console table. "I daresay I've never given it a thought. Now—" He turned and came toward her. "There's something I've been itching to do."

She forced herself not to wilt back like some fainthearted heroine from a ten-penny novel. This was difficult, since he was leering at her in an odiously assessing manner, just as he'd done in the coffeehouse.

He paused and smiled wolfishly. "You don't need to get swoony, ma'am. I am merely going to relieve you of this hideous bonnet."

She gave a sharp cry of protest as his fingers fumbled with the knot beneath her chin. He plucked the offending article from her head and cast it into a nearby coal scuttle.

"That's my only bonnet," she wailed softly, watching it settle beneath a puff of black dust.

"Lord, I hope so . . . there ought to be laws against such things. If I am going to be always running into you, I insist that you wear something less depressing on your head."

"I think you must be mad," she declared. "To be worrying about trivialities like fashion when there is so much else at stake."

He winced painfully. "Fashion is never trivial, Miss Tatlock. Sometimes, as in your case, it can be tragic. But trivial? Never."

Before she could respond to this carelessly drawled pronouncement, he had thrown open the parlor door. He held out one hand. "In here, if you please."

She skirted him cautiously as she entered the room. He sauntered past her and lounged back on the sofa, his arms outspread along the cushions on either side of him. "I wager I gave you quite a fright out there in the street," he observed with a gleeful expression. "It was delicious. In fact, I can't recall the last time I've felt so good."

"Perhaps it was when you kicked a hungry dog or chased off a beggar."

"Mmm, perhaps. But this is today's victory, and it feels very sweet."

"I can just imagine." She paused, then added peevishly, "You took every one of my flyers, you know. And that drawing cost me very dear."

"Then you'll learn not to waste your money in future, ma'am. I know what you're about, by the by. You're trying to embarrass me into dropping the lawsuit. And it won't work. I wonder if it's occurred to you that you might have merely added another log to the fire. You practically came right out and named me this time."

"There you are wrong. Caricature is not considered libelous. I checked."

"A pity your father was not so prudent."

"My father knows a great deal about the courts. He studied law at Oxford, for your information. Well, for the first two years. But then writing essays took hold of him."

He smirked. "And the rest, as they say, is history. But tell me one thing, Miss Tatlock . . . I have been chewing this over since I met you. Why didn't your father come to me himself? Surely a man of his education would be a better advocate for his case than a stripling girl."

"I am nearly four and twenty," she declared.

"A stripling young woman, then. And I wish you would sit down. I am getting a crick in my neck from looking up at you. You're deucedly tall."

"I prefer to stand."

He jumped to his feet and thrust a finger at the chair behind her. "Sit!"

Mercy complied instantly, nearly falling backward, his tone was so peremptory. Goodness, she'd forgotten how intimidating he could be. She had an inkling he could also be very charming on demand, which was possibly even more dangerous. The last thing she needed was to be charmed by a reptile.

Though she would never let him guess it, he was already creeping past her defenses.

He thought he had frightened her out there in the square, but it was much worse than that. He had, in fact, dazzled her.

Before she recognized him, before she realized it was her enemy approaching, she'd been gazing at him, lost in admiration. It was rare in Tiptree to see a man of such masculine beauty riding along the high street. Even here in London, she'd seen few who could compare to Lord Rockleigh Conniston on horseback.

Of course, earlier in the week she had seen him from a distance and had certainly noted his elegant carriage and remarkable height. The first time she'd gotten close to him, in the coffeehouse, the gloom had prevented her from making any accurate assessments of his person. At the Orpheum, she'd been more concerned about not making a fool of herself than in noting his physical attractions.

But the man who'd ridden toward her down the cobbled street had been a vision of bold, nearly mythic proportions, broad shouldered and lean hipped, his black hair sparked to blue by the bright sunlight, his face lit with some inner flame. And it was such a compelling face, high boned and lightly tanned, with a bit of deviltry in the curve of the mouth.

These things she'd noticed before he leapt from his horse. Then, as he stood there virtually toe to toe with her, she'd looked into his eyes and felt her breath catch. She'd never seen him this close in daylight, or she would have been prepared for the shock of his eyes. They were a rare crystalline blue-green, with slivers of gold dappling each iris, like tiny molten fishes playing in the aquamarine. Against his tanned complexion, they'd stood out in startling contrast.

No, she hadn't been frightened by him; spellbound would be more accurate. She had been held immobile by that Mediterranean gaze and by the wicked smile that had curled his lips. That primal response, of feeling instantly in thrall to a man for so shallow a reason as the color of his eyes or the shape of his mouth, had unsettled her.

It was also a dismal excuse for letting him manhandle her across the street and up his steps with only the tamest show of protest on her part. She couldn't lie to herself, either, and pretend she hadn't been thrilled by the contact, by his sheer masculine power.

Even now, as he lounged half across the room from her, she could feel the power of his presence tugging at her. She'd never reacted that way to any man. The sensation was foreign to a woman who made levelheaded objectivity her watchword.

Lord Rockleigh coughed slightly. "Your father, Miss Tatlock?"

"Sorry, I was wool-gathering." She struggled to collect her thoughts. "It's just that I couldn't help noticing . . . you have the most remarkable eyes."

Great heavens, did I just say that out loud?

He shrugged. "I can't take credit for them; they're my father's eyes. And speaking of fathers . . ."

"Yes, of course. You were asking why my father didn't seek you out himself. He has other concerns at the present."

"What is of more concern than a ruinous lawsuit?"

"Family issues." Well, that was the truth. Her whole family was gathering up everything of value in their home to go under the auctioneer's hammer, while her father was furiously petitioning his relations for money to support his defense.

He eyed her speculatively. "My guess is he doesn't know you're here."

Her chin thrust out. "No, he does not. But I will be his advocate with or without his blessing."

"So, you have deceived this paragon of a parent, Miss Tatlock, I am impressed."

She squirmed a little. "It seemed my only course. I wouldn't have done it had the situation not been extreme." Her gaze locked on his face. "See what you have brought me to with your lawsuit? Lying to my father after twenty-three years of upright behavior."

He seemed to consider this notion for a time. "You'd best be careful, ma'am. In my experience, lying quickly becomes habitual, as one untruth begets a thousand. And," he added smoothly, "some habits are the very devil to break."

Mercy spared a moment to wonder that this self-indulgent profligate had *any* experience with breaking bad habits.

"And where does your father think you are at this moment?"

"Visiting his sister in Brighton. She's the widow of a

wealthy baronet. Aunt Clarissa's never approved of Papa's odd starts, as she calls them. But she fancies me, against all reason."

His pale eyes lit up, but he said nothing.

"I told Papa that if I asked her nicely, I might be able to convince my aunt to lend us a small sum. To help with his legal fees, you see."

"So he is in financial straits, then?"

Mercy realized she'd just made a huge tactical error. "I . . . that is, he . . ."

"I knew this already," he interjected softly. "I could not know, however, that his devoted daughter would come winging to London in his defense. And now, having met you, Miss Tatlock, I am amazed to discover you resorting to falsehoods."

"Sometimes, sir, the end justifies the means."

"Ah, the Great Rationalization. I, on the other hand, never resort to rationalization to explain my actions. If I had a motto, it would be something like, 'Never complain, never explain.' I daresay I ought to have it translated into Latin to impress the young ladies at Almack's."

"I doubt young ladies need Latin mottos to find you impressive, sir."

He started back melodramatically. "What? Two compliments in five minutes? Miss Tatlock, I believe London is mellowing you."

Mercy quickly regrouped. "That didn't come out exactly right. I meant that I doubted the young ladies would even understand Latin."

"It won't wash, though it was a masterful effort. And since turnabout is fair play, I will pay you a compliment."

"Ah, no. That is not necessary." She knew she was blushing; her color deepened when he rose from the sofa and approached her.

"Lift your head, if you please," he said, sketching the air with one hand.

She refused, which merely gave him an excuse to tip her head back with his forefinger. "There, now, the morning sun does you great justice. Your hair is a lovely color, rather like tarnished gold."

"Gold doesn't tarnish."

"Hush. Your skin is quite fine, also. You provincial ladies

have it all over the London belles in that department. And your eyes—" He crouched down before her and observed her intently. "Blue . . . no, not quite. Here, turn your head a little. Ah," he said with a sigh, "violet."

He reached out again and, to her alarm, stroked his forefinger over each eyelid in turn.

"Stop that," she hissed, pushing up from her chair. "I will not be pawed by a libertine."

He rose to face her. "I was only trying to bridge the chasm between us, Miss Tatlock, in my own way. You are quite green if you think I have seduction in mind."

"Perhaps I am green. I haven't the inclination to become worldly, thank you. But I am canny enough to know when a rogue is toying with me for his own amusement. Now please, let us get down to our business. Unlike you, I have things to accomplish today."

"Very well. What I have to offer you is something of a barter arrangement."

She sank back into her chair and folded her hands. "I'm listening."

He moved off a few paces. "First off, regarding this duel with your brother—in light of his tender years, perhaps a good thrashing would serve better than a bloodletting."

"You want my father to thrash him? Let me tell you, Father has never once raised a hand to—"

"*I* will do the thrashing," he said serenely. "A simple bout of fisticuffs, perhaps even in Jackson's parlor. That ought to awe the sprat—I might even get in the first blow this time."

Mercy felt an instant rush of relief. Whatever happened now, Toby would be spared.

He leaned toward her from the waist. "Well? You could thank me. I am thinking myself very magnanimous at this moment, especially since your brother was at fault."

"His attack wasn't exactly unprovoked," she pointed out. "I believe you called him a . . . a festering boil on the backside of humanity."

Rockleigh looked nonplussed for a moment, and then a sharp laugh erupted from inside him. And then another. He laughed harder than he had in weeks. What a treat to hear his pithy phrase issuing from the lips of this prickly, starchy young woman.

"Sorry," he said, pressing his knuckles against his mouth to keep from starting up again. "It just got away from me for a minute." He peered down at her. "Don't you ever laugh, Miss Tatlock?"

"Of course I do. Most often when I am not the butt of—"

Rockleigh could not restrain another spurt of laughter.

"Oh, bother . . ." Mercy muttered.

James came in with the tea tray at that moment, and she breathed a little prayer of thanks. Lord Rockleigh's face was devastating when he laughed. All the tightly controlled planes and angles relaxed, and his sneering haughtiness evaporated. He'd appeared younger and, were it possible, even more attractive.

She quickly thrust away this thought and turned to examine the tea tray on the table beside her. James, it appeared, had been extravagant—there were jam buns, cinnamon swirls and spice squares.

"Will you pour, ma'am?" Rockleigh inquired as he pulled a chair closer to their repast and seated himself. "Oh, and James, could you trot off to the shops? I need you to purchase a bonnet."

The footman looked as though his master had asked him to wrestle a wild boar.

"Come now, it's not that difficult," Rockleigh coaxed. "Cream colored or pale yellow. With feathers, perhaps, or a bit of lace. Something lively and pretty."

James fidgeted. "Really, sir, I don't think—"

"I hope this is not on my account, Lord Rockleigh," Mercy said quickly. "Accepting a bonnet from you is out of the question."

He disregarded her. "Just use your own judgment, James. And so you'll know what *not* to buy, take a look in that coal scuttle you left in the hall."

Once James had gone, he turned back to her and smiled amiably. Then his face fell. "Where's my tea, Miss Tatlock?"

"I've a mind to pour it in your lap," she muttered. "But I do try to vary my thrusts."

"Are you angry again? I thought we were reaching an accord."

She looked at him straight on and folded her arms over her chest. "I see this still hasn't filtered into your brain. I am not here in London to take tea or to buy new hats. This is not a pleasure trip. You are the opposition, the man who is seeking to destroy my father. Yet here you sit, trying to be an amusing, engaging host. It's very . . . very distracting."

He spread his hands, palms out. "I'm only trying to keep things civilized. I know I behaved badly"—his face tightened for an instant—"very badly in the coffeehouse. M'best friend is no longer speaking to me over it, if that's any consolation."

Her brows rose at his words, and she felt a smattering of sympathy for him. "Regardless of that, there can be no truce between us, if that is what you're hinting at."

"Even in Parliament, the opposing sides take tea together."

She mulled this over for a bit, then sighed. "Very well."

Rockleigh watched as she poured them each a cup, and then cocked her head over the pastry tray. "Spice cake," he said at once. "And . . . a jam bun."

She forked them onto a plate and passed it to him.

Her hands were not dainty, he noticed, which was in keeping with her unusual height. But they were graceful and elegant, even if there was an ink smudge on her index finger. He'd sat for tea opposite most of the reigning beauties in the *ton*, listening to their mindless prattle, wishing he was a million miles away. Taking tea with Miss Tatlock, on the other hand, made him feet strangely pleased to be right where he was.

Prickly or not, he decided, she was a very companionable woman. Not to mention, she'd made him laugh. Maybe she had stirred up some of that latent Benning blood.

They sipped their tea in silence, though she looked up at him a few times over the rim of her cup. Once she reached out, out of sisterly habit, he was sure, and nearly brushed a stray cake crumb off his chin before he had a chance to raise his napkin. She caught herself in time and quickly diverted her hand to her lap.

But it was too late. The thought of those slim fingers touching his face had set off a clamoring inside him. He had a sudden, unaccountable desire to kiss her. To take that mouth that was so inclined to serious frowns and melt it into sensuous curves. He'd have to go carefully if he followed that inclination; she was not skilled in flirtation or any of the amorous arts. Still, the idea appealed to him. Seducing the daughter of your

sworn enemy was the ultimate challenge, after all. And, when
achieved, the ultimate victory.

She must have sensed the change in him, that he was not
quite the genial host any longer. Her cup chinked down onto its
saucer and she said briskly, "I think we should get on with the
negotiating now."

He crossed his long legs and reclined against the arm of his
chair. "Ah, back to the Parliamentary debate. It was a nice truce
while it lasted."

"We are not debating, Lord Rockleigh. If we were, I would
challenge you to defend your position and tell me what is really
going on in Crowdenscroft."

"But since I won't, there can be no debate."

Her mouth drew up on one side. "You know, that really puz-
zles me. You could end this right here, right now. You obviously aren't suing my father for financial gain, so I am
confounded by your refusal to clear things up."

"Maybe I just enjoy having you dog my footsteps."

She nearly snorted, and then drawled, "Yes, I'd overlooked
that possibility."

"You might be surprised," he purred, which evoked a sigh of
impatience from her.

No, she wasn't going to make this easy for him. And that
made him even more determined to pursue her.

"Now, here are my terms of barter," he said, hitching his
chair even closer to hers, so that their elbows were nearly
touching. "I agree not to shoot a hole in your brother, and in return I want your father to recant. Not only in *The Trumpet,* but
in every newspaper in Kent."

"He won't recant."

"Well, I won't relent."

"Then there's nothing more to be said."

"Stalemate, Miss Tatlock?"

"No, not at all," she said, her fingers gripping the arm of her
chair. "This is just the open declaration of war."

"I might be the last person you want to go to war with,
ma'am. I never stick to the rules. Now, once again I will say
it—you must convince him to print a retraction."

"Impossible," she said. "He won't do it."

"Then it is on his own head. I have tried to be reasonable, for the sake of, shall we say, your violet eyes."

"Don't cozen me, sir. I may be callow but I'm not a fool. And now I suppose you still intend to face Toby over pistols."

He was silent for a time, weighing the need to seek satisfaction with his desire to make a conquest of her. She'd hardly come to his bed if he put a bullet in her brother.

"No," he said at last with a profound sigh. "I've no wish to have a child's death on my conscience."

"Conscience? Ha!" she said, glaring at him openly.

He faced that glare, parrying it with a smile of bemused tolerance. He knew the power of that smile to cajole or to coerce, so he was aware of it the instant she began to weaken. Her expression softened and her hands relaxed in her lap.

They did not speak for a time, but sat looking at each other intently. If not for the heat of their previous discourse, an observer might imagine them to be in accord, so steadfast was each gaze upon the other.

When James came in bearing a floral bandbox, they both immediately looked down.

The footman thrust the box at Rockleigh with a stormy expression. "Next time," he muttered, "I'm giving notice. I swear it, sir." Then he stalked from the room.

Rockleigh set the box on the sofa and slipped off the lid. "Mmm, let's see what we have here."

Mercy turned away. There was nothing of interest to her in that box. Even if Rockleigh Conniston was making little chirps of admiration as he removed the last sheet of tissue, she would not look.

"I have to give James a raise," he pronounced softly. "I'd no idea he had such a good eye." His voice rose a notch. "Well, aren't you even a little bit curious? I know you are a woman of purpose and principle, Miss Tatlock of the Severe Frown, but I think this confection might just appeal to the frivolous side of your nature."

When she didn't move, he added, "Consider it an apology for the way I behaved on Tuesday."

She shifted on her chair. "I certainly cannot leave here without a bonnet. So I will accept it, but only on one condition— that you allow me to pay for it."

He saw the milliner's bill jutting out of the box and quickly tucked it beneath the bottom layer of tissue. "I imagine two guineas should cover it."

Mercy thought that an exorbitant price—in Tiptree, the best milliner charged half that for her creations. She dug the money out of her reticule and crossed over to hand it to him, praying she hadn't just bought a pig in a poke.

She snatched the bonnet out of the box and tugged it down over her coronet of braids without even glancing at it. The satin ribbons were wide, a deep lavender hue. She tied them carelessly under her chin.

"Don't you have a mother, child?" He had taken hold of her arm and now propelled her to the mirror over the fireplace. "Because I've never met a female yet who didn't learn at her mama's knee how to make a pretty bow."

He positioned her directly in front of him, then reached around her to tweak at the knotted mess she'd made. She shut her eyes and tried not to think of those hands beneath her chin or of his body so close behind her. She swore she could feel his heat.

"There," he said. "Open your eyes and behold Madame Stella's handiwork."

"It's just a bonnet," she complained as she opened them. "Just an ordinary, everyday—" Her voiced stopped dead.

"Close your mouth, sweetheart," he whispered, leaning his chin on her shoulder for an instant. "It's ruining the effect."

If this was just a bonnet, she thought as she gazed raptly at her reflection, then the royal barge was a rowboat. It wasn't that the hat was extravagant or overpowering, quite the opposite. It was tasteful, elegant and sublime—a simple inverted dish of fine, biscuit-colored straw with a brim that flared up in the front, where it was adorned with a wafting border of egret feathers in cream and lavender.

It made her look like a duchess . . . or the most exclusive of courtesans.

"This never cost two guineas," she murmured with a frown.

" 'Pon my honor, that's the customary cost."

She looked at his reflection in the mirror, still close behind her own. He was tall enough, broad enough, to make her feel almost delicate. "And how would you know what a lady's bonnet costs?"

He smiled at her slowly, meeting her eyes in the glass. "Oh, it's something I gleaned in my wicked past."

He was holding her gaze now, and, once again, she felt unable to look away. It was as though they were on opposite sides of a window, looking both in and out at each other, not sure of who stood where. Long, potent seconds passed. The air in the room seemed to thicken, and then vibrate.

Mercy knew he felt it too. His teasing smile had faded away, to be replaced by an expression of curious wonder. She saw her own eyes widen and her mouth go a little slack. His breathing grew uneven, while her own increased perceptibly.

When his hands settled lightly onto her shoulders, she didn't even flinch. Not taking his eyes from the mirror, with studied slowness he drew her back until she was nearly against his chest. She felt herself tense then, felt panic scuttle over her spine.

"Sssshh," he whispered, easing her with his hands, running them slowly along her upper arms.

Still watching her intently in the silvered glass, he lowered his head, letting his chin caress the side of her throat. The feel of his slight stubble rasping on her tender skin was shocking, and then strangely stirring.

"*No . . .*" She gave a tiny moan of protest and tried to pull away.

His fingers held her there as he soothed her, murmuring reassurances into her ear. "Sssshh . . . easy. Be easy now."

Those sibilant words were making her whole body tremble. And still he watched her, eyes blazing with an unholy blue-green light. She groaned when he finally pulled her tight against him, saw her own head fall back in surrender, and then the mirror ceased to exist.

His strong fingers curled harder into her shoulders now, letting her feel his strength in deliberate increments. His lips never strayed to her skin; he seemed satisfied with nuzzling her throat with his chin and his cheek, but she found herself praying that he would take her mouth.

He was whispering to her, words she didn't understand or hadn't the wit to comprehend, but they were a honeyflow on her flesh.

"Do you have a name, Miss Tatlock?" he murmured against her ear.

"Mercy," she nearly moaned.

"Mercy, indeed," he echoed hoarsely. She felt him shaking slightly, whether in silent laughter or frustrated desire, she was too unschooled to tell.

"Mercy, Mercy, Mercy," he crooned as his fingers relaxed their grip and slid down to her wrists. He drew her arms behind her so that their entwined hands were trapped between their bodies. Aching for the pressure of his fingers on her shoulders, missing the sensation of being held against his broad, warm chest, she unwittingly arched her body into him.

His indrawn hiss stirred the stray tendrils of hair that drifted beside the lavender bow and made her shiver down to her boot tips.

She was preparing to overlook the urgent proddings of her conscience and allow him full access to any part of her body he desired, when the mantel clock chimed ten. Directly into her left ear. And into his, as well, since his chin was now resting on her shoulder.

"Damn," he muttered as she pulled free of him and darted away.

She halted six feet away, bosom rising in agitation, eyes glassy and wide.

"I must go," she said in a strangled voice. Avoiding his face—which appeared to her suddenly fragile—she began to cast about for her reticule.

"Don't," he said. "I didn't mean . . ."

She stopped her frantic search and spun to him. "Didn't mean what? To touch me? I think you did."

"I didn't mean for you to panic like this."

Her eyes flashed in annoyance. "Do I look like I'm panicked?"

His mouth twisted. "Yes, you do, rather. And your reticule is there by the tea tray."

She fumbled for it, feeling like a complete joke. She might have done better all these years, she thought sourly, to have spent some of her time encouraging the local beaus instead of squandering all her energy on *The Trumpet*. Then she might have a clue of how she was supposed to behave in such an awkward situation.

"You see how green I am?" she cried breathlessly. "I don't know the proper way to do this. To . . . disengage and not make myself ridiculous."

"There is no proper way," he said with a gentleness she didn't think he possessed. "And you are not ridiculous."

It was to be appreciated that he was trying to make it easy for her. And that he was remaining across the room, so she wouldn't be tempted to throw herself back into his arms.

She lifted the bandbox off the sofa, clutching it to her chest like a pasteboard shield. "I truly must be going." When he took a step toward her, she shot him a look of entreaty. "No, please. I can see myself out. I am not that befuddled."

"I am," he said under his breath. It felt as though he'd been struck by a falling building. He really had to get a grip on himself, stop behaving like a schoolboy with his first crush. There was nothing about her so special or so rare that he should be feeling this intoxication, this need to scramble over the furniture and have at her again.

Steady on, he cautioned himself.

She stopped at the door and faced him with one hand on the latch, a wavery smile playing over her mouth. "Thank you for making this . . . situation easier for me. And for finally settling things, which I now assume must be the case. I can't say I'm not relieved."

He was about to ask her what in blazes she was talking about, when she added, "My father will be overjoyed . . . that he can return to his work without your lawsuit hanging over his head."

Rockleigh put his chin up and said with great deliberation, "It is not settled, Miss Tatlock. I'm not sure what was said here to make you think it so, but—"

Her face pinched into a frown. "Not what was said, what was done. I don't understand. You . . . held me . . . and caressed me. You couldn't have done that if you were not feeling some charity toward me. Surely you don't still intend to ruin my father."

His head moved slowly back and forth. "One has nothing to do with the other."

"Well, they should!" she cried.

His black brows rose sardonically as he inquired, "Were you intending to bribe me with your body, Miss Tatlock? Pretty payment, but far less than I'd demand for withdrawing my complaint."

She let go of the latch and took a firm step toward him, her expression livid. "I was starting to believe you had some decency, some humanity. That you were not a depraved, heartless scoundrel. I am more than green, it appears, to have thought that. I am completely witless."

"You're only a trifle naive," he said gruffly. "You'll get over it soon enough."

"I believe I just did," she flung back.

He hitched one shoulder. "Then meeting me has done you some good."

Mercy made an inarticulate sound of rage. "You're right, Lord Rockleigh. This isn't over yet. Now *I* have a score to settle with you, as well."

She slipped through the door and closed it behind her. He was congratulating himself on having escaped her fury relatively unscathed, when there was a loud, resounding thud in the front hall.

She was gone by the time he reached the hallway. And a good thing, too, or he'd have torn her limb from limb. The coal scuttle now lay on its side, just beneath the blackened wall she had heaved it against. Bits of coal were strewn everywhere— over the creamy marble tiles and the Persian runner. The gritty black dust had settled on every polished surface. Her ruined brown bonnet was canted over the bronze bust of Charles II on the console table.

Rockleigh sank down onto the stairs, staring at the shambles around him, not knowing whether to laugh or to weep. Instead, he muttered one sibilant word—"Mercy."

Chapter Five

She was getting tired of walking off her pique at Rockleigh Conniston; this was the second time in five days. If she ever got back home to Tiptree, she'd be a wraith from all this endless walking and fuming. She couldn't recall the last time she'd let her temper get away from her like that. Still, hurling that half-filled coal scuttle against the wall had been incredibly satisfying. The only problem, she now realized, was that Lord High-and-Mighty Conniston wouldn't be the one to clean up after her. No, that chore would fall to James.

Still berating herself over her misguided revenge, she skirted the corner of Hyde Park and made her way along Oxford Street, hoping to distract herself in the noisy bustle of shoppers and vendors. But when she caught her reflection in the window of a yarn shop and saw the delicious bonnet *that man* had given her perched jauntily on her head, she gave an audible moan of dismay. If it hadn't been the most fetching thing she'd ever seen, she'd have thrown it under the wheels of a passing carriage.

Did he seriously think she was a lightskirt, to be accepting presents from him? Oh, she'd paid her two guineas as requested, depleting her purse to do so, but she might as well have given him tuppence. She knew the hat—crafted by the exclusive Madame Stella—cost worlds more than that. To prove this, she pried off the lid of the bandbox and sure enough, there was Madame's bill. After she'd read it, Mercy fell back against the wall of a tobacconist's shop and moaned again. Fifteen guineas! Sweet Mary in heaven. She doubted her entire wardrobe in Tiptree had cost that sum.

Why would he spend so much on a woman who had declared herself his enemy? And what had he been after from her with his teasing and touching, with his easy banter and his shattering caresses?

Nothing, the wise voice in her head replied. Nothing at all. He was amusing himself, passing the time. Furthermore, to a man of his wealth, spending fifteen guineas on a hat was akin to her buying a packet of cracked corn to feed the wild birds.

She eventually settled on a bench in St. James's Park, nibbling on a pasty she'd purchased in the street, hoping that the food might still the churning in her stomach. She focused her attention on the brightly colored waterfowl that inhabited the small lake. Once her anger at Lord Rockleigh subsided a bit, she began to experience another equally strong emotion—shame.

How could she have stood there and let him . . . well, do whatever it was he'd done to her? Not that he'd kissed her or even touched her in any inappropriate ways. He'd merely held her arms, drawn her against him, and drifted his face along her throat. It wasn't precisely decorous behavior, but not the height of scandal either. She fancied couples waltzing in a ballroom might experience a similar level of intimacy without shame. But shame was what she felt.

She feared every stray passersby could discern her fall from grace. It seemed inconceivable that, having been so stirred and tantalized on the inside, she showed no tangible evidence of these things on the outside.

What on the blessed earth had she been thinking? Hanging the posters herself had been her first mistake. Not fleeing from him when he appeared was her second. Going into his house had not been a mistake; it had been a catastrophe.

Knowing she'd suddenly found herself attracted to him should have made her doubly cautious. Instead she had blithely walked into his home and placed herself in his power—although when she'd finally broken away from him, he'd looked so fragile that she sensed for an instant that she was the one with the power.

Was that possible? she wondered. Could a seasoned rake become unbalanced by a woman who'd never even been kissed? It seemed unlikely.

She sat there on her bench, chin on hand, and pondered this. There was a give and take to most human commerce—no one always had the upper hand. Could the dance between the sexes be any different? Men were more usually the pursuers, but that didn't mean that women had no say in the hunt itself. In fact, the prey had nearly as much power as the predator. But only when they knew they were being chased.

Was Lord Rockleigh chasing her? Her heart began to beat an erratic tempo at that notion. Had her quarry turned the tables on her and begun his own campaign of pursuit? Certainly no man before him had ever flirted with her or looked at her with desire in his eyes, not that she'd ever noticed. And she was very observant.

Rockleigh had not only looked at her with sizzling desire—he'd made good on it. And in a manner that still sent occasional shivers tingling along her spine. The man definitely knew what he was about—unhurried, languid, never threatening or demanding. No, he had coaxed and soothed her into responding, and although she was certain his caresses had been lightly given, they had awakened in her something dark and exciting. Passion, she knew now. He had roused her to passion.

Mercy judged herself to be a passionate woman, but her compelling drive to write, to set her thoughts down on paper, was a cool, inert thing compared to the flare of physical heat that had engulfed her when Rockleigh Conniston touched her. She couldn't imagine how she'd react if he ever did anything more intimate. Cosmic fireballs hurtling through the night sky came to mind.

And what of his reaction to her? At first he'd been no more than casually flirtatious. It wasn't long after their eyes met in the mirror, though, that she'd felt something change in him. He'd become—she couldn't exactly get her thoughts around it—urgent, maybe. But urgent only explained the physical part. It was as though something was driving him to draw her closer, not to his body but to what was inside him. There had been need there, as well as desire. And for all that she was a naive pea goose, she believed she knew the difference between the two.

He'd been quite shaken when she pulled free from him—to the point that there was open entreaty in his eyes. Recalling that look now, she felt a budding tenderness toward him. It was gratifying to watch a cautious, well-defended man lower his guard and open himself to a woman. She might be as green as apples in May, but instinct told her that a man could seduce any number of women without once lowering his guard. Rockleigh had given her that gift, whether he knew it or not.

Of course none of this meant he was going to pursue her. Men of his ilk had their choice of beautiful, accomplished women. Lord Rockleigh would never consider her a worthwhile conquest. Not that she wanted to be, she quickly reminded herself. Returning home to Tiptree a fallen woman was not part of her general plan.

Still, there was an undeniable connection between them. All morning she'd seen amusement glinting in his eyes, as though fencing with her entertained him. She didn't mind that; it was exactly the way she felt about him. Somehow, in a span of days, they had become almost amiable opponents.

Her father had such a friend in Tiptree, a banker who was his political and philosophical opposite. They often played chess or fished together. He'd told her once, when she'd asked how he could tolerate such a conservative fellow, that the heat of their discussions added spice to their friendship.

Spice was a very good word to use in conjunction with Rockleigh Conniston.

And then there were those fleeting glimpses of goodness she'd seen in him: his bemused reaction to his footman's aversion to a lady's hatbox, his decision to reduce Toby's punishment to an afternoon of gentlemanly sport. These were hardly qualifications for sainthood, but they displayed some measure of decency.

Still, it ultimately came back to the libel suit, which made moot all her conjecturing on the man. Lord Rockleigh was not an amiable opponent, but an enemy who had vowed to destroy her father. She was no advocate of star-crossed lovers, had no patience with the romantic woes of Romeo and Juliet. Her loyalty could only be to her father and his newspaper. Anything that subverted that loyalty had to be set aside.

She rose from the bench and set off determinedly across the park. Jack's great-aunt lived on the other side, and Mercy decided that a visit to Toby would cheer her. The last time she'd been there, he'd entertained her with tales of Astley's Amphitheater and multiple sightings of the Regent. Toby was having a splendid time in London, which was more than she could say for herself. Furthermore, he would be in high alt when she told him that the duel had been reduced to a bout of fisticuffs in Gentleman Jackson's saloon.

At least one of the Tatlocks, she reflected with a grin, was going to get a legitimate shot at taking down that insufferable man.

It never occurred to her until later that in all her weighing of Rockleigh Conniston's character, she hadn't once factored in his nefarious business in Crowden.

Stanley had not ventured out on the town for four nights running. He feared he couldn't maintain his injured air in Roc's company, and since forgiving his friend was not yet an option, he stayed indoors and occupied himself with reading his collection of travel diaries.

When there was a knock on his door at half past nine, Stanley roused himself from his wing chair beside the window and answered it with a scowl. He'd been scaling the foothills of the Himalayas and was in no mood to give up his trek.

"I've missed you, old fellow," Doncaster said as he sauntered into the room. "You and Conniston, both. Town's woefully short of company." Upon finally noticing Stanley's unwelcoming expression, he merely grinned. "I was in the neighborhood and thought I'd look in on you. I'm still seconding that cub from Kent, the one with the fetching sister, and thought you might have worked out another date for the duel."

"I spoke to Miss Tatlock several days ago. She was not cooperative, and the boy seems to have disappeared."

Doncaster's broad face darkened. "But Conniston hasn't withdrawn the challenge?"

Stanley shook his head.

"Good. I'd like to see if your friend really has the stomach to shoot an infant."

He shifted over to Stanley's drinks tray and examined several bottles before he poured himself a large brandy. Stanley slumped back into his chair, trying not to grumble at the man's gall. "Help yourself to a drink," he drawled airily, waving his hand. "Make yourself at home."

"Thanks, don't mind if I do." Doncaster eased his large frame into the chair opposite Stanley's—the one Roc normally sat in—and brushed a spattering of droplets from the shoulders of his coat. "It's turned into a wretched night out there."

Stanley twitched the edge of the drapery aside with the toe of his slipper. The rain was really no more than a wet, soupy fog.

Doncaster nodded toward the window. "Not much doing out there . . . everyone's running for cover."

Yes, Stanley muttered to himself, *you've made your point. Now what the bleeding hell do you want with me?*

But Doncaster stayed mum, sipping at his brandy and glancing about the small parlor in open curiosity. The man had never been here before. Stanley was sure of that. He didn't make a habit of inviting lurkers into his home.

While Doncaster might have been a gentleman once upon a time, he was currently a mere hanger-on where the *ton* was concerned. Whether it was drunkenness or debauchery or just plain unpleasantness of character that had caught up with him, he had several years ago been ousted from the select homes of Society. His membership in Bacchus predated his fall from favor, and the current owner seemed disinclined to banish him, especially since he managed to lure some of the wealthier members to the club each night with his discreet offerings of opium and other exotic intoxicants. These were not exactly gifts to the titled, however. Doncaster made sure that payment was tendered in gold and well before each client drifted under.

He was proof positive that a man could see his reputation unravel at the same time he watched his purse grow fat. This unsettling notion immediately reminded Stanley of Roc's situation. If that blasted article had any truth in it, then his friend's position in the *ton* would be forfeit. But, by the same token, if trafficking in children was as profitable as one heard, he probably wouldn't care.

It pained Stanley to look upon his loathsome guest and see a shadow of Roc's future.

"I'm not surprised Conniston's avoiding Bacchus," Doncaster remarked as he toyed with the rim of his glass. "Word has it the Duke and Duchess of Barrisford have come to town. Got him by the short hairs by now, no doubt."

"Lord Rockleigh ain't still in leading strings, in case you haven't noticed."

"Yes, but I find it intriguing that the only time his parents leave Devon is when he's gotten himself embroiled in some scandal. Last time I recall it was that business of his fathering a bastard on an admiral's wife."

"That was all a hum," Stanley said staunchly. "Lord Rockleigh was off shooting in Scotland when the lady in question, er, well, you know . . . got with child."

"So what is it this time? What's he done to bring the Barrisfords out of the wilderness?"

Stanley tweaked the brocaded lapels of his dressing gown and made a noncommittal noise. He wished Doncaster would go away. Having him here was akin to entertaining a large, biting insect. He even looked buglike, with his round face, slick, shiny black hair and bright black eyes. Stanley pictured him with two twitching antennae jutting from beneath the fringe of his Brutus, but the image did not serve to amuse him.

"Won't open your budget, eh?" his guest prodded.

"I wouldn't presume to guess why his parents are here." He shifted in his chair so that he could look directly at Doncaster. "I wager you know more of Rockleigh's less savory pastimes than I do. Perhaps I should be asking *you* what he's been up to."

He was rewarded when Doncaster's fingers clenched on his glass. But then the man shrugged and said smoothly, "You're bound to know more than I do, Flemish. I see him around, but you follow him around."

If Stanley was a growling sort of man, he'd have growled just then. No wonder nobody received the fellow.

Doncaster got up to refill his glass at that point and, after he'd done so, he took a walking tour of Stanley's parlor. "This is a cozy little setup you have here."

He bent to examine a painting above the disordered desk, moved on to the bookcase, and then to the mantelpiece, where he admired a pair of Dresden shepherdesses. "I could find you a buyer for these," he said as he took one of them down off the marble shelf. "Got a fellow who pays top dollar for these German pieces."

Stanley nearly shouted at him to put it down. They had been a gift from his grandmother, and he didn't want the Bugman touching them. He breathed a sigh of relief when Doncaster slid the statuette back in place.

But then Doncaster called out, "Ho, what have we here?" as he removed the editorial from under the glass candlestick.

"Put that back," Stanley ordered in a voice not quite his own. "That's none of your concern, Doncaster."

"Looks interesting." He was scanning it even as Stanley came after him and tried to wrestle it away. Doncaster held him off in the manner of a schoolyard bully, using only one hand and a deal of muscle.

Finally he lowered his hand and offered the clipping back to Stanley. "Don't know why you're making such a fuss, Flemish. Anyone can see it's just a lot of trumped-up rubbish. I gather Rockleigh's the man the writer is referring to." He snuck another look at the clipping. "The *Tiptree Trumpet,* eh? Gad, those country papers must be devilish hard up for stories."

"I think you'd better go," Stanley said with a scowl, rubbing at his chest where Doncaster had gotten hold of him.

"Yes, I'll take my leave now. They'll be looking for me at Bacchus."

"I'm sure they will," he said sourly.

"Don't forget about the duel," Doncaster said over his shoulder as he went out into the hallway. "Let me know when Conniston's going to blow a hole in the Kentish cub."

"Bloodthirsty, bloodsucking bug," Stanley intoned once the man was out of earshot.

He hadn't mistaken the gleam in Doncaster's eye when he'd pounced on the clipping. Stanley felt like an idiot for leaving it out in the open.

He wondered if there was any risk to Rockleigh now that Doncaster knew the contents of that libelous bit of newsprint. Probably not. A great many other people had read the thing. It wasn't exactly a state secret. Not to mention, Doncaster had no reason to wish harm to one of his better customers.

Then it occurred to Stanley that perhaps Doncaster was looking to stir up trouble precisely because Roc had stopped being a customer.

"Good for you, Rocky," he said softly, praying that was the case.

*   *   *

Unfortunately for Stanley's prayers, at that moment Rockleigh Conniston was sitting in the card room at Bacchus, impatiently awaiting Doncaster's arrival.

He'd had a miserable day after Mercy Tatlock walked out. It had taken James nearly two hours to clean up the front hall—Roc had himself been compelled to assist him in the end. Then just before supper, James had scalded his arm with a pot of boiling water, and, since the footman was the only house servant left, Roc had found himself not only playing nursemaid, but cook and bottlewasher, as well. James had insisted he could return to work, but Rockleigh had sent him off to his room with orders to rest.

At which point Roc confirmed several things about himself—he could not cook, he was an indifferent washer, and he knew more curses than a sergeant-major. Since supper was a nonstarter, he decided to go to White's for some decent food.

There he ran into his father, who, if he didn't exactly offer him the cut direct, came very close. Roc opted then for Watier's, expecting to meet up with his old friend Clipper Donegan. The doorman told him Mr. Donegan had been called away to Whitehall on a matter of urgent military business.

He'd ended up dining alone with only his thoughts for company. And they were not pleasant companions.

He really believed he'd started to bring Miss Tatlock around that morning. She'd obviously come to the same erroneous conclusion about him. It just went to prove that when he was civil to people, it confused the dickens out of them.

It was some consolation that he'd confiscated her flyers. A number of high sticklers lived on his street, the sort who wouldn't hesitate to go running to his father with the handbills flapping in their . . . well, hands. There were others in the neighborhood who would like nothing more than to see him made ridiculous.

He renewed his vow to increase the pressure on her father. Tomorrow was Sunday, but first thing Monday morning he would visit his solicitor and discover if there wasn't any way to hasten the proceedings. Gad, the courts moved slower than canal barges and were nearly as unwieldy. The English legal system dearly needed a firm kick in the bottom. He took to wondering, over his iced raspberry compote, why that blasted reformer Tatlock wasted his time attacking David, when there was a hulking Goliath like the law to take potshots at.

Of his stirring interlude with Mercy Tatlock he thought very little. It was a trick he had, of being able to put something irksome out of his head. Every time his discipline slipped and he'd start to recall the feel of her under his hands or the soft, utterly beguiling sounds she'd made, he would swiftly shut his mind to them. Just as he'd been able to do with Stanley—pretend he didn't exist. No sense fretting over one prickly friend when there were dozens of amiable fellows about.

He'd been performing that particular trick for years, he saw, not letting himself mourn the loss of the Bower, not letting Torry, or even Trent, know how much he missed the old times with them.

They had been a loose-knit pack back then, but being so close in age, they'd naturally fallen into doing things together—Torrance eternally patient, Trent boldly adventurous and Roc full of studied caution. If they went fishing, Torry was the one who sat for hours in the same place, while Trent splashed noisily up and down the stream. Roc would watch the mayflies flitting above the surface until one of them disappeared, and then cast his lure in that exact spot. He always came home with the most fish.

Their dissimilarities had not been a problem when they were boys. It was only when Torry came of age that the rift began. Roc, at fourteen, couldn't understand how his brother, who was basically a plodder, had suddenly become a person of consequence and a source of such pride to their parents. Then Trent had gone off to begin his military schooling and there was also much made of him whenever he was at home.

Looking back now, Roc could see that he'd been right to feel left out of things. He had been. His mother continued to dote on him and coddle him, but that hadn't been what he'd needed. She loved him, but seemed unable somehow to recognize his own special qualities. His father, whom he had idolized, no longer had time for his youngest son, being too preoccupied with training the fledgling duke in the mysterious ways of crops and livestock, not to mention courtly protocol and county politics.

Rockleigh had an urge to write another letter to Torrance, to ask him what it was really like to be the heir, knowing that your future was neatly laid out for you, like toy soldiers on a mock battlefield. It seemed to him now that there might be comfort in such an arrangement.

Not that he needed comforting, mind. He could find that at any time in the arms of women, or in the company of his friends. Or in the blissful forgetfulness of—

No, he cautioned himself. He wasn't going to think about Doncaster's opium. His mother had pleaded with him to seek out the lighter things, and opium was dark. Deliciously, hypnotically dark.

He pushed back his chair with a soft curse. It had been a hellish day, and he'd do well to return home and go to bed. Maybe he'd rise at dawn and take that headstrong mare into the park again.

In the foyer, he passed a group of young gentlemen he knew slightly. One of them, Havelock he thought it was, glanced at him as he went by and then leaned down and whispered something to his companion. Both men laughed softly.

Roc did an about-face and tapped Havelock on the shoulder. "If I'm to be a source of amusement, I'd prefer to be in on the joke."

Havelock was the toadying sort who would normally preen if Rockleigh deigned to recognize him. Now he stood before him with a broad smirk on his face. "Don't you know, Conniston? Haven't you seen them?"

A tiny blip of fear began to pulsate in Rockleigh's heart. He decided to bluff.

"Oh, that." He sketched his hand in the air. "A trifling inconvenience."

"Well, you're taking it better than I would," another of them remarked. "Especially if my pater was here in town to rip up at me for embarrassing him."

Rockleigh shrugged and moved on. He was nearly to the door when he heard Havelock's voice rise up from the group. "Rakeleigh Care-for-None . . . it fits him like a glove."

He shook off his fear. There was nothing to be alarmed about. Miss Tatlock had told him he'd taken all her flyers. She had a number of vexatious faults, but he doubted that blatant falsehood was among them.

He saw the first handbill as he rounded the corner onto

Berkeley Street. It had been posted at eye level next to an advertisement for stomach powder. The second was hung on a bent lamppost. The third, fourth and fifth were plastered across the doorway of a boarded-up butcher shop. The sixth one he nearly missed—at the corner of Mount Street a hack driver sat waiting for a fare in the nippy night air, a blanket draped over his steaming horse. Some prankster, maybe even the driver himself, had tacked one of the handbills to the side of the blanket, near the horse's tail.

"It doesn't matter," he kept repeating to himself as he hurried away from the hackney. "They're harmless drawings. If caricatures were worth getting agitated over, Prinny would have suffered six apoplexies by now."

It wasn't the handbills themselves that bothered him, however, so much as their venue. While it was one thing to have one's likeness lampooned in *The Times* or showcased on a cartoon in the window of an upper-class bookseller, it was quite another to have it displayed in the commonest of places. Miss Lies-Through-Her-Teeth Tatlock had said that caricature wasn't a libelous act, but surely there had to be some law against posting a gentleman's likeness on a horse's ass.

He stopped counting when he reached thirty. They seemed to be everywhere. He didn't know if they'd been there earlier; he'd been pretty much walking with his chin on his chest. But they were here now, and he couldn't do anything about them, not at this hour of the night. In the morning he'd send James out with a bucket of whitewash to obliterate them. For the present, he'd forget them, just put them out of his thoughts.

A light, mizzling rain had begun to fall; he shrugged up the collar of his greatcoat and kept walking, trying to shake off his anger at Mercy Tatlock—and regretting the fact that he hadn't kissed her properly when he'd had the chance. If he ever got that close to her again, kissing would be the farthest thing from his mind.

He halted at one point to let a group of gentlemen go past him on the sidewalk, and when he looked up, he saw that he was standing in front of Bacchus. Its baroque facade beckoned to him, the lit windows spilling warmth and the promise of comfort down onto the rain-damp street below.

"No," he muttered. "No."

He leaned back against a nearby lamppost and closed his eyes. He was beyond weary from trying to outrun himself. "The Benning side," he intoned. "It's in you somewhere." But there wasn't any lightness in him now, just anger and frustration and a fresh, cutting humiliation. And there was the surcease of all of those things just beyond the etched brass doors of Bacchus.

Something crinkled behind his head. He knew what it was before he even turned around. Another of the handbills. He ripped it down furiously, raking at the pasted bits with his fingernails.

"Damn her," he cried. And louder, "Damn her!"

His greatcoat was already half off when he bounded up the stairs and pushed through the brass doors. He tossed it to the porter and barked, "Doncaster?"

"Not in yet, sir. Although he's expected."

Fine. He would play cards; he would demolish a bottle of claret; he would look for Troy or Vincent or anyone who could distract him until Doncaster arrived.

The play was deep at the faro table, which suited him perfectly. He gambled recklessly and won again and again. And still there was no Doncaster. After an hour, he scraped up his winnings, threw a coin to the pot boy, and said his good nights. The pounding inside his head had grown intolerable. The burning need inside his belly was making him ill, and his mouth was dry as Bengali cotton, in spite of all the wine he'd consumed.

He'd go home to bed as was his original intention. And devil take Doncaster and his seductive poison, that made a man a slave to his own needs.

He swept out the front door and nearly collided with Doncaster on the steps.

"Ho, watch your step, Conniston," he said with a wink. "Last fellow that careened into you out here has to face you over pistols."

"I'd never shoot you, Donnie," he replied with a tight smile. "I wouldn't deprive the world of all your goodness."

Doncaster chortled. "Where're you headed?"

"Home." He went down another two steps.

"Aw, you don't want to go there." He patted the pocket of his waistcoat. "I've got something rare tonight, Conniston. I brought it especially for you."

"Not interested."

Doncaster followed him down to the pavement. "No need for you to sample it in there."

"No need to sample it at all," Roc retorted.

"What's come over you, man? I missed seeing you last night."

"Missed my gold, you mean."

"That too, I won't lie." He draped an arm over Rockleigh's shoulder. "But I'll tell you what . . . I'll let you have this round for free, on me, seeing that you're such a decent sort. I suspect you could use a little distraction tonight. It's a pity that some wag's put up those posters of you all about the town. I went out to use the privy at the Four Bells, and there was one plastered right on the door. Can you imagine?"

Roc groaned softly.

"Now come inside, there's a good fellow. It's plaguey damp out here."

The beauty of it was, there could be a hundred vivid dreams in the space of five minutes or one languid dream that lasted for hours. It was never the same twice. But tonight the dream was strangely skewed, neither vivid nor languid. Doncaster was in it, annoying him with some endless questions about a house out in the country.

"Th' house is for th' boys . . ." Roc mumbled hoarsely. "But iss s-sposed to be a secret. Now go away . . ."

"In a minute, my friend. Tell me about the boys—where do they come from?"

"Everywhere. But nobody wants those boys . . . nobody."

"What happens to them, those nobody boys?"

"We take 'em in, clean 'em up, train 'em to be skillful . . ." Roc grinned up from the midst of his stupor. "But they've got to have . . . good hands . . . must have clever hands."

"And then what?"

"We . . . we find men who want 'em. Men who . . . are pleased to have 'em."

"Lovely," Doncaster murmured. "Bloody lovely." He laid one hand on Roc's head, as if delivering a benediction, and smiled. It was not a heartening smile. "Sleep now, Lord Care-for-None, sleep and dream. You're far blacker than I ever gave you credit for."

Rockleigh's next dream was more satisfying.

Mercy Tatlock was his prisoner in a Turkish harem—one that bore a distinct resemblance to the foyer in his father's town house. She was dressed in a gauzy silk gown that flowed around her, offering flashes of long white legs and supple, rounded arms. She was also wearing the bonnet he'd bought her, which didn't seem at all out of keeping. Lounging back on a cushion on the marble floor, he watched as she took off the delectable hat and undid the braids from around her head. He felt his body tighten as she slid her fingers through the plaits; he sighed deeply as the mass of tarnished gold waves cascaded down, nearly to her waist.

Then she danced for him, swaying in time to an invisible flute player. He watched her body move, slow and sinuous, beneath the sheer material of the gown. Her breasts were hidden by the golden coils of her hair, but as she turned and spun, he caught tantalizing glimpses of her snowy flesh in the candlelight.

The dance brought her closer and closer to where he reclined on the floor. When he finally reached for her, catching her by one braceleted arm, she melted down against him, baring her throat for his kisses. But he wanted her mouth—more than anything he wanted her mouth.

When he tasted her at last, it was like touching velvet for the first time, smooth and soft and unutterably rich. She moaned into his mouth, and he deepened his kiss.

"I'll give you anything," she murmured.

"Anything?" he crooned.

"Yes." She drew back from him, and he could see the spark of heat in her violet eyes. "Especially this—" She'd plucked a long quill pen from her robe and now thrust its deadly tip deep, deep into his chest.

He cried out loudly, clutching at his middle, writhing, twisting in agony.

"God, no! No-o-o!"

Chapter Six

"**R**oc! Rockleigh!"

Someone—he thought it might be Stanley—was shaking him forcefully by the shoulders. He stirred slightly and moaned.

"He's never been like this before," the Stanley voice hissed. "Oh Lord, sir, look at his eyes."

"Let's get him up on his feet," someone else growled softly. He knew *that* voice. *Christ Jesus, it was his father!*

He was hefted onto his feet and dragged along between the two men, forced to walk when all he craved was to lay his head down and seek oblivion. His eyes were open, but he wasn't able to focus on anything, although he could just make out a huddle of men on one side of a long, dark corridor.

"Fetch me some mustard in milk," the duke called out to one of them. "Now!"

Next thing Roc knew, a foul potion was being forced down his throat. He sputtered and fought back. "Swallow it, damn you," his father muttered. "You're too wicked to die."

He managed to gasp out, "I might be too stupid to live."

"That's as may be," the duke said in an easier voice. "And still giving sauce to your old father."

A scant half minute later, Roc was heaving up his guts into a basin. He gagged until he was nearly faint from exhaustion. "Just let me sleep," he moaned.

"Not a chance." The duke lifted him back onto his feet, and they made him walk again, up and down the endless corridor.

Before long he was managing most of the paddling on his own. "He'll do now," Barrisford pronounced.

"Thank God," said the Stanley voice, who was in fact Stanley. "I'll kill that Doncaster when I see him. I swear it, Your Grace."

"I believe that privilege is mine," uttered the duke. "I not only outrank you, Flemish. I believe I can still outshoot you."

Roc twisted away from them both and staggered back a few feet, his hands gripping his head. "What the devil did Doncaster give me?" he groaned as he found a convenient wall to lean against. "Well, whatever it was, he's mine to hunt down. Mine alone." His pale face was awash with deadly intent.

"Still the bantam cock, eh?" Barrisford drawled to Rockleigh.

"Doncaster's up to s-something." He sagged against the wall, trying to stay upright. "He kept asking about the house in Crowden. I . . . I can't recall how much I told him."

"I've a mind to ask you the same thing, boy."

He grimaced. "So you've seen Tatlock's mischief, eh? B'lieve me, it's not what you think. It's . . . it's not what anyone thinks. Damn those Tatlocks for engineering this wretched mess. I could strangle them all . . . one by one."

Barrisford laid a hand on his son's shoulder. "Later. Now I think we'd best take you home."

He snapped his fingers and someone came running with Roc's coat and hat. His father and Stanley bundled him into them, after which they helped him up a narrow flight of stairs into an ornate hall. They were still at Bacchus, Roc noted with surprise. That endless corridor they'd walked him along must have been the two-lane skittles alley in the club's basement.

The duke's Town carriage was drawn up at the curb. He and Stanley settled Roc inside, then began arguing on the pavement. Roc pushed his face against the padding and listened.

"I'll look after him," Stanley was insisting.

"His mother would be best for that job."

"Surely you don't want Her Grace to see him like this? It will break her heart."

While the duke disputed this point, Rockleigh slid across the seat and slipped out the other side of the carriage. The two men were still at it as he wobbled across the rain-slick street and disappeared into the darkness.

There was going to be hell to pay, but he was in no mood

right now for lectures or browbeatings or expressions of disgust. He only wanted a bed. His bed.

It sounded like a heavenly choir singing faintly in the distance. He lay there listening, inert but curious; almost certainly the sound was coming closer. He wondered if he'd died during the night, but then was reassured—if he'd shuffled off this mortal coil, heavenly choirs would definitely *not* be on the program.

Roc opened one eye. The embroidered hangings around his bed were the first thing he saw. James, sitting on a footstool beside him, was the second. "I was worried," James said. "You were . . . not very well last night. It was different from the other times. I thought I'd better keep watch."

"Thank you," Roc said, tentatively testing the use of his four limbs beneath the covers. They still seemed to be attached to his body and susceptible to his brain's commands. "I'm feeling a little better now." He then added, "You're a good fellow, James. I promise I'll never again ask you to buy bonnets."

The footman smiled. "May I ask a favor of you, sir? My name isn't James—it's Walter. Named for my father and proud of it."

"It's a Barrisford tradition," Roc explained, trying to sit up without groaning. The pain in his head—a sharp, constricting clench—was nicely balanced by the aching muscles of his stomach. This was a morning-after like none he'd ever endured. "My family call all their head footmen James. But since I am become a recent advocate of breaking old habits, Walter it shall be."

The footman touched his forelock. "I'll see about getting you some breakfast, if you think you can handle it."

Rockleigh prodded his tender stomach with the flat of his hand. "Maybe toast and tea. Oh, and how are the burns on your arm?"

"They are already healing. You did a good job of it, sir."

After Walter left, Roc lay back against his pillows and listened again to the singing. It was a hymn, one he'd never heard before—not that he was particularly well versed in liturgical music, having avoided the inside of a church since he left Cambridge.

The song had a nice lilt to it.

"He breaks the power of canceled sin... he sets the pris'ner free..."

There was a church on the other side of the square, but he'd never known the voices of the congregation to carry over the park before. It must have something to do with the direction of the wind.

Walter came up with his breakfast, and then, at Roc's insistence, helped him to dress. There was no chance he was going to stay in today and give every gossip in the *ton* proof positive that he had been cowed by those infernal posters.

"His Grace came by earlier with Mr. Flemish," Walter said. "They wouldn't leave until I let them see for themselves that you were properly sleeping it off." He hesitated, twisting the shaving towel he held. After a probing frown from his master, he continued. "His Grace said you needn't bother contacting him until you can tell him the truth about Crowden. He seemed... very much not himself. I mean that he would say something like that to a servant."

"How could he be himself, Walter? Poor man had to save his son's life last night."

"You, sir?" The footman's face had gone pale. "I had no idea."

Roc nodded, and then smiled as he adjusted his neckcloth. "You see me resurrected, don't you? You hear the heavenly choir?"

Walter cocked his head. "Yes, I do. It's much louder here in the front of the house. It sounds almost as if they're standing on the front steps."

A bolt of awareness struck Rockleigh, and his mouth fell open. He brushed past the footman with a muttered apology and hurried down the stairs to the front hall, using the wall for support—he was still not steady on his feet. Flinging the front door open, he stepped out onto the marble steps.

They weren't on the steps, which was small consolation, since they were gathered at the foot of them. Ten or twelve men and women, and one burly giant whom Roc could have sworn he'd bet on during a mill in Withershins.

Their sweet singing never paused as he came gingerly down the steps.

"Oh, who is this gigantic foe, that proudly stalks along.
Overlooks the crowd below, in brazen armor strong . . ."

"Who is responsible for this?" he called out. *As if he didn't know.* "You can't do this . . . it's against the law."

They just kept singing.

"Can my God his wrath forebear?
Me, the chief of sinners, spare?"

"Stop this now," he entreated as he went from singer to singer. He didn't have it in him to shout. "Please . . ."

Already his neighbors had begun to emerge from their homes. Lady Tewksbury, queen of the irises, and Lord Halifax and his rotund wife were now standing on their front steps gawking at the choir. Even ancient Sir Wendell had hobbled out into his garden. He saw Rockleigh and waved. "Very nice," he mouthed.

"Shall I call a constable, sir?" Walter asked from the open doorway as his master returned to the house.

"No," Rockleigh murmured absently—he was now scanning the fenced-in square and the pavement surrounding it for the tallish figure of a woman; he was sure she was hiding here somewhere, enjoying her latest spectacle. But aside from his goggling neighbors, the square seemed deserted.

"I could threaten them with a broom," Walter offered half-heartedly.

"Just let them sing. It might be good for someone's soul."

He went into the house, snatched up his coat and hat, and then, with determined fury blazing in his eyes, he went tottering off along the sidewalk in search of a hack. The refrain of the current hymn echoed in his ears.

"Depth of mercy, can there be . . . mercy still reserved for me?"

Cornelius Gribbings was seated in Mercy's parlor, sharing her Sunday luncheon and helping her cook up new ways to torment Rockleigh Conniston, when the door flew open and the victim in question came striding into the room.

"I would have knocked," he said through his teeth as he

winged his hat onto a side chair, "but that would have given you the opportunity to keep me out. And I will not be kept out, Miss Tatlock. I dashed well will not."

Mercy stood at once, an expression of shock on her face. Rockleigh Conniston looked like a walking wraith—his face drawn and pale, his eyes haunted, like a man who had seen all seven circles of hell. He'd seemed stalwart enough when he exploded into the room, but now that he was closer, she saw that he was trembling visibly.

Gribbings had also risen from the table. "Please, sir. This behavior is not seemly."

"Bugger seemly," Rockleigh snarled.

Gribbings reeled back, his hands fisted, and then he caught Mercy's swiftly repressed look of amusement. He turned to her. "Are you encouraging this black-haired devil?"

She shook her head and muttered, "Sorry. But I've never heard anyone use that expression so aptly."

"I've only just begun, Miss Tatlock," Rockleigh pronounced. "Still warming to my subject, in fact."

Gribbings bristled. "You'll mind your tongue while I'm here, you rascal."

Roc raised one elegant brow. "Then, sir, I suggest you leave."

Mercy quickly took Mr. Gribbings by the arm. "Perhaps you should wait outside for a bit. This might get sticky."

"Then I should stay here. He looks like he's going to throttle you."

"Oh, no," Rockleigh said, moving forward until he loomed over both of them. "I am far past throttling. Maiming and dismembering is more like it."

"He's just being his usual odious self," she whispered to the old man. "It's nothing but a lot of bluster."

She all but dragged Gribbings to the door and prodded him out onto the landing. "If you hear screaming, call the constable. Not until."

Rockleigh's face appeared over her shoulder. "If you do hear screaming, it might just be me. She has that effect on people."

Gribbings watched as Mercy turned to the black-haired devil and raised her face to him until their gazes locked. Lord Rockleigh's eyes challenged her, bright, anticipatory, almost fevered. Her own eyes met that challenge, fearless and openly defiant.

Even an old man like Cornelius Gribbings could recognize what it was that sparked between them. No one was *that* old. He took himself off down the stairs.

Mercy shut the door but made no effort to move away from Rockleigh. "What's wrong with you? You look at your last prayers. I'm surprised you're even standing upright."

"Among other things, I'm feeling distinctly frustrated." He propped his right shoulder against the doorframe to steady himself and sighed deeply. "You're not a bit afraid of me, are you?"

She shook her head. "Not in the way you want me to be. Not intimidated or cowed." When she spoke again, her voice was softer than a blush. "There are other things you stir inside me."

"Don't start with your bafflements, Mercy Tatlock. I had a very bad night. I nearly died." He peered at her intently. "I hope you're happy."

"How could I be happy at such a thing?"

"I thought you'd be pleased to see me in this state. After all, in a roundabout way, you put me here. You see, I did something rash last night because I was angry, and yes, humiliated, by your multitude of handbills."

"Only a hundred."

"Plus your thirteen choir members. Sir Wendell down the row was actually enjoying the performance."

"But you didn't. Enjoy them, I mean."

"You'd like me to admit that . . . let you know you scored another point off me."

"It's not about scoring points, Rockleigh," Goodness, she liked the sound of his name on her tongue. "It's about seeking justice."

She watched him wince, saw his whole face pinch up for an instant. "Sorry. You are not up to this today. The way you flew in here, I was sure we'd get down to a nice heated brangle."

"I'll brangle tomorrow," he said as he pushed away from the door. "Today I have other business with you."

His left arm caught her about her waist, locking her against his hip. His eyes, which had been half focused a moment ago, now bored down into hers, snapping with heat. "I decided last night that I had two choices . . . I could either kill you or kiss you into submission. Now that I'm here, there's no longer any choice."

He tugged her right off her feet and took her mouth—with such complete hunger, she thought dazedly, that he might as well have taken her bones and skin and every little corpuscle.

Her arms had somehow risen to encircle his neck, and, as he raked his mouth over hers, tasting her, drawing on her, she was soon hanging on to him just to keep upright. The desire that had first fanned yesterday in his parlor, which she had never quite banished, now flooded through her, savaging her insides and making her head reel.

As first kisses went, it was outstanding. But it was the ones that came in rapid sequence after it that made her truly understand his frightening power over women.

His lips were at times harshly demanding and at others soft, pliant and gently questing. Their changeability was maddening. She applied herself energetically to the tasting and savoring of his mouth, and was rewarded when he tugged her even tighter against him. She felt the hardened planes of his chest and thighs press into her own soft curves, reshaping them to fit flush against him. She shivered as an exquisite ache of longing ripped through her.

His breathing grew even more ragged as he clenched his fingers in her hair, scattering pins willy-nilly, as a section of her loose chignon came tumbling down.

"I dreamed you murdered me last night," he panted hoarsely, his hand tugging on that fallen lock. "That wasn't a patch on what you're doing to me now." He then clasped her head roughly between his two hands, angling her lips to better fit his mouth.

In the middle of this long, breath-stealing kiss, she felt his hold on her relax. In the next instant, his arms fell away. He sighed her name once, offered her a look of poignant apology and slid to the floor in a dead faint.

She stood looking down at him in shock for one heartbeat, and then fell to her knees. "Damn your eyes, Rockleigh Conniston!" She felt a tearing in her throat as she cradled his head in her arms. "I wanted to embarrass you, not kill you."

Grappling with his limp, heavy arm she searched for a pulse. It was rapid but strong. She stretched along the carpet and tugged the cushion from the wing chair, right out from under his hat, and eased it beneath his head. His hair was night-dark silk under her hands, and she could not resist combing her fingers through it.

She knew it was shallow to be so affected by another's exterior. But even haggard and unconscious, he was still the most beautiful creature she'd ever seen. Although his remarkable eyes might have been obscured, there was much else to admire. The sculpted, sensual mouth, the high-boned cheeks. Even the small jagged scar that marked one temple increased the allure of his face.

"He is a very bad man, Mercy," she told herself out loud, "wicked and profligate. You cannot like him. Admiring his person is one thing, but you've got more sense than to admire his character."

I don't want to kiss his character, a little voice responded.

She patted his cheeks a few times, wondering if she ought to slap him. No, that was for the hysterics. So what did one do for a fainting spell? Too bad Mama wasn't here; she was a dab hand during a medical crisis. Of course, she'd have had a fainting spell of her own had she witnessed her daughter with the profligate's head practically in her lap.

Rockleigh returned to consciousness like a man swimming through marmalade. It was slow, sticky going. Several times the room came into focus, and then faded away again. Then an acrid, unpleasant odor assailed his nostrils, forcing him awake.

"I hope that's not . . . from the bonnet I bought you," he managed to gasp out, eying the burnt feather Mercy was waving about under his nose.

She shook her head. "It's my favorite goose-quill pen."

He recalled his disturbing dream from last night and was now amused by the irony—that her weapon had turned into a restorative.

He tried to sit up, but she set her hands firmly on his chest. "Please wait a bit, sir. I fear you are not at all yourself."

Now there was a monumental understatement. He had come here with every intention of ripping up at her, and instead he'd kissed her. And kissed her. He still wanted to, in fact.

No, he definitely wasn't himself this morning. He wondered who he might be.

And who the devil was she, this Mercy Tatlock? A mystery, a puzzlement, a damned cipher. For one thing, she ought to be furious with him for his outrageous behavior, not kneeling there beside him with tender concern puckering her smooth white brow. He doubted that any man had dared to take liberties with her before this; she could slay ogres with one flash of those magnificent eyes, let alone keep mere mortals at bay. But she'd let him hold her and kiss her . . . and oh, sweet heaven, how she had responded.

His fingers fretted the edge of the paisley shawl she had thrown over him. She laid her hand over his to still those agitated fingers and then drifted it up his sleeve. He watched it with fascinated expectation and was dismayed when it stopped at the point of his shoulder. He'd have given a pony to feel that cool, soft palm against his cheek.

He drew in a sharp breath at that thought and closed his eyes. He dared not look at her—what had once seemed a commonplace face had quite recently become a thing of rare beauty in his eyes. What did it matter if the nose was a bit narrow or the chin molded into a hopelessly stubborn line? Who gave a groat if her hair was an indeterminate shade, neither brown nor blond, when one was barraged with images of it tumbling down from its usual tidy knot to spill over his naked chest and shoulders?

So here at last, he realized, was one thing about Mercy Tatlock that was no mystery—that when he pictured her in his mind, the word naked invariably appeared somewhere in his subsequent thoughts.

Good grief, man, you've wanted women before this, he told himself, trying not to tremble as her cool fingers stroked his wrist. *There's nothing to prevent you from taking her.*

Except that she was kind and honorable and trusting, and he doubted she'd be any of those things once he was through with her. For perhaps the first time in his life, he examined the possible consequences of his actions and was distressed by them.

He made a soft growling noise deep in his throat and felt her fingers tighten.

"Are you going to be sick? Shall I fetch a basin?"

"No chance," he replied, forcing himself to look up at her. "I am hollowed out like a gourd after last night."

"I would normally hesitate to ask you what occurred then," she said, "but I fancy the fact that you are lying on my carpet gives me that right."

"I told you, I did something foolish, trusted someone I knew better than to trust. I let down my guard."

Her eyes narrowed. "You have enemies in London?"

"You mean besides you?" He grinned up at her, and then added, "No more than the usual number, only a dozen or so."

She sat there looking thoughtful. "Is one of them Mr. Doncaster, by any chance?"

Roc leaned up slightly in surprise. "Why would you think that?"

"Something he said to my brother that morning in the park. That you were long overdue for your comeuppance. It surprised me. I assumed he was part of your circle of friends."

" 'Was' is the key word there. *Was* part of it."

He lay back down and shut his eyes again. He knew she was looking at him, could almost feel the sweet whisper of her gaze drifting across his face. And then, there it was, a light finger touch upon his brow, soothing, down over his temple to his cheek.

His hands slipped beneath the edge of the shawl, and he clenched them until his nails were nearly embedded in his palms. *Restraint,* he told himself intently. *If you leap up and try to wrestle her to the carpet, you'll get nothing but a clout on the head for your troubles.*

Still, it might be worth it.

Her hand drew away and he heard a faint, wistful sigh. He wondered which of them had produced it.

"Perhaps I should get you something to drink," she said. He opened his eyes then, saw her bite her lip as she untangled her long legs and got to her feet. "You can see I'm not very good at this nursing business."

"Pretend I'm a manuscript page that needs editing," he drawled. "That should inspire you."

She chuckled softly. "Be careful or I'll send you back for a rewrite." She crossed the room and spread her hands over a disordered heap of pages that covered half the table. "That is going to be the fate of Mr. Hannibal and his elephants here."

"I thought it was the Romans did him in."

She shook her head with great solemnity. "This time around

it was a fool of a biographer. I fear the fellow did most of his research in a tavern."

He watched as she poured out a clear liquid from a stone pitcher, then shifted up onto his elbows when she returned and knelt beside him. She held the glass to his mouth, and he took a deep swallow. And then sputtered, "Accchh! What in blazes is this?"

"Lemonade?"

"I thought you were going to bring me a drink."

She sighed. "There are no alcoholic spirits here. Mr. Gribbings is a strict Methodist. That was part of his church choir you met this morning." She again set the rim against his mouth. "Now please drink."

He thrust the lemonade away, threw off the shawl and forced himself to struggle to his feet. His beguilement was rapidly evaporating. What on earth had he been doing there, lying on a threadbare carpet in this shabby room? He reminded himself he wanted no part of these people, especially this prim young woman with her mundane Methodist connections. She would be worse for his constitution than any potion Doncaster could concoct. No, she was not for him, and there was an end to it.

His head spun as he achieved his full height, but he motioned her brusquely away as she came forward to steady him. "No, stay back."

"Very well," she said stiffly. "Fall on your backside again, I don't care. Next time I won't waste a perfectly good quill pen on you." She turned away from him and set a rapid course for a doorway on the other side of the room.

He was perplexed; it wasn't like her to leave the field of battle. "Miss Tatlock?" he called out.

She halted only when she had reached the door. "Sorry, but I believe our interview is concluded, Lord Rockleigh."

He himself couldn't have improved on her supercilious tone. But why did it trouble him, that look of icy contempt in her eyes? He reminded himself that he wanted no part of her. Then instantly acknowledged it for a lie. There were a great many parts of her he wanted. Dewy mouth, satin skin, ripe breast, sleek waist, and long—God help him—the longest legs.

He gave a little cough. "I didn't mean to sound so uncommon rude just now."

"No matter," she said evenly. "For a time there I'd forgotten with whom I was dealing. But you brought me up sharp soon enough. Perhaps I should thank you."

"Stop that," he said irritably. Her hand reached for the door latch. "No, don't leave."

Was that a note of pleading he'd heard in his voice? A tone of supplication? Well, then pigs would surely fly.

She put her chin up. "Why not?"

He made his way gingerly to the wing chair, dispossessed his hat, and then sank down onto it with a deep sigh. He was facing away from her now; he didn't have to witness the cold, hard thing in her eyes. But he knew she lingered there behind him, primed for flight.

"Perhaps I can explain," he said softly, addressing his words to a faded watercolor on the far wall. "I don't make a very good object of charity. I am not used to such things. Although I liked it, I liked it enormously." He was aware that he was no longer referring to her charity. Under his breath he added, "And I should not. I dare not."

"I can't credit that you are without your comforters, Lord Rockleigh." Her tone was no longer brittle, merely arch.

"But as you might have observed, I rarely invite kindness."

"I couldn't very well ignore you," she said, "lying there in a great heap on my floor. Besides, you only needed a bit of looking after."

The coach driver's words came echoing back to him. *You need looking after, sir.* They had incensed him at the time, but now they took on a whole new meaning. It wasn't so bad, really, having a soft-voiced, sweet-smelling, tenderhearted woman looking after you. Rather made a man long for more.

I must have struck my head when I fell, he muttered to himself. That was the only way to explain away these moonstruck musings. Or perhaps Doncaster's foul potion was still addling his wits.

Oh, damnation! He'd forgotten all about Doncaster. He still had a self-proclaimed reckoning with the wretch. But he was much more inclined to sit in this shabby, badly sprung wing chair, which seemed to have lost its cushion—no, there it was on the floor—than to brave the perils of the London streets on a sunny Sunday afternoon.

"You're still not faring very well, are you?"

He looked up, startled. Mercy was now standing beside his chair, looking down at him with a tiny frown.

"Because," she continued, "for all your bad humor, you've always been consistent during our encounters. Beastly, the day we met. Smug at the theater. Vexing in your parlor. But this morning you have quite spun me around with the speed of your mercurial changes." She peered down at him. "In the space of five minutes you have gone from surly to contrite to contemplative."

"I will not bandy words with a newspaperman's daughter," he replied tartly. "I know when I am outclassed."

She crouched beside his chair, one slim hand on the upholstered arm. "It might ease your mind if I tell you something."

His hooded gaze lowered to her face. She wasn't smiling, but a tiny dimple had appeared high on her cheek. "What?"

She drew in a breath and shut her eyes for an instant. "I liked it enormously, too."

He felt something lance through him—jubilation, excitation, a compelling jumble of frightening new feelings. It was absurd that such a puny confession had the power to stir him, but it did more than that. It nearly overwhelmed him.

But hadn't he just convinced himself that she was poison? Men of his class, whatever their vices, did not dally with gently bred females. It was too risky, especially if a man intended to stay clear of parson's mousetrap for the next decade or two. Women such as Mercy Tatlock had mothers who put bulldogs to shame—fierce, tenacious creatures who came armed with special licenses and were supported by whole regiments of outraged relations.

He leaned toward her and said silkily, "I'd be quite happy to oblige you again."

To his relief, she recoiled. But then her face broke into a grin. "You do love to posture, don't you? Lord Rockleigh, the world-weary man-about-town. Lord Rockleigh, the predatory host. Even, I fear, the petulant child." He grimaced at that. "But do you know, I believe that for about three minutes back there, you entirely forgot to posture."

"You mean while I was unconscious?"

"No, paperwit," she chided him, "when you kissed me. That

was the first honest response you've ever given me. Oh, there was a moment in your parlor when I believed you'd let down your guard, but now, this morning, I truly saw it come crashing to the ground."

"That was *me* that crashed to the ground, if you will recall."

"You are being purposely obtuse," she said with a pout. "And there is something else I need to tell you."

"What? That you enjoy my kisses? Hardly news—half the women in London can give me references."

"See? You're doing it again . . . playacting the callous libertine. I don't wonder Miss Wellesley's father couldn't find some use for you in his troupe."

He stared at her, his expression a study in incredulity. "Are you making fun of me, Miss Tatlock?"

"Yes," she said with a dry chuckle. "And getting a bit of my own back. As I said earlier, you don't frighten me a bit. It came to me yesterday after I'd marched from your house—and by the way, please tender my regrets to your footman about the coal scuttle. Anyway, as infuriating and arrogant as you've been"— she poked him in the arm several times for emphasis—"I've also seen occasional glimpses of humanity in you."

"Mere lapses," he retorted smoothly, flashing her a devilish look. "I will apply myself anew to eradicating them."

"Too late," she said. "Once that door opens, it's nearly impossible to close it again."

"Oh, fiddle," he said. "You are demented, ma'am."

"I have a theory," she continued, undaunted by his deepening scowl, "that you are not so much a blackguard as a lost soul. When people lose their direction in life, they forfeit some of their humanity. They might do wicked things, but that does not mean they themselves are wicked. Just lost."

"And you, I take it, have decided to help me find my . . . my direction."

Her dimple showed again for an instant. "That's hardly my place now, is it?"

"No." He tamped down a small pang of disappointment.

"But you might just find your own way, if someone holds up a light."

He pushed up from his chair. "You sound like a mewling Methodist now."

She shrugged as she rose to face him. "Papa and I are in agreement . . . those labels are mostly irrelevant; one religion is very much like another when you get down to basics. It's how we play things out with each other that really matters."

"I hardly think this is a fitting conversation to be sharing with a man who's made it clear he wants to seduce you."

Mercy rocked back on her heels and made a disparaging noise. "Seduce me? You've already kissed me right into next year. I daresay there is not a lot more to be accomplished in that area."

With one step he closed the gap between them and murmured darkly, "Oh, you think not?"

She did not step back from him, but her face had tensed with uncertainty. And some curiosity.

He caught her by the chin and said softly, dangerously, "Then watch."

Holding her with his gaze, he drifted his fingers slowly down her throat, over the sheer tucker to the rounded neckline of her gown. He watched her violet eyes darken to black as his splayed hand continued over the curve of her pristine bodice until it reached the flutter of ribbons gathered beneath her breast. As his fingers tightened over those ribbons, he tugged her forward, lowering his head and letting his mouth caress her just above his fisted hand.

The noise she made was barely audible and incredibly stirring. He shifted his mouth to the filmy tucker, so reminiscent of the sheer robe she had worn in his dream. He tasted her through the fabric, warm, vanilla-scented, softer than a fawn's gaze, and then nudged aside the scrap of muslin. When his mouth touched down on her skin, on the first swell of her breast, she shuddered against him. His arms immediately slid around her, tightening not in passion, he was startled to realize, but in an effort to reassure.

"Sweet Mercy," he sighed against her breast. And then raised his head to nuzzle her mouth, setting his tongue into the subtle declivity of her lips, drawing it back and forth with slow, studied languor. She opened for him, sighing, head fallen back as he kissed her now in earnest. Deep, penetrating kisses that were making his heart pound as his blood surged through his body at a killing pace.

She was clutching his arms now, her fingers curled tightly into the fabric of his coat. Those hands, those strong capable hands, so unlike the perfumed hands of titled ladies or the clever hands of whores, were making him wild with fanciful imaginings. He wanted to be naked with her—there was that word again—and he wanted her touching him everywhere. *Everywhere.*

But her hands never strayed from his coat sleeve, as much as he silently willed them to. It was clear she had a great deal to learn, for all her grasp of Hannibal and his elephants. There were some things a woman could not discover in a pile of foolscap.

"Let me have the keeping of you," he said in a harsh, urgent whisper. "I can take you to places you've never dreamed of. Bring you such pleasure, such completion—"

"No!" she cried abruptly, struggling out of his hold. "Now you *are* frightening me. Rail at me if you must. Curse me, even, for that is what I am used to from you. But do not patronize me. It is beneath even you, Lord Rockleigh."

He swung away from her—stifling a groan at such rapid movement. Patronizing her had been the last thing on his mind. Becoming her patron . . . well, that was a different matter entirely.

"Fiend take you," he bit out. "You are the most exasperating woman I have ever met."

"Good!" she crowed, her eyes ablaze. "That's the real Lord Rockleigh speaking. Not some wretched coxcomb."

He dragged a hand through his hair, clenching his fingers around a waving strand and tugging at it in pure frustration. "What do you want with me, Mercy Tatlock? You humiliate me and alienate my best friend; you send church singers to wake me and rude brothers to pummel me. You cloud my days and haunt my nights. What in the name of heaven do you want from me?"

She crossed her arms and looked him straight in the eye. "Drop the lawsuit."

He opened his mouth to cry "Never!" but couldn't get it out.

He paced across the room, his emotions in turmoil. She had played him like the most skilled coquette, letting him think he was in command of the situation, and then had neatly turned the tables on him. He ached for her, had such a mindless, clamoring need to feel her body beneath him, and in the same instant he wanted to strike out at her with something heavy and lethal.

He went to the table and poured himself a glass of the vile lemonade, swallowing it down in several long gulps. For all its tartness, it eased the raw pain in his throat. He had to gain some control over himself. This felt like the longest morning of his life. To end it, all he had to do was walk through the door. But that portal seemed miles away.

When he had the strength, he would cross the tattered carpet and make his final farewell to her. He would put Mercy Tatlock and her hellborn clan out of his mind. Let his solicitor make a settlement with her father, tender him a small sum of gold in return for an admission of guilt. And then his life would be his own again.

He set the glass down and looked across to her. He could have sworn her mouth was still rosy from his kisses. But there was now an expression of open caution on her face that hadn't been there before, not even when he'd come rampaging through her front door.

She'd been starting to care for him—he was aware of that. Lord knew, a woman didn't kiss a man that way if she held him in distaste. But now her approval had been withdrawn. The merry light that frequently danced in her fine eyes when they were together had been extinguished.

All it lacked now was the coup de grace, the final stroke, and his disturbing connection to Mercy Tatlock would be severed.

"I am not lost, as you have proposed, Miss Tatlock," he said in a clipped, remote voice. "The plain truth of it is that I *am* a blackguard. Have been for most of my life, in fact. I drink and gamble to excess, and I enjoy the company of whores. I have even been known to take opium on occasion. So now you see, the playacting is at an end. Never fear. I will not have the chance to patronize you . . . if there's a God, I will never have to see you again. You may be a finer creature than I am, Avery Tatlock may be a saint among men, but I find the both of you extremely tiresome. My solicitor will make an arrangement with your father . . . something agreeable to all parties."

He moved forward and bent to pluck his hat from the floor. "As for your brother, if you would give me his direction, I promise he will come to no harm at my hands. Meeting him at Jackson's is merely a matter of satisfying my honor, if a blackguard can lay claim to such a thing."

In a constricted voice, Mercy told him the address, and with a nod he went out to the landing. She moved toward him, hands outstretched, as if to aid him down the stairs, but he halted her with a warning look. He no longer required her tender care.

He lingered for a moment, gazing at her in silence, and when he spoke at last, his voice was barely more than a whisper. "You told me once that you pitied me, Miss Tatlock of the Violet Eyes. I advise you to save your precious pity for a man who gives a damn about such things."

Chapter Seven

H e was gone down the stairs, off along the pavement, before
Mercy quoted softly into the empty hallway, "Methinks
the gentleman doth protest too much."

It was an old newspaperman's adage that where there was
smoke, there was usually fire. Lord Rockleigh had smoldered
and flared, and Mercy didn't believe for an instant that she
could have ignited such heated anger in him if he had become
completely indifferent to her.

Not that such knowledge did her a bit of good.

She went back into the parlor and sank down onto the wing
chair. And then, with a soft curse of annoyance, reached down and
took up the cushion. She had meant to place it beneath her, but instead cradled it in her arms. *He* had laid his head upon it, and she
now imagined that same head nestled against her breast, the rich,
dark hair caressing her skin, his mouth soft, easing into sleep.

Though she had drawn back when he'd made his insulting
offer, she was still trembling inside from the potent effect of his
touch. It had never occurred to her until this moment that one's
body had a will of its own when presented with a man of Lord
Rockleigh's allure.

It was something, she supposed, to be going home with any
sort of offer in her pocket. It was the first one she'd had from a
man, though not of the variety most maiden ladies dreamed
about. Not the ones in Tiptree, at any rate.

Maybe she should be flattered. Lord Rockleigh doubtless
dallied with any number of women, but she had a feeling most
of them were no more than fleeting fancies. She sensed he was
too restless by nature and too easily bored to light on any one

branch for very long. It might be something to congratulate herself on, that he'd actually spoken of keeping her, which implied an arrangement extending over a period of time.

She wagered she'd have amused him for the sum total of a week, and then she too would be cast off—disgraced, penniless and, if truth were told, heartbroken.

There was an unwelcome, unfamiliar constriction inside her chest, something pressing along her breastbone, making it difficult to breathe. It was as he'd said—the time for playacting was over. She couldn't pretend any longer that what she felt for him was merely a stimulating physical attraction. Somehow she'd let herself stray into very dangerous territory. One did not place one's unfledged heart at the feet of a rake, especially one who had just made his dishonorable intentions clear. He would trample it as surely as his dandified double had trampled Lady Justice in the drawing.

And how had this happened in less than a week? How had she gone from levelheaded to completely dunderheaded in so short a span? Her mother had not prepared her for such a thing. Mama's advice usually amounted to pointing out that her gloves did not match or that her hem was coming down in the back. As for insight on the male sex, well, she'd once overheard her mother lamenting to her bosom bow, Mrs. Hatcher, that Mercy was more likely to throw herself in front of the Dover coach than ever let a man come close enough to court her.

Ironically, in Rockleigh Conniston, Mercy had found a man to enact both sides of her mother's lament—he'd not only gotten close, but he also made her feel as though the coach had already driven over her. Several times.

Her father, bless him, had told her she was under no pressure to marry, not so long as she preferred another course. It had seemed an idle pronouncement at the time; it never occurred to Mercy that she wouldn't spend her life working at *The Trumpet*. Though she still lived at Boxwood with her family, she'd turned the old gardener's cottage into her own private sanctuary. She had solitude when she required it, and at any time could avail herself of the lively goings-on in the main house.

It had seemed an ideal life . . . until last Tuesday, when she had walked into a coffeehouse and come face-to-face with her own fallibility.

Even if Lord Rockleigh was now willing to negotiate with her father, he'd already taken his pound of flesh from her. The cost of seeking justice had been high, she thought bitterly. Much too high, if it meant she was to spend the rest of her life pining for a man who thought of her only as a plaything.

She leaned back in the chair and shut her eyes, willing the image of Rockleigh Conniston to leave her in peace. But as was the case after their first encounter, it refused to be banished. She could number his faults and condemn his idle way of life, but she could not make him go away. Not from inside her head; he dwelled there in a sort of shimmering haze, where she was able to glimpse only an occasional flash of white teeth and aquamarine eyes. Or sometimes hear a soft, whispering echo of her own name being spoken over and over.

Ah, but what did any of this matter? There was nothing to prevent her from returning to Tiptree now, and so she would, the instant Toby was free of his obligation to the man.

She rose and set the cushion back in place on the chair seat. She still had seven chapters of the Carthaginian Disaster to get through before she left London. It was the least she could do to repay Mr. Gribbings for his hospitality.

Doncaster was nowhere to be found. It was as if he had disappeared from the face of the planet. Of course, the first place Rockleigh checked was his lodgings in Soho, but there had been no response to his knock. Roc had then ridden all over London, asking after Doncaster at all his regular haunts: Bacchus, of course, The Four Bells in Stepney, the Fox and Fig in Pimlico, and at several brothels in the East End. No one had seen him since last night.

It was nearing dark when Rockleigh returned to Soho. Doncaster's man met him at the door this time, but said he was not at liberty to reveal his master's whereabouts. A significant coin changed hands, and the servant then muttered something about a very discreet house party in the Lake District, coupled with the name of an infamous, but highly inventive countess. Rockleigh would have, at one time, driven much farther than Windermere to be in her company.

He complimented the man on his master's choice of entertainment and went back down to the street, feeling an overwhelming sense of relief. If Doncaster was planning something underhanded, it likely had nothing to do with Crowdenscroft or Kent. Not if the rascal was on his way north.

Stanley was waiting in the parlor when he arrived home. "Are we speaking yet?" Roc inquired urbanely. "Or should I call in my footman to act as intermediary?"

"You look like hell," Stanley said without getting up from his chair.

"That's an answer of sorts. The truth is, I feel even worse than I look. Whatever it was that Doncaster gave me last night—"

"It wasn't just the opium this time, was it?" Stanley's chin had thrust out. "Something even more dangerous, I wager."

Roc settled back onto the sofa, closed his eyes and sighed in relief at being off his feet at last.

Stanley growled softly. "Well? You may as well tell me."

Roc opened one eye. "I have no idea what it was."

"Maybe something you ate reacted badly to the opium. I recall one time when I dined on poached oysters directly after drinking a glass of negus. Let me tell you, I was—"

"I didn't take opium last night," Roc interjected curtly. "I will probably never go near the stuff again, not if it means trafficking with Doncaster."

"There's a blessing, then," Stanley said. "You ought to tell your father. He's convinced you are the king of vice after seeing the state you were in last night."

"Oh, and whose fault is it that he saw me, my little talebearer?"

Stanley shrugged. "If I hadn't written to him, if he hadn't come to London, you might be a corpus by now. Just thought I ought to remind you of that."

"And what did bring the two of you to Bacchus? I've been mulling that over in my head all day, along with the dozen or so other irritations that have cropped up."

"I was worried . . . Doncaster came to my rooms last night."

"The devil he did—"

"And started asking questions about you, about what trouble you'd gotten into now, that your father had to come out from Devon." Stanley paused melodramatically. "Then he read that damned news clipping that was on my mantel. Took himself off after that, looking like the cat that licked the cream."

"Ah, it begins to make sense now. It explains why he was asking me about Crowden last night. And why he slipped me something—in my brandy, I assume—that addled me enough so that I couldn't resist his questioning. Though what he was after—"

"Belladonna," Stanley exclaimed.

"Who?" Roc gaped at him for an instant. "Oh, you mean the poisonous plant. I thought you were referring to a person."

"Listen, Roc. M'sister told me once that ladies used to put belladonna in their eyes to make them bright. Your eyes were like that last night. Strangely bright . . . sickly bright, like a man with a fever."

Roc gave this some thought. From what he knew about belladonna, it might just have been Doncaster's choice. The poison, he recalled reading somewhere, was used to subdue pain-crazed farm animals, and unless he was mistaken, witches had once employed it to conjure up the devil. All he'd managed to conjure up last night had been Mercy Tatlock and her deadly quill. Close enough.

"But why drug me, Stanley?" he asked at last. "Why would Doncaster care about some foolish allegations about a place down in Kent?"

Stanley pursed his mouth into a contemplative moue and stroked at his chin. "He's from Kent, you know. From Dover actually." He looked down sheepishly when Roc made no comment. "Sorry. I have this dashed annoying ability to remember things people have mentioned in passing. Where they were born, who their great-uncle begat, useless nonsense really. Wish I could remember where I left my diamond stickpin."

"No," Roc was saying slowly, "not nonsense. We've both heard rumors that Doncaster's involved himself in some pretty questionable dealings. Not just the opium trade . . . but money-lending and fencing stolen goods."

Stanley recalled the way the man had practically drooled over his Dresden shepherdesses. "It's not a huge leap then," he said, "to imagine him selling children to brothels."

"A rather small leap," Roc pronounced. "But he's missed his mark this time. He has no idea of what's really going on in Crowdenscroft."

Stanley rolled his eyes and drawled, "Yes, Doncaster and the rest of the civilized world."

Roc ruffled his crown with the base of his hand. "But it makes no sense. His man told me he's left London, gone north to Lady Trey's house party. Why bother to drug me, if he's not going to use the information I gave him? I can't sort it out. My brain is overtaxed, and I'm too damned tired."

"He's probably decided to play least-in-sight in case you died last night. The porter at Bacchus saw Doncaster and another man half carrying you out of one of the card rooms. He refused any assistance, said you'd just had too much brandy. He left you in a storeroom in the cellar, by the way. The only reason your father and I searched for you was because your greatcoat was still with the porter."

Roc hadn't known that part; he had a skin-crawling feeling that Doncaster really had meant for him to die. But he still had no idea why. He looked across to Stanley. "And how did you and my father hook up? You never finished telling me."

"I thought about Doncaster's face when he read the clipping. Like a spider who'd spotted a nice fresh fly." He shuddered theatrically. "I just wanted to find you and warn you that he was up to something. I met your father by the merest chance, coming out of White's."

"And you told him about the clipping?" There was no censure in his tone.

"No, he knew already. Lady Blythedale sent it to him weeks ago." Stanley's voice lowered several notches. "He's done with you, Roc. He told me so himself, after we'd made sure you'd gotten home from Bacchus in one piece. He swore he wouldn't put your mother through the pain or worry any longer, and that unless you had a first-class explanation for what happened last night, he was going to scratch your name right out of the family Bible."

Roc didn't say anything for a long while. Stanley fidgeted in his chair, and then said softly, "He was so afraid at Bacchus, afraid you weren't going to make it. I saw the panic in his eyes, the fear of losing you. I doubt my own father could have mustered such concern, and you know he dotes on me."

"His Grace don't care for me," Roc said gruffly. "Not in that way. He just didn't want a scandal in the family, not with Torry about to wed."

"You're wrong," Stanley said. He rose and took a few steps forward. "Dead wrong."

Roc hitched one shoulder. "And how is it you know so much about it?"

"Because," Stanley replied slowly, "I expect it was the same look I had in my own eyes."

"Oh." Roc felt himself begin to blush, felt the unaccustomed heat rise from his neckcloth. And then he was on his feet, grinning and shaking Stanley by both arms. "Well, then, I say thank God for you, old fellow. Thank God for you *and* for my father."

Now Stanley was blushing. "You've a stout constitution, Roc. I doubt the poison would have done you in." He grinned. "The duke said you were too wicked to die."

Roc's face sobered instantly. He drew away from his friend and returned to the sofa, perching on the edge of the cushions. "Am I, Stanley?" he asked earnestly. "Am I truly too wicked? You see, I've spent a large part of the day thinking about that very thing. To the point of wondering if I had a deathbed conversion last night."

"More like a skittles alley conversion." Stanley chuckled. "You weren't nowhere near your bed." Then he glanced away and said awkwardly, "Dash it, I can't judge you, Rocky. You're my best friend. Have been since the day you knocked Sir Kevin's brute of a son off his pony for calling me Flem Face. I never saw such a row."

"I remember *that*," Roc said, rubbing at the small scar over his temple. "We both ended up bloodied, but I finally convinced him to apologize to you."

Stanley grinned. "So you see, you aren't wicked."

"Well, I might not have been back then . . . what was I, ten at the time? It's what I've become since that troubles me. I suppose you've seen those posters plastered all over London."

"Mmm. There was one outside Melville's. Your father tried to pull it down."

"That," he said with a wry twist of his mouth, "was the work of your plucky Miss Tatlock. This morning there were church singers caterwauling on my front steps. I can hardly wait to see what tomorrow brings."

No, he reminded himself, he needn't worry any longer. He was done with her. There would be no more taunting posters or embarrassing hymn recitals. No more dreadful bonnets or taxing debates, no more sublime, heated kisses or stirring caress—

Roc started out of his revery. "What was that?"

"I was just wondering—are Miss Tatlock's barbs the reason you're suddenly so preoccupied with your own wickedness?"

Roc gave a dry, mirthless laugh. "She thinks I am a lost soul."

Stanley almost nodded in agreement, but caught himself in time. "I take it that you've encountered her since that episode in the coffeehouse."

"More times than mortal man can withstand. She is a menace to my sanity. But," he added, "you will be happy to learn I intend to negotiate with her father. It was easier than having her pop out of the woodwork at every turn."

"Clever girl," Stanley said, half under his breath. Miss Tatlock had obviously found a way to bring Rockleigh around. He wondered what else she had managed to do to his friend. Rockleigh looked as though he had gone nine brutal rounds with Clobber Reese, and Stanley suspected that not all of that wear was the result of Doncaster's little gift.

"So she's going to get her way after all," he said aloud.

"That's not what I meant," Roc protested. "I haven't given up. Negotiating isn't the same thing as relenting. Not by a long shot."

"She really has gotten under your skin," Stanley observed as he settled back in his chair. He was enjoying the spectacle of Rockleigh Conniston without his habitual mantle of disdain.

"She certainly has not. She's a gadfly, no more."

"She must have done something more than tweak you, Roc, to have gotten your back up. What is it . . . come on, tell me."

Running a hand wearily over his face, Rockleigh muttered, "Nothing . . . oh, everything. It's like having your conscience spring into life and dog your footsteps. I feel as though I've acquired my own personal Hannah More."

Stanley smiled into his palm. "Um, you may not have noticed this, Roc, since you have no sisters, but that's what decent women do. They think it's their job to keep a fellow on the straight and narrow."

"It's intolerable. I wonder men can bear the notion of marriage."

"Perhaps you should write to Bryce on that score," Stanley said. "He hardly had the look of a martyr when he sailed from Portsmouth with Lady Jemima."

Rockleigh had observed this same phenomenon himself. But Lady J was a peach, a rare pearl, a good 'un. There were few women like her in the breadth of England.

"Miss Tatlock is hardly in the same league with Jemima Bryce," Roc countered. "She is a nonentity. Probably quite content with her narrow little life. Happy toiling for her father's paper, happy with her parish choir and her utterly boring town."

"I've observed that some people don't need much to make them happy."

Rockleigh's voice took on a thoughtful, faraway tone. "And *some* people have everything they could possibly desire, the world at their fingertips, and a life of ease in the greatest city in the land."

"And they are not happy?" Stanley probed gently.

There was a long pause. "No," Roc said at last with a ragged sigh. "They are not."

Stanley knew he was not the brightest bud on the rosebush, but it was occurring to him that something had altered Rockleigh Conniston almost beyond recognition. His face was haggard, his complexion paler than normal, but it was his eyes that drew Stanley's scrutiny. Their expression was almost bleak, yet at the same time very human, possibly even vulnerable. Stanley, who'd always had a problem looking straight into them, now felt compelled to do exactly that.

However, he didn't think this was a good time to tax Roc about this radical change. Furthermore, from the tone of his conversation, Stanley had a feeling his friend was already aware of it.

"And what of Miss Tatlock's brother?" he asked cautiously.

"I'm off to see him in the morning. We'll settle our differences in Jackson's Parlor, and then I'll buy him an ice at Gunter's, or whatever in blazes you do to amuse a sprat."

Stanley smiled impishly. "I think you might be right, Roc."

"About what? Gunter's?"

"About the deathbed conversion. You actually sounded like a rather decent fellow just now."

Rockleigh put his hands over his face and groaned.

Toby and Jack looked up from their game of piquet as the butler came into the sitting room. "Lord Rockleigh Conniston," he intoned roundly, as though he'd been waiting his entire life to utter just those words.

Roc stepped past him into the room, and both young men sprang to their feet, knocking into the table and scattering playing cards all over the carpet.

"Gentlemen," he said with a nod. He bent down to retrieve a card that had landed near his boot and set the knave of spades face up on the table.

"Lord Rockleigh," Toby croaked, trying unsuccessfully to hide his expression of horrified shock.

Roc nearly grinned. He'd wager the boy's sister had never worn such an expression in her life. "I'm not planning to shoot you here in the sitting room, you young hothead. Not planning to shoot you at all."

"I know that," Toby managed to get out. "M'sister told me. I . . . I just wasn't expecting you to call on me . . . in person. I, uh, understood you had a second."

"Oh, Mr. Flemish is out of things now, since it's merely to be a bout of fisticuffs. A man doesn't need a second if there's no bloodshed involved."

The color began creeping back into Toby's fair-skinned face.

"We're off to Jackson's if you've no other plans for this morning." Roc eyed Toby's companion, a lanky youth with waving yellow hair, who was at the moment trying to sidle away from the drapery behind which he'd fled. "You're welcome to come along, too."

He gave Roc a weak smile. "Thank you. I would like that above anything. I've heard you're one of the only men who's actually knocked Mr. Jackson onto the ropes."

"Don't believe everything you hear, Mr.—"

"Skillens. Jack Skillens."

Roc took them both under his wing. It was a novel experience; as the youngest child in his own family, Roc was unaccustomed to playing the role of mentor. He found the boys' enthusiasm, as he introduced them to the venerable science of pugilism, to be amusing and strangely gratifying. He discovered that Toby did indeed have a splendid right uppercut, and that Jack, while not so gifted as his friend, was tall enough to achieve a respectable reach.

A small group of Roc's acquaintances wandered up to the edge of the ring, while he was squared off against Toby. Lord Vincent seemed amused beyond all reason, remarking to the other gentlemen in a lazy drawl that Conniston had obviously been reduced to plundering the nursery to find opponents.

Even though he and Vincent had been friends since Eton, Roc's first instinct was to shoot back a cutting remark. Instead, he simply smiled benignly down at the man.

To his surprise, Toby spoke up. "I'm long enough out of the nursery to know when someone's done me an honor." He added with a wry grin, "Anyway, I believe Lord Rockleigh required some new recruits. He's had his fill of besting the Town beaus."

There was a rise of laughter from the men beyond the ropes. Vincent sketched a bow to Toby, and they all moved on.

Roc was impressed. An hour ago the boy had been stammering in distress, and now here he stood, bantering effortlessly with one of the *ton*'s sharpest wits. But then, he should have expected such a thing; Toby was a Tatlock, after all. Roc doubted there was a wag on the planet who could get in the last word with any of them.

At one o'clock they found themselves outside Jackson's, well pleased with the morning's work. It was only a momentary aberration, Roc swore later, that made him invite Toby and Jack to Watier's to take luncheon with him.

Toby kept his eyes on his plate while they dined, while Jack gazed about with open curiosity and attempted to display his worldliness in a mildly self-consequential manner.

"Is that Lord North over there? I hear he's going to give Liverpool trouble on the military appropriations bill. And, I say, is that Sir Robert Poole rising from his table? He came to Dover last year and spoke at our school. A fine orator, we all thought so. Whiggish sentiments, but I suppose that's to be expected from a reformer."

While Jack rambled, Roc passed the time observing his other guest. Toby's hair was a shade or two darker than Mercy's, and his eyes were more blue than violet, but in manner and voice he was so like his sister that Roc frequently felt a painful tugging in his chest. It hadn't occurred to him that Toby would be such a tangible reminder of a woman he wanted only to forget.

He turned his attention back to Jack, inquiring if he intended a career in politics. This was a mistake. The boy launched into a one-sided conversation on the failings of the government, the unrest in Ireland and the lack of financial restraint displayed by the Regent.

Roc was aware that Toby had several times kicked his friend's leg under the table, but Jack went right on talking, trying desperately to prove his mettle.

Seventeen-year-old boys, Rockleigh thought wonderingly. Eager, impressionable and wide-eyed, yet perched right on the cusp of adulthood. He tried to recollect what he was like at that age. Surely he'd not been as callow as these two. He'd had his first woman by then, and had also discovered the sweet allure of wine and brandy.

Neither of his guests, on the other hand, was much interested in the fine claret he'd ordered. Nor did they appear to notice, after the three of them left the club, a very tasty group of ladybirds who were strolling along Piccadilly. It would have been easy to label them bumpkins or rubes, but Roc had a feeling they were nothing more than innocents—abroad in the capital for perhaps the first time and maybe a little cautious of the depravity that lingered on the fringes of the city.

When they reached Hyde Park, Rockleigh touched his hat to them, preparing to depart for home. Toby whispered something to Jack, who made his own farewells, and then went strolling off into the park.

"I wanted to have a word alone with you, sir," Toby said. Rockleigh assumed an expression of alert interest. "It's about m'sister."

Rockleigh's expression faltered slightly.

Toby's brow furrowed as he searched for words. "You see," he said at last, "I know she's been playing pranks on you to get you to change your mind about the lawsuit." He cast a questioning look at Rockleigh. "But you haven't, sir, have you?"

Roc shook his head slowly from side to side, his gaze unwavering.

Toby rolled his eyes heavenward. "Knew it was a daft notion when she told me. What this needed was man-to-man dealing. But I let her go her way, because she's older, and truth to tell, she's clever for a female."

"No one who's met her would ever question that."

"But she hasn't had a normal upbringing," the boy continued. "I managed to, somehow, and so did Bitsy and Ralph."

"And Bitsy and Ralph are?"

"My younger sister and brother. But Mercy's always been, well, too much like my father. She was a handful for Mama, even as a child. She wouldn't paint, wouldn't stitch—she nailed the lid of the sewing box shut, in fact. I've been hearing tales of her domestic crimes since I was breeched. So my father saw to her for the most part. Got her interested in history and philosophy, started her reading Rousseau and Voltaire and Lord knows what other radical things. As a result, Mercy's got very unorthodox ideas about the gentry; she's practically a Republican."

"I take it you don't share these views."

"Father calls me the Little Conservative. I am probably something of a disappointment to him. He was hoping I'd follow in his footsteps. Not sure what I want to do, though. I'm mad for science and math, but I've got my university years to decide, I suppose."

Since Rockleigh had been out of Cambridge for nearly a decade and still had no idea what he wanted to do with his life, he chose not to comment on this apparently cavalier approach to one's future. He also had another startling insight—if he'd kept up with his plan of ruining Tatlock, this merry, promising young fellow would not ever have gotten those university years.

"Sorry to go off on a tangent like that," Toby said, tucking his hands behind him. "My point is, I know you are a man of the world, and Mercy isn't. I mean a woman of the world."

He grew flustered and displayed the same propensity for blushing as his sister. Rockleigh thought it endearingly youthful.

"Dash it all, you know what I mean," Toby muttered. "She ain't well up on things."

"So I have noticed. And is this, then, the brotherly warning that I am not to take advantage of that unworldliness?"

Toby shifted on his feet. "It's all that Doncaster's fault."

Roc leaned forward intently, intrigued by this non sequitur.

"He said some very flattering things to me about Mercy's appearance. Rather surprised me. I mean, at home we all think of her as a sad romp."

Rockleigh looked straight at him. "Your sister is one of the loveliest women to set foot in London in the last ten years. Believe me, I know."

Toby worried his lip. "I was afraid you were going to say that."

"You're not going to hit me, are you, young Tatlock? Because then I'd have to seek satisfaction, and I don't think Mr. Flemish could handle the pressure of being my second again in so short a span of time."

Toby shook off the notion. "That's not what I'm worried about. I know you'd never take advantage of her. No, here is what troubles me—you add together all these things about Mercy: she's not fledged, she's been raised to think life is nothing but an exchange of ideas on paper, *and* she's pretty, to boot. Now how could a woman like that possibly have a chance of winning you over, Lord Rockleigh?"

Oh, you'd be surprised, young Tatlock.

Toby continued his diatribe, quite unaware of the amusement in Roc's eyes. "It was an idiotic notion to think she could move you. But you see, I'm so used to her getting her way. She bosses us all something fearful. Even my father." His face tightened. "I wager she's tried to boss you too, sir."

"Innumerable times," Rockleigh drawled.

Toby's voice rose. "Well, that's a dashed shame. Because I can see she was wrong about you. You are no panderer or dupe of panderers."

Rockleigh thought the latter had a nice lurid ring to it. Perhaps the boy had a vocation in newspapers after all.

"Unfortunately," said Roc in a calming tone, "she was merely echoing your father's sentiments. Who can blame a child for displaying such filial loyalty?"

"I'm his child, as well. And you shall deal with me now. Mercy's had her turn and clearly bungled it. Handbills and church choirs . . ." He blew out a disdainful breath. "I expect she'd have resorted next to a troop of Morris men to plague you in the streets."

Roc looked a bit rattled by that notion. Morris men always unsettled him. There was something about all those disharmonious bells.

He offered Toby a half-moon smile. "Then let us negotiate like gentlemen. I have no wish to harm your family. My only desire is to have my name and the reputation of my house cleared. So I will offer your father a generous sum of money to recant. Whatever amount he requires to soothe his newspaper-man's pride."

Roc was not expecting the boy's look of outrage. "You think you can *buy* my father? Is that your solution?"

So much for gentlemanly negotiating, Roc thought wryly. "Not buy him, exactly. Just grease the wheels of justice a bit. I understand it's done all the time."

"Not in Tiptree, it's not," Toby said darkly. He thought a minute, chin on chest, then looked up. "I have a better idea, Lord Rockleigh. Why don't we drive down to Crowden and pay a visit to your estate? I can write to my father to meet us there, and then he will see that there is nothing remarkable going on."

"So you truly don't believe his inflammatory tale of children sold into vice?"

Toby drew himself up. "I fancy I am as good a judge of char-acter as the next fellow. You are not the sort of man who would involve himself in such a distasteful business."

Rockleigh bowed slightly. "You honor me, young Tatlock. And I must say, you're easier to convince than your sister." His eyes narrowed. "But I'm afraid no one is getting near that house."

"But it would put an end to the matter." Toby was practically dancing with frustration. "You must see that. Father will recant at once if the truth is laid before him."

Gad, the boy was starting to sound just like his sister.

"He will recant if I make it worth his while. There's not a man born who won't come around eventually for a bit of the ready."

Roc could have almost predicted Toby's next words.

"You obviously don't know my father."

Toby found Jack walking along a deserted path. He related his conversation with Lord Rockleigh, and then added stoutly, "There's nothing for it, Jack. I've got to go down to Crowden."

Jack stopped plucking at a patch of tall grass and stared at him. "That's a corkbrained idea. You don't still believe Lord Rockleigh is involved with—"

"Of course not. But whatever he's hiding on his estate—and he is still being very mysterious—I swear it's nothing illegal. If I can prove to my father that he's wrong about Lord Rockleigh, then he'll have to admit it, and we won't lose our home. You

see, Bitsy's been writing to us . . . she says that Papa was un-
able to raise even a groat from his relations. And of course,
Mercy and I are supposed to be off in Brighton petitioning Aunt
Clarissa for money, which we are not."

"Maybe you'd have done better to go do down to Brighton
than let your sister tangle with Lord Rockleigh."

Toby made a rude noise. "That clutch-fisted old harridan
wouldn't give sixpence to a saint. She was just the only excuse
we could think of to leave the house without our parents getting
the wind up."

"And what of Mercy? Will she be all right here by herself?"

Toby reminded him that he'd hardly been playing watchdog
to his sister this past week. "And she's come to no harm, in
spite of it. Anyway, Mr. Gribbings will look after her. My going
to Crowdenscroft will fix everything. Then Mercy can go home
to Boxwood."

"I don't like it. Suppose there are smugglers in that house . . .
it's near enough to the coast for that to be a possibility. Or
maybe Conniston's harboring French spies."

Toby shot him a look of disgust. "You just spent hours with
the man. Did he strike you as that sort of scoundrel?"

"You weren't so keen on him when you drew his cork outside his club."

"I didn't know him then, not like I do now. Besides, he was
in his cups at the time."

Jack began pacing up and down the path, the tails of his coat
dancing in time with his loping strides. "Well, I suppose going
down there does make sense. You don't want to lose your
chance to go to university, and you certainly don't want your
family put out on the street." He fidgeted with his single fob.
"Here's a thought . . . we'll tell my great-aunt that we're off to
Hampton Court for a few days—I've told her I wanted to visit
the place. That will explain our absence."

"*Our* absence?"

Jack grinned. "I am not letting you go off without me, Tobe.
Not with your temper to get you into trouble at every turn. Besides, I happen to know where my aunt's butler keeps a brace
of very fine pistols. We can't go into a den of smugglers un-
armed, now, can we?"

*   *   *

Rockleigh went directly home and slept for the rest of the afternoon. He had still not regained his normal vigor; he'd spent yesterday haring all over London in search of Doncaster, and though his time with Toby and Jack had not precisely been tiring, it had been a strain.

Just before he fell asleep, when his will was at its weakest, he allowed himself a splendid daydream about Mercy Tatlock. It wasn't a made-up daydream; rather, it was a recapitulation of their last encounter. And only the good parts.

He recalled the way her skin tasted and how she smelled of vanilla; he heard again the tiny, ragged noise she'd made when he kissed the rise of her breast. He was too weary to waste time regretting that he'd probably never get to savor those particular delights again; just imagining them was enough. It was pleasant to pretend that he was not alone in his bed, that she was there beside him, curled into him, drowsing. He'd wrap a strand of her hair around his hand and gently draw her head back so that he could whisper into her ear. Such things he'd tell her—his childhood dreams of adventuring abroad, the rollicking times he'd shared with Torry and Trent. He'd describe his home to her, the tall chimneys soaring up, backlit by the sun, the wild green moor plummeting down to the edge of the sea, the look of his father's wheat fields just before a storm, when the tassels bent double in the wind like a rippling golden blanket. And then they'd sleep, bodies molded together, breathing in tandem, and he'd be happy and content.

So vivid were these imaginings that when he awoke several hours later, he reached for her across the wide bed. And when he realized she was not there, would never be there, he felt a pain of such depth in his chest that he could barely draw breath.

He lay there, staring at the shadows on the ceiling, wondering if it was possible to win her favor. She wouldn't be impressed by the offer of a fine small house or a curricle and pair, the usual inducements a man held out to potential conquests. He could buy her books, he mused, rare volumes of Dante and Milton. No, he decided, too starchy. She already had plenty of starch. What he wanted was to unstarch her.

Of course, the logical gift would be dropping his case against Avery Tatlock. But that came very close to using her father's plight to lever her out of her virtue, which sounded tawdry, even to him. Still, there had to be some way he could bring her to his bed.

He realized, as he mulled over various methods of seduction, that Mercy could never return home once he'd taken her into his keeping. Tatlock, for all his radical Republican leanings, was still a father and would surely not be of such liberal inclinations when it came to his own progeny. Roc suspected it would be no different if he had children. He'd not want them succumbing to the temptations of London, not even the ones he currently enjoyed.

"Perdition!" he muttered aloud. "Did I just think that?"

He rolled over and buried his face in the pillow. What was happening to him? Had Doncaster's potion bewitched him into a dreary state of goodness? He wrestled with his conscience, tried to force it back down into the moldy cellar where it had dwelled these past fifteen years. But it eluded his grip, grinning at him with open insolence.

He had not been the one to let it out into daylight—he was sure of that. No, someone else had come along and done the deed. Someone who was interfering and obstinate and bossy.

If he wanted a woman so badly, there were dozens he could choose from, highborn and low-. What he didn't want was a woman in the middle—one not high enough to wed with, nor low enough to bed. And that was why he was in a state of miserable confusion, he saw now. He'd chosen exactly the wrong woman.

Roc reminded himself firmly of his lifelong rule—to never covet something he couldn't possess. He would simply unchoose her. How difficult could that be?

Chapter Eight

Toby called on Mercy the next morning. She was still laboring across the Alps with Hannibal and was glad of the interruption. A walk along the river, she announced, was just what she required to clear her head. Toby couldn't know that there were more troublesome phantoms lurking in there than a barbarian general with a yen to sack Rome.

Her brother gave her a glowing report of his encounter with Lord Rockleigh as they strolled along the Thames. She tried not to let her jealousy show. Rockleigh had apparently treated Toby to a heaping dose of charm and generosity—two things he rarely bothered to bestow on her.

Once they were back in her parlor having tea, Toby mentioned in an offhand manner that he and Jack were traveling to Hampton Court for a few days.

"That's a bit of a blow. I was hoping we'd be able to return home tomorrow—I'll have completed Mr. Gribbings's book by then. When will you be back?"

"Thursday, perhaps. Friday, at the latest. So I take it you've given up your fight here in London."

"Not exactly." She meshed her hands on the tabletop. "The last time I saw Lord Rockleigh, he assured me he would arrange a satisfactory solution."

Toby gave her a cryptic smile. "And did he tell you what that was?"

"No, but one has to work these things out with lawyers. I'm sure he'll withdraw his complaint, and then Papa can write something flattering about the Barrisfords to appease him."

"No," Toby pronounced. "That is *not* what Conniston is

planning to do." He then proceeded to tell his sister exactly what he *was* planning to do.

Needless to say, she was a trifle incensed.

"But don't worry," Toby continued quickly, "I've got some plans of my own to settle this matter." He patted her hand reassuringly. "You just let me handle it, Merce. Your methods only made him angry." His eyes lit up. "I told him he was lucky you weren't planning any more pranks, or he'd have Morris men to contend with, at the very least." He chuckled. "Morris men."

"I agreed to stop baiting him," she said between her teeth, "because he led me to believe he was seeking a fair resolution, not about to resort to bribery."

"Oh, don't tell me you're going to start up again with your torments. Please, Mercy. Promise me you're not. He's . . . he's not of our world. You can't know what their consequence means to men of his breeding."

"That is exactly why I did it."

"Well, I think what you've been doing to him is akin to putting a cracker hat on a high-blooded horse—it demeans the prankster more than the victim."

Since it had never occurred to Mercy to look at things quite that way, she was impressed by her brother's insight. Still, it wasn't enough to make her back down from Rockleigh. Not after what Toby had just told her.

She sat in silence for a time. "I promise not to demean myself with him. There, does that satisfy you? Honestly, Toby, you'd think the man had sprouted wings and flown around the dome of St. Paul's doing somersaults, you're that impressed with him."

"And why shouldn't I be?" he asked as he rose from the table and pulled on his gloves. "He taught me the most punishing overhand blow. It was a stunner—I never saw the like." Then he grinned wickedly. "You ought to be equally impressed by him. He called you one of the loveliest women in London."

"Insufferable," she muttered, keeping her blush at bay by sheer force of will.

Toby crossed over to his sister, who was still in midsimmer, and kissed her carelessly on one cheek. "I'd best be going. Jack's off hiring a gig, and he should be outside any time now."

He stopped at the doorway. "Now stay out of trouble, there's a good girl."

She waited until he was down the stairs before she hurled her teacup across the room. It shattered nicely against the mortared stone of the firebreast. It was not *her* teacup to shatter, but that didn't trouble her just then. She had more irksome problems on her mind.

Rockleigh had to admit he was enjoying himself. These embassy balls were usually notable for a lack of fresh air and an overabundance of royal dukes. Tonight, however, someone had had the forethought to open French doors in the ballroom. Furthermore, there wasn't a royal duke in sight, although Prinny himself had threatened to appear.

Roc had danced and flirted with several married ladies, and only those in the ever-decreasing ranks of women with whom he had not yet dallied. He knew a number of his former conquests were eying him speculatively, but a wise man never went back for seconds at the banquet table. It invariably led to all sorts of internal complications.

Just before supper, he managed to slip into the garden with Lady Beatrice Townsend, she of the sloe eyes and divine decolletage. Her husband was off buttonholing Liverpool in the card room, so the coast was clear for some exploratory groundwork—so to speak.

Lady Beatrice turned to him halfway along the path and tittered into her fan.

He set one hand over his heart. "Your laughter is enchanting, Bea. But I wish you would share the jest."

"I probably shouldn't laugh, Rockleigh, but it was vastly amusing. Lady Tewksbury told me earlier about the raggedy people singing hymns on your front steps." She shook a finger at him. "Have you been naughty, Roc, dallying with some vicar's daughter?"

"Hardly," he said. "Those singers merely lost their way. My footman sent them about their business."

She tittered again. "That's not what Lady Tewksbury said. She told me your footman invited them in for tea . . . at least that is what *her* footman heard. And servants, in my experience, always know the truth of things."

Rockleigh hadn't a clue what she was talking about, but made a mental note to shake the truth of things out of Walter.

He shrugged in unconcern. "It hardly matters," he said smoothly, "not when the moon is turning your hair to ebony and your skin to ivory. You could be a statue of Aphrodite, not one made of cold marble, but of warm flesh and—"

"Speaking of works of art," she interjected with a throb of amusement, "I couldn't help noticing those handbills that were scattered all around town. A rather good likeness of you, didn't you think?"

Rockleigh bit back his annoyance. "Those of us in the public eye are prime targets for wags and jokesters. Prinny himself is often the subject of lampoons."

"But," she added, "I wager Prinny's never found a gaggle of church singers on the steps of Carlton House." She tapped him playfully with her fan. "It sounds as though you've made an odd sort of enemy." Her eyes narrowed. "I wonder who it could be."

"No one of any consequence, I assure you. Now"—he closed the gap between them and slid one arm about her waist—"let us forget everything but that we are here together, alone at last."

She sighed as he kissed the side of her throat, but then shifted her head away. "Yes, you make love very nicely, Roc. But you've given me little encouragement these past weeks. I'm not sure I shouldn't punish you for it. Townsend has asked me to spend next month with him in Brighton . . . and it would serve you right if I agreed to it."

He tightened his hold on her. "You think I wouldn't come to Brighton to be with you. I'd travel to the ends of the earth to—"

"Oh, pooh," she said with a delicate scowl. "You don't even visit your dear mama here in town. I saw Her Grace last night at the Derwents' musicale, and she told me so herself. You are not a very attentive son, so why should I expect you to be an attentive lover?"

His arms instantly dropped away from her, evoking a look of surprise from the lady. He knew she was teasing him, that she had every intention of allowing him liberties. But he was no longer sure he wanted to take them. Not with a woman who had no doubt laughed at him behind his back. One who had, furthermore, discussed his filial shortcomings with his mama.

He had never shied away from scandalous behavior, never allowed his conduct to be swayed by the standards of others. His morals were not anyone's business but his own. And so he had gone blithely about his life, immune to the general tattle that insisted he was a heartless profligate. He suspected the label lent him a sort of cachet with women.

But he was not immune to this—to being regarded as a prime joke. Mercy's ridicule had clearly pervaded even the loftiest echelons of the *ton*. It was intolerable. *She* was intolerable.

Lady Bea gave an impatient sigh, and then slid her arms around him. "Rockleigh? I was only having a bit of fun. No one's taking those things seriously. Well, most of us aren't. And what does it matter if a few of your . . . your rivals in the *ton* are making merry over them?"

She moved closer, and by force of habit he drew his arms around her. But he might as well have been holding a dressmaker's mannequin, for all the passion he could muster.

He gently disengaged himself and stepped back. "Sorry, Bea. I am not feeling myself tonight. Must be something I ate. The . . . er, poached oysters, maybe." He sketched her a rapid bow and, with a troubled expression, made his escape from the garden.

"Poached oysters?" she echoed into the quiet night. "But we haven't even gone in to supper yet."

There was a note from Mercy awaiting him when he got home, asking to meet with him the following afternoon at a tea-house on Oxford Street. At least she'd acquired enough Town bronze not to suggest Melville's.

Still, the note filled him with misgiving. His encounter with Lady Beatrice was still too fresh in his mind. He didn't think he could forgive Mercy for the damage she had done to his consequence.

Then his anger at her faded a little; she'd had so few weapons at her disposal, he almost had to admire how she'd found the perfect one to wound him. And now she was conducting her battle in a more businesslike manner, sending proper notes instead of setting him up for ridicule. However, it was best if he ignored her request; he had nothing more to say to her. It was in his lawyer's hands now—he'd written to him that very morning about resolving the matter.

He tore the note into tiny pieces and handed them to Walter. Walter appeared disappointed. Since the note had not been sealed, Roc could only assume the footman had read it.

"Don't give me that hangdog look," he said brusquely. "You *know* what happens whenever I have anything to do with her. Annoying handbills, upturned scuttles, poisonous potions, pious psalm singers. She is a one-woman plague, my friend. Now I am going to bed."

The teahouse was nearly empty. Roc settled himself at a table in the bow window and began perusing his copy of *The Times*. Sir Robert Poole was to speak in the Commons on Friday, and Roc thought he might take a look-in. Poole could be counted on to stir things up, and Rockleigh needed a distraction.

Well, besides the one that was about to occur in the street outside.

He was idly scanning the lastest crim cons, when Mercy passed by his window. He tossed down the paper and hurried to the door; he didn't want to miss a moment of this.

By the time he reached the threshold, the Morris dancers had come capering out of the alley. Bells jangling, voices raised in rich baritone harmony, they completely encircled Mercy before she had a chance to enter the teahouse.

She stood there, unmoving, as the six men danced around her, singing an ancient song honoring the Queen of the May. The words had been altered slightly, however; it was the "Queen of Mayhem" they now saluted.

Rockleigh lounged in the open doorway observing the sight with relish. Mercy's cheeks were flushed, her hands crossed on her chest, as the Morris men wove a pattern around her, white handkerchiefs whipping and snapping through the air.

A small crowd had gathered on either side of the spectacle; most of the onlookers wore expressions of amusement and, in some cases, overt sympathy for the woman at the center of the ring. Roc's gaze slid again to Mercy.

She was looking directly at him. And she was laughing. There was nothing but delight glittering in her eyes.

His own face tightened. How infuriating of her not to be put out, not to be humiliated and embarrassed. No, she stood there reveling in the performance as though she were an onlooker and not the object of the joke.

When the dancers had finished their song, Mercy shook each of their hands, and with one eye on Rockleigh said loudly, "And now you shall come in and have tea. You must be parched after such a rousing performance, and I'm sure Lord Rockleigh will foot the bill."

They filed past him, grinning and a bit red-faced, Mercy bringing up the rear.

"Thank you," she said as she stopped before him, "that was very entertaining. There's nothing I like so much as a stout troop of Morris men." And then, with a brilliant smile, she went into the shop.

"Damnation," he said under his breath.

They both knew she'd taught him a lesson, given him a stellar example of how a well-bred person handled potential humiliation—with grace and good humor.

Blast her eyes!

He stalked back into the teahouse and sat down opposite her. "If you think you've scored another point off me, let me just tell you that—"

"Rockleigh?"

He looked up instantly. His mother was standing beside the table with two other females slightly behind her. It was the Blythedale tabbies, mother and daughter. He nearly groaned as he rose to his feet and bowed.

His mother dimpled. "We were shopping for Jessica's trousseau at the milliners across the street and heard the commotion outside. I just had to come out and watch. You know how amusing I find Morris dancers. Lady Blythedale saw you hiding in the doorway."

"I wasn't hiding," he muttered.

Lady Blythedale commenced to coughing slightly. His mother turned to her at once. "Yes, Drusilla?"

Lady Blythedale whispered something to the duchess, something which made Her Grace's brows knit. "Of course she isn't," she replied in an undertone. "He certainly wouldn't."

Rockleigh knew instantly what Lady Blythedale was implying: that Mercy was not a woman the duchess should be seen with in public, that is to say, one of his ladybirds.

He looked across to Mercy, who was watching the three women with an expression of alert interest. Her delectable new bonnet was set atop a soft chignon, and her gown of cream-colored muslin, though not precisely stylish, fit her slim body in a way that must surely invite masculine admiration. Over her arms was draped the paisley shawl she'd used to cover him in her parlor.

She was the picture of simple, fresh femininity. His gaze strayed to the two Blythedale women, with their small eyes and hawklike noses. Their dark hair had been dressed alike beneath their plumed bonnets, in a manner that was far too fussy for an afternoon of shopping.

He reached out and took his mother's hand. "Mama, may I introduce Miss Tatlock? Miss Tatlock, my mother, the Duchess of Barrisford. Oh, and I believe that's Lady Blythedale behind her, with her daughter, Miss Blythedale."

Lady Blythedale nearly hissed. Her daughter's mouth formed into a peevish frown as she pointedly looked away from Mercy. "Really, Mama, I must get back to my shopping. I vow I will be extremely put out if someone else buys that length of primrose sarcenet."

His mother, meanwhile, had offered her hand to Mercy, who looked at it for an instant with terror in her eyes, then took it and shook it several times.

The duchess grinned. "Delighted, Miss Tatlock." And then her face fell. She turned to whisper to her son. "But isn't that the name of . . .? You know, the newspaper piece."

"We must be going," he said abruptly as he navigated his way around the three women. "Come, Miss Tatlock, let me see you to your lodgings."

When Mercy didn't budge, he leaned down and practically lifted her from her seat. "You don't want to know those two women," he said under his breath. "No one does."

He threw some coins on the table to cover the bill for the Morris men, and with a swift nod to his mother, he led Mercy from the place.

Lady Blythedale sniffed. "No better than she should be, I expect. And that hat! Fit only for the commonest sort of woman."

The duchess noted the fearful creation of feathers and fruit that sat poised on Lady Blythedale's elaborate coiffure and said a bit combatively, "I thought it was a very pretty hat."

The baroness patted her hand. "But you spend so much time in the country, dear Abigail, you are not quite abreast of the current styles. But let us not distress ourselves by discussing your youngest son's unfortunate taste in women. Torrance's taste is, thank heaven, impeccable." She cast a fond look at her pinch-faced daughter. "Now my Jess shall have her sarcenet before another moment passes, eh, puss?"

The three women crossed the street and returned to the hunt for trousseau treasures. Her Grace, however, had developed a pounding headache and had no heart for it.

Poor Torry, was all she could think, to shackle himself to such a dragon's daughter.

Mercy was strangely quiet as they walked. Rockleigh kept looking down at her, but didn't know quite what to say. He felt sad for some reason. And angry with good reason. How dared those Blythedale cats not acknowledge her!

Finally, in desperation, he said, "I'm sorry."

She stopped walking and turned to face him. "I didn't mind, honestly. I do like Morris men. And it's nothing more than I deserved for tormenting you this past week."

"I wasn't talking about the Morris men. I was referring to the fact that Lady Blythedale and her daughter gave you the cut direct."

"Did they? How remarkable." She started forward again. "I just thought they were being mildly disagreeable. Shopping has that same effect on me."

"My brother Torrance is to marry Miss Blythedale, heaven help him."

She gave a little skip to keep up with his long strides. "You never speak of your family, you know."

He was about to reply that since he rarely thought about them, it was pointless to speak about them. Then he realized that wasn't true any longer. He had found himself thinking about them a great deal lately.

"Torrance is the heir," he said. "He's a right old stick-in-the-mud, but I still don't wish that harpy on him. Trent is next in line; he's off on the Peninsula with Wellington."

"Were you supposed to enter the Church? I believe that's the traditional role for third sons."

Now it was his turn to stop and face her. "Miss Tatlock, having known me for, what is it, eight days, can you honestly see me wearing a surplice and stole?"

She did a curious thing then. She raised her hand and cupped his cheek for an instant. His breathing hitched.

"Do you want the truth? I can see you doing anything at all . . . except wasting your life on the pursuit of empty pleasures." Her nose crinkled. "Goodness, that sounded horribly prosy. Let me say it another way. You made quite an impression on my brother. You did him a great kindness, not only by taking him to Jackson's and asking him to dine at your club. You gave him your undivided attention and offered him a deal of tolerance. I doubt you scowled at him even once."

"I save my scowls for you, Miss Tatlock," he murmured. Gad, he wished she would touch him again.

She smiled up at him, and he felt his heart soar. "I have two other siblings at home."

"Toby told me. You've not exactly been forthcoming about your family either, Mercy." His eyes teased her.

"So you see, I know how tiresome the younger ones can be at times. But you treated Toby so well, I can't help thinking you've a benevolent streak in you somewhere."

Roc shrugged lightly. "He amused me, he and Jack both. Though Master Skillens professes a great understanding of things he clearly knows nothing about."

"Toby's brought him home to Boxwood several times. Papa says that Jack's often wrong, but never, ever in doubt."

"Precisely. Ah, here we are at your lodgings. Has your brother returned here, now that the dread threat of meeting me has been removed?"

She made a face. "No, now he's gone haring off to Hampton Court with Jack. I suppose I should be glad that *one* of us is enjoying their time away from home."

He offered her a commiserating smile. "Well, shall I come up? I assume you still need to speak with me. Or was that note a ruse to get me away from my house so you could have your minions paint grotesques all over the facade?"

"No," she said, repressing a chuckle. "My minions have all retired. I promised my brother not to trouble you any longer."

Ah, if that were only the case, he thought wistfully. He had a sinking feeling she'd be troubling him long after she left London.

"I do need to talk to you though," she said, "and it's best done in private."

He wasn't sure he trusted himself to be private with her. Confound the Blythedales for forcing him from the teahouse. In such a public place he would have had to mind his manners. In her little parlor, there were no such restrictions.

He followed her up the stairs and waited in the wing chair while she set out several spice squares on a plate. Instead of lemonade, she offered him a glass of buttermilk. "Don't turn up your nose," she warned him. "It's quite nourishing."

"I'll just have the cake, if it's all the same," he said, eying the glass of yellowish liquid with something akin to revulsion.

She settled opposite him on an ottoman, nibbling on her cake. "I'm very angry at you," she said conversationally. "Very angry indeed."

"And that is why you are feeding me and offering me healthful potions?"

"No, I am merely trying to distract myself from my anger. But it's there, Lord Rockleigh, make no mistake."

"And you're angry this time over . . . ?"

She sighed and set her plate on the floor. "Toby told me you now intend to offer my father a sum of money to recant."

"Yes, I do. In addition, I will pay any legal costs he has incurred. I was thinking of something in the range of, shall we say, one hundred pounds?"

"Excuse me," she bit out. "That is called bribery. As my brother would say, 'It ain't done.' "

"Five hundred pounds?"

"This is beginning to unsettle me," she cried, springing up from her seat. "Who wants you to pay that much money to keep my father quiet? Do the men who leased the house from you have some hold on you? Have you gotten in over your head with this, Rockleigh? Is that why you aren't free to explain any of it?"

"Sweet heaven, you've a fertile imagination." He rose at once to confront her. "Nobody owns me or has a hold over me. I answer to no one but myself on a good day."

She paced away from him, fretting with the cuff of her gown. When she spun back to face him, her expression was purposeful. "I rarely go into Crowden, but six weeks ago I went there to pay a sick call on a woman, one of my sopranos in the Tiptree parish choir. Afterward, I stopped in at the dry goods store and met a boy of perhaps seven or eight. We fell into talking; he said his name was Perkin . . . from Romney. He told me he was newly come to Crowden to live in the big house. I was curious about that, so I asked him what he was doing there. 'I'm to learn my manners,' he said, 'and then some gentleman will want me.'"

"You couldn't deduce that perhaps he was being trained to go into service?"

"That was my impression, naturally. But then a burly man came along and saw me talking to the boy. He dragged him out of the shop without a word. The door was propped open, and so I overheard him tell the boy to keep his bleedin' gob shut. Er, those were his words."

"Of course."

"And then he said, 'You know the rules . . . you'll be back on the streets faster than a cat can spit if you forget them again.' I wanted to run after the boy and take him away from that rough man. Instead, I started to keep watch on Crowdenscroft."

Rockleigh's brows lowered. "Where you saw, as you said, unkempt boys going in and well-dressed boys coming out. Airtight proof of white slavery, Miss Tatlock. I congratulate you."

She ground her teeth audibly. "Your sarcasm solves nothing."

He moved closer. "And your curiosity will be your downfall one day. I'm surprised your fond father lets you creep around neglected old estates. But maybe he was creeping around with you, since he wrote that fanciful piece."

"I do much of his research."

"But not the actual writing."

"Some of it."

She wouldn't look at him now, and it got him thinking. "But not this piece, right, Miss Tatlock? You didn't write this outrageously off-the-mark editorial."

"My father is chief of staff at *The Trumpet*. He writes the editorials."

He stepped even closer, his eyes narrowed. "But who wrote this one?"

"Whose name is on the lawsuit?"

"Don't try to flummox me, Mercy."

Her mouth turned mutinous. "I know what I saw. I know what I heard. You don't train children to be servants in such secrecy. There's no reason for warning boys to keep quiet unless they're involved in something illicit."

He crossed his arms over his chest, his face a study of smirking delight. "Well, well, well," he purred. "So you wrote the editorial after all. No wonder you defend it so hotly."

She set her fisted hands against her eyes for a moment. When she lowered them, her face was pale. "My father's taking the blame for it," she cried softly. "Doesn't that tell you what sort of man he is? He had nothing to do with it from the start. I wrote it out of righteous anger one night after coming home from Crowden. I left it on Papa's desk, hoping he would use it. One of the pressmen found it and inserted it in the paper by accident."

"And your father didn't filet you for it afterward?"

"Not right after. He thought it was rather good. Just a bit inflammatory, he said."

"Just a bit," he echoed darkly. "Were you aware, ma'am, that a week after that piece appeared, some twenty townsmen from Crowden marched out to my estate after dark? Fortunately, my groundskeepers managed to prevent them from entering, but you can imagine what the sight did to the people who live there."

"Oh, bother!" she cried. "That was all I could think of when I heard about it. Little Perkin and the other boys . . . they must have been so frightened."

He set his palm against his brow and shook his head. "Lord keep me from meddlesome women," he murmured. But when he looked up at her again, his eyes were less harsh. "I will tell you this much, and I hope it will send you back to your wretched Tiptree. There are people I am trying to protect in that house. The boys work for them. Nothing illegal. Nothing illicit."

"It still makes no sense. What sort of work are they doing that requires ruffians to stand guard? And why would Lord Care-for-None concern himself with protecting anyone? I don't believe you. It's just the sort of thing a scoundrel would make up, a scoundrel who . . . who forces his kisses on unwilling women."

"Unwilling?" His mouth twisted. "As I recall it, you were plastered to me like one of your pestilential handbills."

Her bosom swelled in affront. "Plastered? I never was. I was . . . merely carried away by the novelty of the experience."

"Novelty?" he echoed.

"Yes," she said, regaining her composure slightly. "That's all it was. I've been thinking about it, you see. I've never done anything so . . . so rash. But then it came to me, that it was rather like the first time I ate a honey bun. It tasted so delicious, I wanted to eat a hundred. But after nine or ten, you start to lose your appetite. And they are not very good for you, are they? So the novelty wears off, and you become indifferent to them."

"You're not indifferent to me, Mercy," he murmured. "Or unwilling, either."

She steadied her hands on the back of the wing chair. "I may not have been the last time you were here. But I am now. Quite indifferent. And still angry."

"Hang your anger," he said as he moved to face her above the chair back, leaning to press his hands over hers. "I am trying to help you and your family, you ungrateful little shrew. And salve my pride into the bargain. Can't I have that? Won't you let me have at least that?"

His pale eyes entreated her, and she was not proof against that look. But she could not soften her heart, not for all the azure eyes in the kingdom. "Shall I tell my father to back down? Admit that his daughter is a misguided, zealous fool? What about *our* pride, Lord Rockleigh? Or doesn't that matter to men of your ilk?"

"You're not a fool, Mercy—you just drew the wrong conclusions." His hands slid slowly up from her wrists to her elbows, where they lingered, his fingers stroking the fabric of her gown. She recalled that time before the mirror when he had caressed her that way, just before he nuzzled her throat. She wanted to feel his lips on her skin again, to feel that shivery spark of heat that only he could evoke. Her anger at him faded away, replaced by something even stronger. Desire.

She shook it off—she'd vowed she would not let him beguile her—and pulled back from his touch. "We seem to do nothing, you and I, but go around and around. I am nearly dizzy from it."

He studied her quietly for a time. "Back there on the street," he responded softly at last, "you said I'd been benevolent to your brother. You told me there was nothing I could not achieve. So tell me this now—do you truly think I could condone the selling of children into vice?"

Her voice broke. "I don't want to believe it. It shreds me inside to even think it. I have seen you let down your guard with me, Rockleigh. But I've let down my own considerable guard, as well. I surely don't want to believe I made myself vulnerable to a monster."

"I am not a monster," he said evenly.

"No, just a gentleman of the *ton*." She grinned weakly. "You see, I haven't forgotten our first encounter."

"Neither have I." His voice had gone quite husky. "Nor any of the other times we've been together."

Her gaze rose to his face, and what she saw there made her breathing falter. She made a tiny choking noise; he instantly skirted the chair and moved behind her. When his hands gripped her shoulders, it took every ounce of will not to lean into him.

"God help me, you're like a fever in my blood," he murmured against her hair. "A torment I cannot stop. And when you are gone from London, I fear even then it won't be over."

"Oh, Roc," Mercy said, ducking her head away from his seductive whispers. "We both know there's no point to this. There can't ever be any—"

His hands tightened almost painfully on her shoulders. "Listen to me, Mercy. If I promise to drop the case, say you will let me—"

"Don't!" She pushed roughly away from him. "Don't say the words, or I will have such a disgust of you . . . I am reconciled to the offer you made me on Sunday. I understand enough about your life not to hate you for demeaning me. But don't you dare bargain with me for my—"

He cut her off. " 'Pon my honor, that's not what I was doing. I'm not that much of a knave. I only wanted to know if I could call on you once you returned home, after I've settled things with your father."

"Where's the sense in that?" she asked, wondering all the while how she could sound so calm when her heart was drumming a violent tattoo in her chest. "Won't that just make the torment worse?"

For both of us, she added silently.

His mouth tightened for an instant. "I realize now that if there was anything more . . . more intimate between us, it would sully the things I admire in you." He gave her a rueful smile. "It's a fine muddle I've gotten myself into." Drawing in a deep breath, he added, "No, you're right. I suppose it's wisest to part now. Seeing you surrounded by the Tatlock clan might be more than I can weather."

"We're not so bad as all that," she said, rallying slightly.

"No," he murmured, letting his gaze travel over her face like a lover's touch. "I don't believe you are."

Mercy moved to the door and held it open while he retrieved his hat from the wall rack. The fabric of his coat was molded to his shoulders, and it moved with him like a second skin. She nearly sobbed. He was grace and beauty and everything fine she'd ever dreamed of. And he was leaving.

"I'll see what I can do to ease things with my lawyer," he said as he went past her.

"Good-bye," she said in a dry, rasping voice.

He turned, but didn't say a word, just stood looking into her eyes. It was the bleakest moment of her life, losing him, letting him go. It was also the most rewarding moment—all her pain and bewilderment was echoed tenfold in his startling blue gaze.

I care about you very much, her heart whispered into the strained silence.

I know, his responded. *I know.*

Chapter Nine

Rockleigh made the night his own with a vengeance. He delighted a number of hostesses by appearing briefly at their entertainments, and he even made a rare foray into Almack's. The hopeful mamas regarded him with eager eyes, while hiding any niggling doubts about his character behind their fluttering fans. Their daughters welcomed him with dimpled smiles and assessing looks.

Weighing my purse, to a woman, damn them, he observed under his breath.

Stanley was there; they spoke a few words behind a pillar. But his friend seemed preoccupied with a diminutive brunette who was chatting animatedly with a group of young men. A few minutes later, Roc saw Stanley dance by with the young lady in his arms. She barely came up to his shoulder. Would wonders never cease? Stanley had never, to Roc's knowledge, been in the petticoat line. But then his friend probably had a deal of free time on his hands now that the two of them had stopped living in each other's pockets.

"I've been replaced by a simpering Lilliputian," he muttered as he went to find a drink. He cast one look at the watery punch and the listless tea cakes and decided he'd be better off at a lady's charity luncheon. There, at least, he might stand a chance of getting a glass of ratafia.

He sketched a departing wave to Stanley—who seemed barely to notice as he strolled beside his new conquest—and left the assembly rooms with the beginnings of a throbbing headache. It was full blown by the time he reached Madame Montcalm's three-story house.

There were several likely-looking prospects in the parlor, all of them in appealing states of undress. He chose one at random, a blond-haired Juno in a gauze wrapper, and held out his hand. She preened a little as she went to him, then shot a look of triumph over her shoulder at the women behind her before she ducked under the flounced drapery that separated parlor and hall.

"Gor, our Annie's the lucky one tonight," a tall redhead muttered to her companion, a ringleted brunette in a Nile-green negligee. "A lady can always count on Lord Roc to make things interestin'. And from what I hear, he's not been near a brothel in donkey's years."

"And he hasn't set up a new mistress, neither, not since Belle DeWitt and Josie DuValle tangled over him last month on the steps of Covent Garden."

Both women looked up at the ceiling with open envy. Whatever was about to transpire in the room above them, Annie was sure to be the better off for it, one way or another.

Roc observed the woman on the bed. As was the custom at Madame Montcalm's, the whore was cleaner than most. He thought he caught a gleam of intelligence in her dark eyes. Or perhaps it was avarice. What did it matter? They were all avaricious—though he did not mind it if *these* ladies weighed his purse; it was part of their business after all.

He began to undo his neckcloth. Annie crawled up from the bed and relieved him of the task.

"So fine, sir," she murmured as she drew the length of linen several times around her right wrist. Her left hand, meanwhile, had begun to trace its way down his chest to his lean belly. "So very fine."

He stepped back abruptly, barely concealing his revulsion at her light, teasing touch. Her hands were clean, but the nails were chipped, gnawed down to the quick in some places. And there wasn't an ink smudge in sight.

He controlled an incipient shudder. Something was terribly wrong. He needed more to drink. He needed more time. He needed—No! He'd sworn he wasn't going to say it. He was never going to say that name again. *She* was no different from this woman, no better, no prettier. So why should a whore's hands make him ill? Why should *her* undainty, capable hands fill him with longing?

Annie was looking at him with a certain amount of professional tolerance. "S'been a while then, has it? Some parts get a bit rusty. Your Annie can fix that. A little grease for the axle.. . ."

She reached for him again, her aim frighteningly acute. He nearly leapt back out of range.

"Not tonight, Annie, I'm afraid," he said quickly, tugging his neckcloth away from her. "There's something I've forgotten. Something I must do."

He threw a handful of notes onto the canopied bed and backed out of the room. The servants' stairs were at the end of the hall, and he hurried down them, groping his way out into the back of the house. After stumbling past an assortment of castoff furniture, he reached a high plank fence, coming smack up against it in the dark. And then he just stood there, face pressed to the damp wood, shivering and afraid.

His body was fine; he could have taken his pleasure with Annie and perhaps a few of her friends, as well. No, it was the resounding, doomsaying thud in his chest that was making him quake with fear. All he saw, there in the thick, stifling darkness, was the broken gate, the shattered barrier. All he felt was the certainty that his rock-solid heart, which he'd have sworn was inviolable, had been breeched.

He could not deny it any longer; it shouted and railed to be heard. At the same time it whispered to him for surcease, for a completion that had nothing to do with the bodies of whores or titled ladies and everything to do with discovering a warm, bright haven in a cold, ugly world.

"Mercy," he uttered hoarsely, saying aloud the name he had foresworn. "Sweet Mercy, what have you done to me?"

His mother was still up, expecting his father's return, no doubt. Rockleigh wondered how a man could wander idly through the Town when such a woman awaited him at home. These were new revelations to him, he realized, but there was a logic to them he'd never before appreciated.

She looked up from her desk and laid down her pen as he came into the room. More of those endless letters, he saw. He wondered how the head gardener's daughter was faring, off in Ireland. She'd been a pretty snip of a thing, though it had been strictly hands off for him and his brothers. The gardener was not a man you wanted to cross.

"This is a surprise," said the duchess as he slouched into a chair without a word. "I'd been wondering when you would find time to pay me a visit. I barely managed to have three words with you this afternoon."

"I'm sorry about that," he said. "The Blythedales are a royal pain."

"Yes," she answered with a little sigh. "I'm beginning to notice."

"At any rate, I wasn't sure I'd be welcome here. Stanley says Father is about to obliterate my name from the family ranks."

"Your father is not . . . happy with you at present. Not that I blame him; I heard some of what happened the other night at Bacchus."

"It wasn't opium, Mama," he said earnestly. "I promise I've left all that behind me." His chin sank down onto his chest. "Got a new vice now."

He'd announced this in such a drawling, sarcastic tone that she wasn't sure if he was asking for help or just trying to tweak her.

"You can be extremely provoking, Rocky. And you forget yourself, if you think your Mama cares to hear about your newest *chère amie* or your latest gambling losses."

He glanced up at her from over the folds of his neckcloth. "It's not that kind of vice. Oh, it grips me, right enough. Calls to me and won't let go for an instant. What's the word? Obsession?"

"I think you must be foxed."

He grinned at her. "Were it only that simple. A man can sleep off a night on the town. This thing that holds me . . . there are not enough nights in a hundred centuries to free me from it."

She rose and went to him, setting her hand on his shoulder. "This sounds serious." She could barely repress a smile. It had come to him at last, she saw, and was wise enough to know that he would put up the devil of a fight.

She'd had some suspicion that afternoon in the teahouse—

she'd seen the anger in his eyes when Drusilla and her daughter had snubbed his companion. That wasn't like her Rocky at all; he never stirred himself for anyone. Yet righteous fury had sizzled there for an instant, just before he whisked the young woman away under his protective arm. A Miss Tatlock, she recalled. Daughter, perhaps, to the man who had accused her son of a heinous crime. She'd been intrigued at the time.

Now the truth was right under her nose, sulking in a chair.

"Is this something you'd like to talk about?"

"No."

"You're just teasing me then, giving me the meager details so that I can lie awake all night and puzzle it out."

He shifted forward and looked up at her. "I don't expect you to puzzle it out, Mama. I haven't been able to do that in over a week's time. I . . . I was just hoping His Grace was here so I could ask him to forgive me. I put him through hell the other night. No man should do that to another, let alone his own father."

She nodded once. "I'll tender your apology. It might hold more weight coming from me."

Rockleigh's face tightened into an expression of dismay. "Never say he takes it out on you? My misdeeds, my scandals? Tell me he doesn't blame you because you intercede for me."

The duchess nearly rolled her eyes. "Good heavens, child. His Grace dotes on your mama." She settled in a chair beside his. "You're muddled in your head if you've ever believed otherwise."

"Yes," he said, again leaning back against the cushions. "I'm all muddled in my head. I don't know what to think about anything."

With a patient sigh, she reached out to him and touched her fingers to his lean cheek. "Maybe you shouldn't think. There's that Conniston side again, assessing everything."

His gaze shifted up to her face. "I think I've found my Benning side, Mama."

"Amen," she whispered softly. And then, with the relentlessness of mothers since man first crawled up from the swamp, she said brightly, "Now tell me about this Miss Tatlock you introduced me to this afternoon."

"Oh, no," he said, struggling to his feet. "There's nothing to be said on that score. She's going back to Tiptree and good riddance to her."

"And why, pray, did she have a personal escort of Morris men?"

"I owed her a bit of payback, is all. A harmless jest. You saw her face—she enjoyed it."

"I saw your face, as well. It made you unhappy. It also made you unhappy when Lady Blythedale ignored her. It seems that in one instant you were trying to make her look foolish, and in the next you were ready to slay dragons for her."

"Someone should slay *those* two dragons," he muttered. "Sanctimonious harpies. She's worth a dozen of them." His hand fisted in the disordered mess of his neckcloth. He cast a beseeching look at her. *Please,* his eyes entreated, *please don't make me say it.*

"You've said enough," she answered softly—and saw that she had startled him with her acuity. "Perhaps you should go now. It's been a difficult day. Rather more revelations than either of us were expecting."

It was a toss-up. He could go to White's and find Stanley—they'd made a sketchy plan at Almack's to meet there at the end of the evening—or he could go home. If he saw Stanley, he feared he'd have to listen to a lot of moonstruck prattling about the petite brunette. Then again, Stanley might have to listen to a parcel of besotted musings about a tall, tawny-haired bluestocking. It could go either way.

No, he'd be wiser to seek his own bed. Maybe he could induce Walter to clout him over the head with a poker and put him temporarily out of his misery.

However, Walter was not there when he arrived home. He called out from the front hall, then shouted his way through the house. His footman had apparently left him to his own devices, curse the fellow!

Roc was in his bedroom, tugging himself out of his coat, when Walter appeared in the doorway, breathless and disheveled. "Sir, I'm sorry I wasn't here. I've been out to White's and Watier's looking for you . . . the courier said it was urgent." He sagged against the doorframe and held out a sealed letter.

Rockleigh's heart missed a beat. He knew that odd scrawling script, even though he hadn't seen it in months. He took the note from Walter and guided him into a chair. "Sit and catch your breath, my friend. You did very well."

Roc sat on the edge of the bed and scanned the note. It was worse, much worse than he imagined. "Have you an ounce of strength left, Walter? Because I need you to run about London some more. You can take my mare. It's . . . it's life or death, I'm afraid."

Walter drew himself to his feet. "I'm your man, Lord Rockleigh."

Roc smiled grimly. What had he done to deserve such loyalty? "You are indeed. Now I want you to drink a bit of brandy before you leave. Meanwhile, I'll write down the places you need to go."

"I'll see to it, no fear," Walter said.

No, Roc thought with a shiver, *a great deal of fear.*

Mercy heard the noise as if from a great distance. Iron spikes being driven into wooden planks. Great axes hewing towering oaks. *Bang! Bang! Bang!*

She struggled up from deep sleep, tugging at the sheets that had twisted around her legs. There it was again, a steady, insistent banging that made her heart race. No good ever came of late-night visitors.

She fumbled for her robe, and then, cursing when she could not find it, went out into the parlor clad only in her nightgown. Crossing cautiously to the door in the darkness, she opened it and stepped onto the landing. The night banger was down at street level, hammering at the lower door, which Mr. Gribbings kept locked at night. Grasping the wooden railing, she crept down the unlit stairs like a blind woman in a tilted tunnel.

"Who is it?" she called through the door.

"Mercy, please! Let me in."

His voice was muffled, but not enough to keep her pulse from faltering at the sound of it. *He must be drunk,* was her first thought. Or addled by that drug he'd boasted of using.

She was halfway up the stairs when she heard him call out, "It's Toby! I must speak with you about Toby."

When she unlocked the door, he nearly carried her up the stairs with the force of his urgency. She quickly lit a candle and spun to face him. He was dressed for travel, wearing a long driving coat and topboots.

"Sit down," he ordered, motioning to the wing chair.

"But—" What she saw in his face made her knees turn to jelly. She sank into the chair with a soft whimper.

"Your brother," he said in a controlled voice, "did not go to Hampton Court. He went down to Crowdenscroft to poke his nose into my affairs." He set his hands on her wrists. "He's been hurt, Mercy. Shot, it appears. He's alive, but not conscious. I don't know much more than that."

Mercy took the piece of paper he now held out to her. She read the words, but it took fully two minutes before they made any sense to her.

> *Sir, there has been another commotion here. A young gentleman was shot outside the grounds this morning—he is most grievously wounded. We brought him inside and sent for the doctor from Crowden. The young man revived enough to say his name was Tatlock. Tobias, I think. Then he asked after someone named Jack, but there is no sign of another boy. The doctor is not reassuring me and the patient has not stirred again. This is a sorry thing. It would be best if you came down here yourself.*

It was signed only with the initial *G.*

She looked up at him. "Who is this man, this G?"

"You'll find out soon enough. Get some things together. I've got my curricle outside, if that street arab who's holding my horses hasn't stolen it. You're going to get your wish, Mercy. You're going to see the inside of Crowdenscroft. The doctor should already be on his way."

She rose at once from her chair. "What doctor?"

"I sent Walter to fetch my father's town coach and then to wake up Sir Ryan Digby. He's a friend of Trent's, an ex-army surgeon who has a practice in London. My brother swears by him, claims there's nothing he doesn't know about bullet wounds." He took Mercy by the shoulders and shook her gently. "Toby will have the best care, sweetheart. I promise."

She gazed up at him with hollow eyes. "Did your men shoot him, do you think, the ones who patrol the grounds?"

"I doubt that's the case. But he shouldn't have been creeping around down there."

Why would Toby lie to me? she wondered dismally. But the answer came soon enough. One lie begets a thousand, Rockleigh had warned her. She'd lied to Papa; now her brother had lied to her. And Lord Rockleigh, was he lying as well? Covering up for his hired bullies?

She shook off her shock-induced paralysis and turned toward the table—she'd need to leave a message for Mr. Gribbings. Something that wouldn't worry him overmuch.

"He won't die," Rockleigh called out softly as she folded her note to the old man. "Not with you there to boss him back to life. Now hurry and pack. We've a night of travel ahead of us."

She hung on gamely to the side of his curricle as they raced out of London. Rockleigh's bays were fresh and full of the devil. She had a feeling that he was not the sort of callous owner to spring his horses out of caprice, but she appreciated that he was getting every bit of speed from them now.

They stopped fifteen miles out of town to change horses, but she didn't alight from the carriage. She heard Rockleigh charge the ostler to walk his horses for an hour before they were stabled, and then he climbed back into the seat and set his whip to the new pair.

Towns flashed past, then long stretches of countryside. The roads grew increasingly bumpier the farther they got from London. She clutched his arm several times when they rounded curves at an almost reckless speed. At one point he muttered something about them both breaking their necks, and after that, he restrained his horses to a less hair-raising pace.

If only she'd learned to drive a pair, Mercy lamented; she could have spelled him. It had to be exhausting, staying alert on such a dark night with the full moon often obscured by clouds.

As worried as she was over Toby, she couldn't help but marvel at Rockleigh's skill and strength. For a man she'd judged idle and devoid of active pursuits, he possessed a remarkable stamina. He seemed, during the final stage of their journey when she began to make out familiar landmarks in the inky darkness, to be urging the tired horses onward with the force of his will alone.

They went through Crowden at a scant trot, passing along the small high street, past the butcher and the baker and the dry-goods store where she'd met Perkin from Romney. The estate was perhaps a mile beyond the village, and it was the longest mile Mercy had ever traversed. Rockleigh had tucked her hand under his arm some miles back, and now he moved it so that it rested over his heart. She nestled it against the softness of his neckcloth, feeling the heat of him and the strength.

"Not long now," he whispered, leaning down to rest his head upon hers for an instant. She moved right up against him, offering him the support of her own strong back and the warmth of her body.

They came to the high stone wall that surrounded Crowden-scroft, and then the double gate was looming before them, wrought iron tipped with spaded points, all ornately gone to rust.

Rockleigh cursed under his breath as his stiffened fingers awkwardly drew a large key from his coat pocket. "Can you open it?" he asked. "I dare not leave the horses."

As if these weary beasts are going anywhere, she thought as she climbed down. The lock opened easily, and she pushed both sides of the gate wide. He drove the curricle through them and then drew up his horses. "Lock it," he said grimly. "Please."

Once she was seated again in the carriage, he shifted around. "Whatever we find in there," he said gruffly, "I want you to know I'm sorry. It shouldn't ever have come to this."

"No," she said, forcing herself to turn away from the misery in his voice. "It shouldn't."

But then she shifted back to him—she couldn't help herself. He was hurting just as she was. He cared now, almost as much as she did. "It's not your fault, Rockleigh. Toby's nearly a man grown. He made his own choices, even if they turned out to be dangerous, foolish ones."

"Thank you," he said softly. "I needed to hear you say that."

She expected him to take up the reins again, but he sat there looking down at his hands. "There's something else I should tell you. Inside that house are certain things that you might not care for or approve of. I'm asking you to be tolerant, Mercy."

"All I care is that Toby's there. Nothing else matters."

He touched her sleeve briefly, then set his horses in motion once again.

When they pulled up to the shallow, covered porch, a burly man in gaiters came out of the house. "The boy's still breathing," he announced at once. "We weren't expecting you so soon, sir. You made good time."

"Is the surgeon here yet, Finney?"

"Aye." The big man gave a quick grin. "He made better time."

Rockleigh nodded, then explained to Mercy, "My father keeps his own cattle on the Dover route, prime goers. I knew Digby would need to make haste."

She had wondered why he hadn't availed himself of his father's coach; now she understood—he'd given the faster vehicle to the doctor. She ought to thank him, but she had no more words. Only a gnawing, desperate desire to see her brother.

Roc lifted her down and set her on the top step of the porch. A woman had come to stand in the open doorway; she was silhouetted by the soft light from the hall behind her. Her belly was greatly distended beneath her gown; she appeared to be only weeks away from her confinement. Rockleigh went forward immediately, took her hands and spoke to her in an undertone.

At the sight of them together, Mercy's chest constricted painfully. This now explained all his secrecy about Crowdenscroft. He'd been trying to protect this woman. A woman who was likely carrying his child. A discarded mistress—or, she revised mentally as she saw Rockleigh bend his head toward her, not quite so discarded. Just exiled to the country, not unlike many *ton* wives, while she increased.

What other explanation could there be? No, she argued, she was done with rushing into judgment. But Rockleigh's warning, spoken less than five minutes earlier, now made complete sense. She wondered how much tolerance she could manage.

Rockleigh motioned her forward and made a swift introduction. Mercy was too shaken to catch the woman's name. She did observe that she was blond-haired and not so young, perhaps thirty-two or -three. Her eyes were bright, intelligent, but her mouth was drawn down slightly by some perpetual sadness.

Mercy knew she ought to make a polite greeting, but she was too weary to thrust away her suspicions. They crowded her and would not let her breathe. She felt light-headed, as though she might at any second collapse onto the flags of the hall. Another part of her wanted to swing around and berate Rockleigh for daring to bring her here.

Ah, but Toby was here. Rockleigh'd had no choice.

"Where is my brother?" she asked the woman abruptly. Then her voice softened. "Please, I must see him."

"Of course. I will take you to him."

"I'm sorry," Mercy said as they ascended an oak staircase. "I didn't quite catch your name."

"It's Sally Banner," the woman said with a bob of her head.

She had not called herself *Mrs.* Banner, Mercy thought archly.

Oh, Lord, when did I turn into such a horrid cat? This woman has probably been looking after Toby. How can I dislike her, even if she is carrying Rockleigh's—

No, she wasn't going to let her feelings intrude here. It was none of her concern. Rockleigh Conniston was none of her concern.

She followed Sally Banner along a dark corridor. They passed a number of doorways until they reached a passage that led to the rear of the house. "The boys sleep in this wing," Sally said over her shoulder. "It's also where we have an infirmary of sorts. With so many boys about, it's rather a necessity. We put your brother in here."

The room was lit by several branches of candles and contained three beds. An auburn-haired, narrow-shouldered man in a fine black coat was bent over the center bed. He looked up in surprise as they came into the room.

"I'm his sister," Mercy said. "How is he?"

The man's face was grave. "It's hard to tell, ma'am. Though the doctor from Crowden stopped the flow of blood, he was afraid to extract the pistol ball—I fear it's lodged near your brother's spine. I can remove it, but he could end up with a paralysis."

"And if you don't remove it?"

"The wound may fester and poison his blood."

"And he will die?"

He only nodded once.

"Remove it." It was Rockleigh's voice. He'd come up behind them. "Do it, Digby. Trent says you've the hands of an angel, with no mucking about."

"May I see him first?" Mercy asked, with uncharacteristic hesitance. The sickroom and all its trappings were foreign to her. She had a sudden wish that Mama was there beside her.

"Of course," Sir Ryan said. "He's still not come to, but I expect that's from loss of blood. They tell me he was lying in a pool of it when they found him." He looked as though he was about to apologize for bringing up such a distasteful subject, but Mercy had already gone past him to kneel beside the narrow bed.

Toby was lying on his side facing her, his shirt gone and a blanket covering his lower limbs. She stroked her hand along his pale cheek. "Oh, Tobe," she whispered. "Mercy's here now. It's going to be all right. Everything's going to be fine. I'm watching over you. We're all watching over you."

She found his hand, limp beneath the edge of the blanket, and squeezed it. There was no response. She moved away from the bed, trading places with Sir Ryan, who began to set out his instruments. "I'll need someone to assist me," he said, looking up at Rockleigh.

Sally Banner stepped forward. "I can help, sir. I was raised in a cantonment. I know my way around a surgery."

Mercy was about to volunteer, as well, but Rockleigh caught her by the arm and drew her from the room. "No, Sally will do what needs to be done. I have to talk to you alone."

She pulled away from him. "I'm not sure I have anything to say to you. Did you see him in there? Bloodless, broken."

"But you said out in the drive . . . ?"

"That was before I saw that woman, your—"

He set his hand over her mouth and tugged her along the passage. "Mercy, my patience has limits. Even with you." He squared her up before a doorway. "Now listen to me. I want to send for your parents. They need to be here in case . . . in case he—"

"In case he dies?" she bit out. "Well, he isn't going to die. You said it yourself: Sir Ryan is a miracle worker. My parents have been under a terrible strain these past weeks, which I lay at your door. And now you want them to come to this house? To have all its unpleasant secrets laid before them?"

"What in blazes has that to do with your brother?"

But she wasn't heeding him. "I swear, the instant Toby can be moved, I will take him away from this place."

"As you like, Miss Tatlock," he said with incredible control. "That is certainly your decision to make." He indicated the door behind her. "This is your room. You would do well to keep the door locked when you are inside. If you hear something scratching at the panel, call out. If no one answers, don't open it."

She had a mind to ask him if there were lunatics ranging about the place as well as his exiled mistresses. Instead, she brushed past him and went inside. She drew off her cloak and lay down on the bed, nearly numb with weariness. The hours they'd spent on the road had become a blur. She forced herself to make the last hour a blur, as well, to focus all her thoughts on the still, silent figure of her brother. However, there was little she could to aid him but pray, and that seemed a feeble thing in this dark hour.

Chapter Ten

Rockleigh went back outside, needing to deal with his anguish and his anger in private. The sight of Toby's still form had shaken him to the core. What a bloody irony it was, that the one noble act he'd performed in his lifetime had now turned around to strike at him and those he cared about.

Oh, he could tell himself that Toby had brought this disaster down on his own head, but Roc knew differently. One word of explanation back in London to Mercy or her brother, and this tragedy would have been averted. But because of his blind arrogance, his lifelong caution, he'd refused to explain. And had inadvertently sent a young man into danger.

He stalked around the perimeter of the estate, passing in sequence the two guards who patrolled the grounds. As he neared the stable block, a loud, guttural howling arose in the night. He raised his head as the noise was repeated, even louder this time, and his eyes widened.

A small, oddly dressed figure broke from the stable, running low to the ground, sometimes on two legs, sometimes on all fours. Six feet from him, it launched itself into the air and careened into his chest.

"Bulbul!" he cried, rubbing at the long, furry arms that had wrapped themselves tightly around his neck. He felt his anger begin to subside almost instantly. "Ah, my sweet Bulbul."

"She misses you, Rock-lee," came a soft melodic voice from the shadows of the stable.

Roc half turned toward that voice. "I see you're both hiding out here."

"Your secrets remain safely out of doors, Rock-lee, as long as there are strangers in the house."

"What nonsense is this?" he said as he lowered Bulbul to the ground. She grunted in displeasure and danced around him, lifting her arms. "No, vixen," he chided, "mind your manners." She showed her teeth, and then moved away, crouching down and tugging at the hem of the drab coat she wore over her bare, hairy legs.

The man moved forward into the spill of light from the stable doorway. He was tall, nearly as tall as Roc, his skin smooth and dark, like polished mahogany. The hair that waved over his brow was jet black. Back in India, where his own skin had darkened to a fine shade of teak, Roc often thought they could be taken for brothers.

"I'm sorry this has fallen on your shoulders, Gupta. The boy's father is the one who published that blasted newspaper piece. I met young Tatlock in London. I refused to bring him down here, so I gather he decided to have a look on his own. Trying to vindicate me, perhaps." Roc's face twisted. "No sign of his friend yet?"

Gupta shook his head. "We found an abandoned gig down the road, the horse gone missing."

"Tell me what happened yesterday. The boy's sister is here—she'll need to know."

"There were men outside the gates Tuesday night and the night before. Quiet they were, sneaking about. Bulbul scared them off the first time. But last night, very late it was, we heard shots being fired. Two shots, I think. Bulbul was shrieking out on the lawn—she woke up the whole house. I went outside the gates with Finnigan and Harris—they are good, steady men you hired, my friend. Bulbul led Finney to the ravine across the road, and that's where he found the boy."

"Any idea who those men were?"

"Not from the town. The doctor from Crowden was making calls Tuesday night and said he didn't see one soul on the roads. No, those men were not from the village."

"Dover," Rockleigh spat out.

"Why do you say that in such a way?"

"Because I've been a blind fool, Gupta. Because a man I

have every reason to mistrust is behind this. And he hails from Dover."

"Will the boy live, do you think? Maybe he saw the man who shot him."

"Toby doesn't need to describe him," Rockleigh said with a grim smile. "This has the feel of Doncaster, the smell of him. Still, I'd better ride to Dover as soon as it's light. I need to find some proof of my suspicions before I call in the authorities." He tugged on the sleeve of Gupta's coat. "Now come back inside; the boys will need you. You're my strong right arm, remember?"

Gupta smiled, a flash of white in the darkness. "And what of the young man's sister? Will she not be alarmed by me?"

"Ho, Miss Tatlock? You get on her good side, my friend, and you won't find a better advocate. You—um, might want to keep Bulbul away from the house, though. I don't know how Mercy feels about baboons."

Mercy started awake to an echoing howl and instantly feared it must be coming from Toby. Except it had not sounded even remotely human. But something had made that bloodcurdling noise. Unless she'd been dreaming.

She glanced down at her bodice watch and realized she had only been asleep for ten minutes. Whatever it was that had awakened her, she was glad of it. She'd never meant to sleep; she needed to stay alert, ready to rush to her brother's bedside, in case he didn't—

She raised one hand to her mouth to halt her shivery, panicked breathing. What had happened to all her fortitude and her clearheadedness? Even her mother, who was at times distressingly volatile, always managed to stay calm during family medical emergencies. It was only this recent financial emergency that had sent her into a decline.

All Mercy could feel was a sick anguish in her belly. She might have vented her anger on Rockleigh, but she blamed herself fully as much. If only she hadn't written that cursed editorial. Oh, and why hadn't she stayed in Tiptree and fought her battle with Rockleigh Conniston from a distance, with letters and threats of countersuits? But she'd been so certain she couldn't fail in person, not with right on her side.

What was it Mr. Gribbings had said about Hannibal? *He believed himself invincible. Anyone who thinks that is ripe for a fall.*

Only she hadn't been the one to fall; it had been Toby.

Mercy forced herself to get up. She wouldn't lie there like a fainthearted child; she'd been raised to have more pluck than that. And so what if she wasn't accustomed to the sickroom—she'd at least be there with Toby.

She opened the door to the infirmary slowly, not wanting to startle anyone inside. Sally Banner looked up from dabbing at the blood that was welling up in Toby's wound. Sir Ryan never raised his eyes as he probed the ragged hole with a long metal forcep. They'd moved Toby to the right-hand bed, Mercy saw, and placed several clean sheets beneath him. The top layer was already bright with his blood.

She made a strangling noise deep in her throat.

"There's no one to see to you if you faint," Sir Ryan said warningly under his breath. And then, "Ah, there. Got it!" He dropped the misshapen piece of metal into a basin. "More gauze, Sally, there's too much blood. I need to see if the rib's splintered."

Mercy forced back her dizziness and went swiftly to the pile of medical supplies on the table between the two beds. She handed several gauze pads to Sally, who immediately pressed them firmly against her brother's back.

"Thank you," Sally said. "I think the worst is over now."

Sir Ryan worked on Toby for several more minutes and then stood up with a satisfied expression. "Doesn't appear to be any bone damage. And I believe I've cleaned out any stray bits of fabric." His gaze shifted to Mercy. "They're always the devil in a pistol wound."

She watched as he closed up the oozing hole with catgut stitches, far neater than any she'd ever been able to manage on her samplers. Roc's brother was right—Sir Ryan Digby was a gifted surgeon.

He covered the wound liberally with basilicum ointment, and then he and Sally bound a wide linen bandage around Toby's waist. "Only time will tell now," Sir Ryan said as he cleaned the blood from his hands in the basin of water on the washstand.

"I'll get Finney to move him back to his own bed," Sally said.

"No, I'll carry him."

Mercy turned abruptly. Rockleigh was leaning against the doorframe. "It's the least I can do," he said as he moved past her with a wry look, "since this seems to be a committee effort."

As he lifted Toby from the bloodstained bed, the sheet over his lower body started to slide off. "Perhaps you ladies should excuse us," he said quickly as he grabbed at the length of linen.

"Men!" Sally was grinning as she ushered Mercy from the room. "As if I'd never seen a young gentleman's limbs before."

Considering Sally's present condition, Mercy suspected she'd seen rather more than that.

They stood there in the hallway and an awkward silence fell between them. Finally Mercy said, "He seems a very capable surgeon. And my brother surely owes his life to him. I hope Toby won't go off hotheaded into any more misadventures for a long, long time."

"They *are* hotheaded at that age," Sally agreed. "I was a governess in India, and I watched a number of my charges grow up. The good news is they do get past that age."

And then they turn into Lord Rockleigh Conniston, Mercy nearly added.

Sally touched her sleeve. "I was thinking of having some tea before I start breakfast for the boys. Would you like a cup?"

"No, I can't think of food. And I want to stay close by in case he wakes up."

Sally nodded and then moved away. Her gait was ungainly now and slow, although she'd moved along briskly enough earlier, when she'd led Mercy up here. This couldn't be good for her, Mercy reflected. All this stress and turmoil. Not good for mother or child.

She called out, "Thank you for all you've done."

Sally turned back. "I'd do anything for Lord Rockleigh, Miss Tatlock. I owe him a debt that can never be repaid."

And what about what he owes you? Mercy wanted to cry out. Dash it all, the woman was practically a saint, carrying his child without complaint and looking after Toby and the other boys. She wondered how such a good woman came to care for such a wicked man. She might as well ask herself the same question, she realized bitterly. Rockleigh had a surfeit of decent women in thrall to him; she wondered if there were others, hidden away in various holdings around the country.

How foolish she'd been to think she was special to him. He merely had a hunger for her, the way he hungered for brandy or for opium. She was just another stimulant in his empty, pointless life.

She forced away these unhappy musings. Toby had to be at the center of her thoughts now.

Ah, but the pain of realization was so keen . . . she felt wounded in a deep, hidden place, somewhere so remote that even the miracle-working Sir Ryan could not aid her.

Mercy checked on her brother throughout the day, but he never stirred. Sally had told her that a bit of fever was to be expected, but the sight of his flushed face filled her with misgiving. She managed to choke down a light luncheon of soup and bread in her room, but that had been only to keep her strength up; she had no appetite at all.

The times she wasn't sitting with Toby, she spent napping or reading a book of sonnets she had found in her night table. There was something about Crowdenscroft that unsettled her, and she had no desire to explore anything except the corridor between bedroom and sickroom.

She had never found the place especially appealing during her weeklong vigil in April, when she'd kept watch from the hill across the road. Even though the house was built in the Jacobean mode, a style she favored, it seemed closed in on itself, like a miser guarding his gold.

Now that she'd gotten inside the place, it still disturbed her, though for no reason she could fathom. The room she'd been given was neatly appointed, and the other rooms she'd seen were clean and in good repair. Unlike the exterior, which bore the sorry appearance of long neglect, the grass growing wild on the lawns, the hedges untrimmed, the paint on the wooden window frames flaking and patchy.

This dichotomy perplexed her. Why bother to fix up the interior and leave the outside to the elements? What purpose did it serve? Ah, but she knew these small towns in Kent. The instant a run-down estate showed signs of refurbishment, everyone from the vicar to the local seamstress would come calling. Rockleigh clearly wanted no one calling on Crowdenscroft. And so the grounds and house had continued to present an unwelcoming aspect to any one who passed by.

She took a moment to wonder where Rockleigh had gotten to. He hadn't looked in on her brother all day, and it was getting on toward dusk. She wouldn't blame him if he'd spent the day asleep. He'd set a killing pace last night. It still impressed her, the hard steel she'd glimpsed beneath that languid exterior. Whatever his morals, and she judged them to be only slightly higher than a tomcat's, he had come through for her.

The way a friend would, she realized, though she hadn't any close friends to judge by. Once they'd left Mrs. Filbert's academy, all her school friends had gone off to London or to Bath to meet marriageable men. She had gone home to Tiptree to meet long-winded politicians, disagreeable landlords and parsimonious advertisers.

That she had been shortchanged somehow was only now occurring to her. Rockleigh had teased her that the new bonnet might appeal to the frivolous side of her nature. She realized now, as she set down her book, that she didn't have a frivolous side. A wishful side, perhaps, and certainly a humorous side. But there were never thoughts of gaiety or lighthearted pursuits inside her head.

"I'm an old tombstone," she thought wretchedly. "No wonder he doesn't want me."

It was nearing seven when Mercy went to the sickroom to spell Sally. She wasn't there, but a young boy was sitting on the bed next to Toby's. With a shock, she realized it was Perkin, the child she'd met in Crowden.

"I was prayin' on him," the boy said. "But quiet like. Mizz Sally says we need to pray ifn we want good things to happen. I surely don't want this here boy to die."

"Neither do I," Mercy said gently.

Perkin reminded her of Toby at that age, in spite of his badly cut hair and his ill-fitting clothing. He also made her think of Ralph and Bitsy, on the other side of the ridge, barely three miles away.

Should she send for her father? she wondered for the hundredth time. Would he ever forgive her if Toby died? She forced back tears that would serve no purpose.

A small hand crept into hers. "Mizz Sally says iss awright to cry." He tugged Mercy down onto the bed and then surprised her by crawling into her lap. "We'll watch over him," the boy said, nestling against her. "So he knows inside him that he iss not alone."

It was dusk when Rockleigh returned to the house, nearing total exhaustion and barely able to keep upright in the saddle. He had spent the day canvassing Dover's lowest haunts, its brothels and workhouses and waterfront taverns. He'd even ventured into a mollie house, one of the discreet brothels that offered strictly male companionship. He knew such places existed in London, but his own appetites had always drawn him to other establishments. The house in Dover had been more refined that he'd expected, and to his relief there had been no children on display.

He had opened more than a few doors by pretending to be the very thing that Mercy's editorial had accused him of—a procurer in search of prey. He'd looked the part, right enough, as he made his rounds, unshaven, unwashed, unkempt.

It didn't take long to discover, in these unsavory places, that any craving could be fed if the price was right. He'd finally eked out a few names, those of the shadowy connections who sold children of both sexes to men of tainted appetite. He soon felt tainted himself, even if he was only playing a part.

It had been worth it, though; he'd learned enough to put the pieces of the puzzle together. Doncaster's name had been whispered to him more than once, most distressingly at a workhouse run by a pouch-bellied, greasy-haired man. The children in the desolate yard had ranged in age from three or four, clinging to their mother's skirts, to twelve or thirteen, standing alone and trying to muster an expression of hardened cockiness. All were gray-faced and whip-thin.

The man had assured Rockleigh in a low voice that someone named Doncaster had been there looking for "goods" to sell in London. "IIe an' his men come here less than a month ago.

Rough-lookin' lot, they was. But," he'd added with a wink, "he paid a fair price."

Rockleigh saw now that he'd been doing the devil's own work in trying to shut down Tatlock's paper. There were sordid, ugly things in the world that were far more deserving of ruination than an idealistic man with a compulsion to instigate change.

Finney was patrolling near the front of the house when Rockleigh came down the drive; he hurried over and helped him dismount. Roc dragged himself through the front door—and found himself surrounded by boys. They quickly shifted away, cowed perhaps by his great height or his haunted, hollow-eyed expression. Still, it had been the same the other two times he'd been down here. Although he knew this was a different group of boys, they nonetheless gave him a wide berth.

A week ago he'd have called them a parcel of ungrateful brats—it was his money, after all, that funded their schooling. Now he looked at them with new eyes, saw how helpless they were against any who wished them harm, how beaten down by life some of them still seemed. He thanked heaven that they were safe inside this place and not fodder for the likes of Doncaster.

One bold fellow did come forward, asking if he could take his hat. Rockleigh placed his fine beaver over the boy's cowlicked hair. The boy gave him a wide grin as the hat sank down over his eyes.

"You need a bit of meat on you," Roc said, propping the brim up with one finger.

"They all need a bit of meat on them," Sally remarked, coming up beside him.

The boys clustered around her, leaning toward her. They were so damned hungry for affection, for a simple, kindly touch. In India, he'd watched Bulbul's mother risk her own life to protect her from poachers—which was more than he could say for some human parents. It made him want to despise his own kind.

"We were just going in to supper." Sally's eyes assessed him. "You look about done in. Would you like a tray in your room?"

"If I can make it that far," he said with a feeble grin.

To his surprise, a dozen small hands reached out for him. "Let me help you, sir." "Lean on me." "It's not too far." Someone came through the crowd and set his hand on Roc's shoulder. "Let your strong right arm help you."

Roc smiled. Gupta sent the boys off with Sally, and then guided him up the stairs. Roc's head was spinning and his legs could barely carry his weight, which was not surprising, since he'd been up since yesterday morning.

"How is the boy?" Roc inquired as they made their way along the corridor.

"Sleeping still. Not too feverish. Sally says he'll be out of the woods by tomorrow."

"And what of Miss Tatlock?"

"I've not seen her. She hasn't been downstairs all day, and I don't think she's eaten or drunk anything."

"Nerves," said Roc. "I know just how she feels."

At the door to his room, he pulled Gupta close and told him what he'd discovered in Dover. "Keep a close watch tonight, you and Bulbul and your men. Doncaster's still out there somewhere. I can feel it. I fear he thinks these boys are his for the taking."

"No cudgels, eh? Carbines and pistols?"

"That might be best. And don't let the boys outside after supper. They won't like it . . . have Sally play for them. They can always be counted on to sing."

"But how will you sleep then?"

"Like the dead, my friend, never fear."

Rockleigh decided to look in on Toby before he collapsed into oblivion. He found Mercy there, sound asleep on the bed next to Toby's. Her chignon was falling down in the back, her cheeks becomingly flushed. A young boy of perhaps seven was sprawled in a relaxed heap on her lap, one arm around her waist, the other dangling over the edge of the bed.

The sight of them tweaked at him, making him imagine a future he had no right to hope for. But that didn't prevent his brain from conjuring a picture of his own child asleep in Mercy's arms, its dark head cradled tenderly against her breast.

"Never thought to see it."

It took Rockleigh about ten seconds to realize that the voice had come from the bed in front of him. Toby was gazing up at him with fevered, glittering eyes. But his mouth had formed into a grin.

He went forward at once and knelt down. "How are you?"

"Been better," Toby said weakly. He pointed with his chin. "I just can't get over Mercy with a grubby sprat in her lap. Nearly shocked me back under."

"No," Roc said, gripping Toby's hand. "Don't go back under just yet. Let me explain what's happened." Toby nodded. "You're at my house in Crowden. You were shot outside the gates, and then carried inside."

"I remember some of that."

"The surgeon's removed the pistol ball, but it was very near your spine."

"M'buck feels like someone's been at it with a red-hot poker."

"I know damned little about this, Toby, but tell me one thing. Can you move your feet?"

At the end of the bed, the coverlet twitched.

"Bully!" Roc said softly.

"Can't keep a Tatlock down."

"One more thing, and then you must sleep. Do you have any idea who it was that shot you?"

"Not a clue. There were a number of men. They sounded rough. Jack . . . er, he tripped and his pistol went off. Next thing . . . shots started spitting around us." His eyes narrowed anxiously. "I say, any chance Jack could sit with me? I need to apologize for dragging him into this."

Rockleigh stood up and began fiddling with a stoppered bottle on the night table. "Not a good idea just now." He certainly couldn't tell Toby that Jack had disappeared. "Now swallow a spoonful of this draft the doctor left for you, and go back to sleep. We'll sort things out later."

"What about Mother Hubbard?" Toby asked with a grin.

Roc let his gaze wander over Mercy again. How he envied the child who was nestled against her. He had a sinking suspicion he'd never get that close to her again.

"Let her sleep," he said at last. "She's had a rough time of it. And she'll awake to good news." He ruffled Toby's hair gently. "Very good news."

*   *   *

Roc fell into his bed at last and was asleep almost instantly. But then his dreams began to fret at him. He'd seen too much filth this day for his sleep to be easy. He tossed himself awake—and was unable to relax again, feeling edgy and afraid for his charges. Toby was healing but still as weak as a kitten. Sally couldn't afford any more shocks, and though Gupta and his men were capable, Roc didn't like the idea of any of them being at risk. And then there was Mercy. He had a notion she would be an asset if it came to a fight. A woman with a cool head and the light of battle in her eyes. An interesting combination.

He mulled over his options and decided it was best to confer with Gupta; he'd need his friend's permission before he brought in reinforcements. He dressed himself again, missing Walter's skillful touch with a neckcloth, and went out into the hall.

Sir Ryan was coming toward him along the corridor. "You look like hell, man."

"I've been hearing that a lot lately. But thank you for the professional opinion."

Sir Ryan chuckled. "I was just coming to find you. I have to get back to London in the morning, unfortunately. I've other patients to tend. The boy is doing better than I expected, though. Youth alone is sometimes the best medicine."

Rockleigh was glad Digby would be staying the night—it couldn't hurt to have a medical man around if things turned ugly.

He found Finney in the front hall, sent him in search of Gupta and then made his way to the library, where he settled at the long table. His gaze drifted over the room. The leather spines of the books were now lustrous, the dark woodwork of the stacks gleaming. He'd paid to have most of the heavy labor done to make the interior of the house habitable, but Gupta and Sally had not spared their efforts on the smaller details. He wouldn't be ashamed for his mother to see her old home now. Well, the inside of it, at any rate.

Gupta knocked once and came into the room, an expression of disapproval on his face. "You were supposed to be sleeping, Rock-lee."

"Couldn't." Roc shrugged and then sighed. "Nerves, as I

said earlier. And too many bad dreams." He motioned Gupta to a seat, and then proceeded to explain his plan.

"It's up to you, though. If you don't want any strangers here, then so be it. We'll deal with Doncaster on our own."

Gupta lowered his head and tapped his fingers on the varnished surface of the table. "Will they be coming into the house?"

"I'll explain that they must restrict themselves to the kitchen and front hall. It will probably only be for a night or two. Doncaster's not a patient man."

"Very well," Gupta said. "Anything to protect the women and the boys."

"If we make it through the night unmolested, I'll start rounding up volunteers tomorrow morning. And I know just the place to start."

Chapter Eleven

Mercy awoke this time to the distant sound of singing. She had a moment of confusion, thinking she was in London, watching the Methodist choir on Rockleigh's front steps. Only she hadn't been there to witness it, hadn't wanted to risk his anger again. And she wasn't in London any longer—she was in Crowdenscroft, in the house of secrets. At some point she knew she'd have to abandon her vigil, go downstairs and discover exactly what it was that Rockleigh's boys were doing here. Clearly not what she'd thought.

She shifted the sleeping child off her lap. Perkin didn't even stir as she pulled a loose blanket over him. She had a sudden longing to be home at Boxwood with her own young siblings, Ralph plaguing her with his endless drawings of birds and Bitsy mooning over the handsome boy who lived across the lane. She wanted Mama scolding her for burning the toast and Papa grinning at her fondly, declaring he preferred it dark. Most of all, she wanted to see Toby, running to the brook with his fishing line or doing nimble tricks on the back of his old chestnut mare as he rode through the orchard beside the house.

She knew, though, that that simple, domestic picture would shatter like a dropped mirror if Toby did not get better.

Once this ordeal was over, if he recovered, she swore she would never stray from home again. It would become her refuge from Lord Rockleigh, a place to heal her own wounds. She had work there to divert her, in the front room of a newspaper office, and a life she'd enjoyed until Rockleigh had come into it and made her long for something more.

However, there couldn't be more, not with him. And not, she

feared now, with anyone else. He'd bound her to him, in some manner that did not allow for successors or replacements.

That notion seemed so bleak, so oppressive and so foreign to her instincts—which prompted her always to fight back—that she made a new resolve. As soon as she had any reassurance that Toby was recovering, she would confront Rockleigh. She had to exorcise him from her thoughts; perhaps in the heat of righteous anger she could burn away her pain and regain a piece of her soul.

Kneeling beside Toby's bed, she felt his brow. It was now blessedly cool to the touch. She bent down and kissed his cheek, heard him murmur in his sleep.

Then his eyes opened. He was smiling.

Roc was giving Gupta his final instructions when Mercy appeared at the library door. It was obvious from her narrowed, questioning eyes that this was her first glimpse of his companion.

"Miss Tatlock," he said. "This is my good friend, Gupta Bannerjee."

"Sir." She had the grace to curtsy, but her face now gave nothing away. She turned to Roc and said quickly, "Finney said I would find you here. I wanted to tell you that my brother woke up a few minutes ago and is alert and talking." She stopped and caught her breath. "I thought you might like to know."

"I did know," he said. "I looked in on him as soon as I returned from Dover. He was actually rather chatty. You were, um, asleep at the time."

She took a few steps into the room. "Did you just say you'd been to Dover and back? Heavens, Roc, no wonder you look half dead." She recovered herself. "I mean, Lord Rockleigh."

"That's better," he said. "You wouldn't want to be overly familiar."

Gupta's bright eyes moved from his friend to Miss Tatlock, and a glimmer of understanding shone in them for an instant. "I will leave you to your guest, Rock-lee. I am needed outside."

As he approached Mercy, she drew her skirts back. It might have been just to ease his passing, Roc knew, not necessarily a display of distaste. For the first time in memory, he could read nothing in her face. He'd been prepared for overt caution or even dismay regarding Gupta, but he didn't know what to make of the shuttered expression she now wore.

He leaned back against the table and crossed his arms. "You don't appear very happy, ma'am, for a woman who's just had her brother returned to her."

"Of course I am happy," she said in a subdued voice. "I am ecstatic."

He nearly chuckled. He wondered how she'd look if she were truly cast down.

She stood there unmoving near the opened door, her face still unreadable, her body tensed for flight. He pushed away from the table and went swiftly around her, closing the door before she could make her escape. "Something's bothering you," he said as he herded her forward into the room. "Something more than Toby."

She spun to face him. "Do I appear to be distressed?"

"No, you don't appear to be anything at all. And that's what's troubling me. Your face is usually a reliable map, Mercy, to everything that's going on inside you." His gaze prodded her. "What is it you're hiding?"

Her eyes began to darken. He wagered that any second now she'd start spitting at him, just like old times. So he was not at all prepared when she drew in a great shuddering breath and began to weep.

Three or four fat tears rolled down her cheeks. She swiped at them impatiently with the back of her hand and his heart twisted at the sight. He'd never have taken her for a crying woman. Showed all he knew.

"Ah, Merce, it's going to be all right." He took a step forward, his hands held out to her. "He's improving every minute. And maybe you're just letting your fears come out, now that the crisis has passed."

"You don't understand," she said with a watery sniffle.

"Tell me, then," he said gently. "What don't I understand?"

"Anything," she said raggedly.

She tried to move away from him, but he caught her wrist and held it firm. "Be a little weak, Mercy," he said gruffly. "Be a little frail. I won't think the less of you for it."

"I *am* weak and frail," she moaned, and then looked at him reproachfully. "I ought to despise you, Rockleigh Conniston."

Her voice rose. "But I can't, you see. Because there is something in here, inside me"—she thumped at her chest with one fisted hand—"that is so . . . so linked to you, so tied to you, that hating you would be like hating myself."

He dropped her hand and drew back from her slightly. "What have you discovered, Mercy, that you are convinced you must hate me for it?"

She blinked several times. "Are you so lost to common decency that you can't know?"

He could think of several things that might have upset her, several things that quite probably would upset her when she learned of them, but there was nothing so heinous that it would make her detest him. At least he prayed not.

"Are you still blaming me over Toby?" When she shook her head, he said, "Then I think you'd better tell me. I'm a bit weary to be playing guessing games."

She drew in a deep breath and said haltingly, "Knowing how . . . how I feel about you, you must see how hurtful it is to me . . . to be here in this house."

His face tightened. "Damn it, Mercy, how does this hurt you? You are making no sense at all. And how *do* you feel about me? One minute you want to hate me; the next you are spouting some mumbo jumbo about how we are linked together."

She drew herself up, her eyes flashing dangerously. "It's clearly only a one-way link, Lord Rockleigh. I see that now. So thank you, you have just set me free."

With a muffled curse, he shifted away from her, paced to the long window and stood frowning out at the night sky. The moon was again obscured behind a scrim of clouds. The darkness would work in favor of Doncaster's men if they were planning an attack. But he had a more pressing problem to deal with just now. His stalwart Mercy had come undone over something. Devil take women—they could twist a man until he was a corkscrew of confused feelings.

The answer came to him before long. He'd shivered in the backyard of a brothel two nights ago and felt the same whirl of dizzying, baffling emotions. And she was fighting them just as he had. Because she was frightened and because they were so new to her. Furthermore, she didn't have a mother close by— well she did, actually, but not within speaking distance—to soothe her as he'd had. So he'd just have to be the one to do it. And that was new to *him,* taking on the responsibility for someone else's feelings.

"It's not a one-sided link," he said softly without moving from the window. "And I'm sorry I called it mumbo jumbo. I make light of things that I don't want to acknowledge. Only one of my many failings."

He waited for some response. When she remained silent, he forced himself to go on. "You said just now that I don't understand. I think I understand a great deal. You and I . . . something happened between us, something neither of us expected or, I suspect, even wanted. We began as enemies and then . . . oh, I don't know . . . it changed. And now neither of us is easy with what it's become."

"What has it become?" she asked in a small voice.

He turned to her, his head angled to one side. "Don't you know, sweetheart? Don't you know what it is that links us together?"

"Irritation?" she said with a tiny glint of amusement in her eyes. Then they turned bleak again. "No," she said, almost to herself. "I can't banter with you. There is no place to be playful, not any longer."

He crossed back to her and touched her hand. "Please, Merce . . . I can't watch you like this. You must tell me straight out what is wrong."

"Very well." She pressed her hands to her face for a moment. "But it's very difficult to speak of. And besides," she added, looking at him over her fingers, "she's been so kind to Toby. I cannot help but like her, in spite of everything."

"Ah. You're referring to Sally." He rubbed at his chin fretfully. "I was hoping you wouldn't find it so distressing. After all, knowing of your radical upbringing, I'd hoped you would be more generous."

"Generous?" She echoed. "You must think me a saint. Or a half-wit."

He winced. "I know it's an . . . unusual arrangement. It began in India, as you've no doubt guessed."

"And then you brought her here to England?"

His eyes narrowed slightly. "No, Gupta brought her here. A year after I'd returned from India, there they were on my doorstep in London. I was surprised, to say the least. But quite happy to see—"

"Please, spare me," she cried softly. "Have a little care for my feelings. I . . . I know Sally must be foremost in your thoughts, as the mother of your child, but—"

"What!"

Rockleigh stood thunderstruck for five heartbeats—and then gave a great whooping shout of laughter. "My child?" he cried almost gleefully. He moved forward and caught her by the hands, sweeping her in a wide half circle. "Oh, sweet Mercy, is that what your tears were about?"

"Stop it!" She dug in her heels and tried to pull free.

"Mercy, Mercy . . . You are never going to live this one down. Ten, twenty years from now I will still be grinning every time I think of it." He pulled her close and tipped her head back with his chin. "Look at me. No, don't glare, look. Sally Banner is not my . . . lover. She is Gupta Bannerjee's wife. Has been for nearly four years."

Mercy, wide eyed, echoed, "Gupta's wife?"

"Yes, his wife." He stroked the hair back from her brow. "I can excuse some of your confusion, as they've recently taken to calling themselves Banner—it was easier for the boys to say. But if you'd gone downstairs today, you'd have seen them together and known the truth of it at once. They rarely take their eyes off each other, especially now, with the baby coming."

She stood there, trembling with relief. A crushing weight had rolled off her chest. Toby was healing and Rockleigh was not a scoundrel. Well, not a greater scoundrel than she already knew him to be. She wished she'd been paying better attention when he'd spoken just now, when he'd mentioned the thing that linked them together. She had her own theory on that.

Rockleigh mistook her silence for censure. His eyes grew anxious. "You don't approve of their marriage, then? I was afraid of that. You're a prim English lady at heart, for all your—"

"Rockleigh," she interrupted him. "I know I am starchy and bossy and"—she swallowed hard—"often misguided in my conclusions. But I have never, ever been inclined against people because of the color of their skin. My father's been writing antislavery tracts since before I was born." She stroked his sleeve. "And I understand now why all the secrecy was necessary."

"Do you?" His eyes probed her face. "Can you?"

"They've been forced away, haven't they, from every place they've lived. We English are not a very tolerant people, not of those who are different or marked. So you offered them a haven here at Crowdenscroft."

"Bravo, Miss Tatlock," he said softly, his voice tinged with respect. "You've gotten it on the first try. There is always a problem when East meets West. They have encountered prejudice and ignorance wherever they've lived. India, England, it hasn't mattered."

"What about in Kent?"

He gave her a long look. "They were doing just fine, keeping very much to themselves, until an interfering baggage wrote an inflammatory editorial. No, don't look so forlorn. I was teasing. It was only a matter of time before one of the boys let something slip."

She looked down at the toes of her slippers, peeping from beneath her hem. "Still, I'm sorry I've caused so much trouble for them. Especially since I know now that they are your friends."

"They didn't start out as friends, exactly. Sally was a governess in Calcutta, in the compound where I was staying. Gupta was always about, looking for stray children to rescue. You see, he'd been an orphan himself, born to an English soldier and a Pathan mother. The blighter never married her, and she died of some scourge, typhus or cholera. But Gupta learned a trade and did well for himself; he was very skilled, very enterprising."

"And how did he come to be your good friend?"

"I was sitting out on the veranda one night at dusk, smoking a cheroot. He was passing the time with me over the railing. I'd always thought he was quite special—it's hard for a man with no caste to make his way in that place. Anyway, something moved out of the shadows beneath my chair. It was a cobra, instantly reared up and ready to strike. Before I could react, Gupta killed it—Pathans are fairly deadly with a knife. He saved my life, Mercy. And then he went back to talking to me as though nothing had occurred. I nearly fainted." He coughed slightly. "And you know I hate that like the devil."

"Yes, I know." Her gaze moved boldly along the length of

his thigh. "It would have bitten you there," she said, then raised her eyes to his face. "And you would be dead."

"Mmm. Almost instantly, I'm afraid."

"I have to thank Gupta."

"Do you?" His voice held a note of relief and something else, as well.

"For keeping you alive. Just think how tame my life would have been if we'd never met."

He smiled down at her as he traced his fingers over her cheek. "So are you better now? No more crying or upsetments? Good, because there's something I need to tell you. There, ah, might be trouble outside tonight. Remember Doncaster from London? He and his men have been watching the house at night. I believe one of them may have shot Toby by mistake."

"Doncaster?" She didn't try to hide her shock. "I recall you said you'd had a falling out with him. But what does he want with Crowdenscroft?"

"I discovered in Dover that he's up to his thick neck in some pretty unsavory business. There's something he wants in this house, and I fear he means to take it by force."

She was about to ask him to explain, but the answer came to her almost at once. Doncaster was after the boys, Rockleigh's homeless boys. For the same wicked purpose she'd written about so scathingly in her editorial.

She looked at him and bit her lip. "I brought him here, didn't I?"

His mouth tightened for an instant. "Perhaps. I know he saw your news clipping in Stanley Flemish's rooms. That same night at Bacchus he fed me some foul poison and began questioning me about this place and about the boys. I don't recall exactly what I told him, but it's clear he's now trying to cut himself in on what he believes is my profitable business, trading in children."

"That was the night you told me you'd almost died." She moaned and set her hands over her face. "Oh, Roc, I've blundered beyond all forgiveness."

He drew her hands down and held them between his palms. "You couldn't know any of this when you wrote that editorial. I only found out today what he was really up to."

"But he shot Toby! And it's my fault."

"Mercy, we can't spend eternity berating ourselves over what we did or didn't do. Let it go now. I've been overly cautious. You've been overly zealous. Those aren't crimes, necessarily—we were acting on our natures."

Her mouth twisted into a tremulous frown. "I'd always thought I had a good, decent nature. Now I find that I am full of false righteousness and stubborn pride. It's very lowering."

"Yes, it is," he said. "I've come face-to-face with a few of my own shortcomings these past days."

He released her hands and stepped away from her. "Now, I've got to get to my bed before I fall down."

She watched him make his way from the library, a man carrying a weighty burden. Even with his shoulders sagging and his face drawn, he still drew her to him. Maybe more so now, when he was a little weak and frail himself, not so overpoweringly virile or full of his own consequence.

She went in search of a meal—her appetite had miraculously returned—and found Sally sitting in the kitchen. Mercy saw immediately that her color was not good. After brewing her a strong cup of tea, she sat down across from her with a slice of meat pie and attempted to distract her with questions about India. But the pain that pinched her face every so often was troubling.

"I shouldn't worry about those men outside," Mercy said soothingly. "I doubt Lord Rockleigh would have gone to bed if he truly thought we were in danger."

Sally nodded. "And Gupta knows quite a bit about soldiering. He had friends in the army who taught him to shoot and such."

Mercy stared down at her plate. "I don't know if you've learned of this or not, but I'm the person who wrote that wretched editorial. The one that's caused every one of our problems."

When she looked up, Sally's sad mouth was smiling. "Don't fret, Miss Tatlock. My husband would say that we are all of us entangled in the Wheel of Life and that everything that happens has a purpose."

Mercy grinned back at her. "That, Mrs. Bannerjee, remains to be seen."

Chapter Twelve

Dawn was just breaking when Mercy scratched on the door to Rockleigh's bedroom. When there was no response, she opened it and tiptoed inside.

She'd barely been asleep an hour last night when things started heating up. It had been quite a time, all things considered, and thank heaven Sir Ryan had been here. In spite of having been an army surgeon, he still possessed those miracle-working hands.

She'd never in her life felt so weary as she did right now. Or so elated.

She could make out Rockleigh's bed in the pinkish light that filtered through the partially opened drapes. He was sprawled diagonally across his mattress and he didn't appear to be wearing any clothing. Fortunately, his lower body was covered by a cotton spread.

She crossed to the middle of room and stood there with her hands on her hips. "Ahem."

He opened one eye and observed her for a time. "This isn't how I picture it," he finally drawled with a sleepy yawn, "when I imagine you coming into my room. No, not at all the way I picture it."

"I see you've recovered your sense of the ridiculous."

"It came back to me the instant I knew your brother was going to recover. I gather we didn't have any unwanted visitors last night." He paused and looked past her toward the door. "Unless Doncaster has forced you into my room at pistol point. If that's the case, I must thank him."

"I don't suppose it occurs to you that there might have been another sort of trouble here last night."

"What occurs to me, Miss Tatlock," he said in the midst of a sinuous stretch, "is that you are irretrievably ruined now. It's not good *ton* to badger a man in his bedroom. Aside from that, what else is troubling you? Toby's not suffered a relapse, I hope."

"He's eating his breakfast as we speak."

He narrowed his eyes and peered at the mantel clock. "Good heavens, it's only six o'clock. Do you always rise this early? Because I have to warn you, I cannot possibly—"

"Aren't you even curious why I'm here at six o'clock in the morning?"

She almost smiled when he quoted slyly, "My curiosity is at an all-time low." Then he added, as he hiked himself up onto one elbow, "But I have every faith that you will not leave me in peace until you have explained."

"Oh," she said lightly as she approached his bed. "I have a new motto—'never complain, never explain.' Except that right now I do have something to complain about. About the way you managed to sleep through an entire household crisis last night."

"Crisis? What happened? Not Doncaster scaling the walls? Then whatever it was, it will keep. All I really want is to go back to sleep." He rolled over and plumped a pillow against each ear.

She marched up to the bed and tried to tug the nearest pillow away. He held firm and told her in muffled accents to go to the devil. She was about to make a heated reply, when there was a noticeable scratching at his bedroom door. It then creaked open and a strange, dwarfish creature crept into the room. Mercy watched assessingly as it half stood and craned its head around.

She wasn't sure what imp of impropriety invaded her brain then—she could have justifiably chalked it up to lack of sleep or, less justifiably, to the stirring vision of Rockleigh's naked, sleep-warmed torso. Whatever her reasons, when the creature greeted her with a guttural hoot and came scurrying eagerly toward her, Mercy gave a bloodcurdling, theatrical shriek and launched herself onto the bed.

Practically on top of Lord Rockleigh.

She pummeled his back with one fist. "Look! Oh, Roc, look! There is some sort of creeping animal on the rug. And it's wearing a little coat."

He raised his head from the pillows and clucked softly. "Easy, sweetheart, don't let her frighten you."

She huffed. "I'm not *that* frightened."

"I was speaking to Bulbul. She hates it when people shriek at her." He grunted softly. "And could you please move your knee? It's poking into my back."

Mercy didn't move an inch. Meanwhile, the creature in the drab coat was reaching over the side of the bed toward her hand. Mercy shot her a conspiratorial look of warning, and the long fingers retreated.

"It occurs to me," she said, snuggling her face for an instant against his shoulder, "that this is a house of madness."

Rockleigh twisted around under the covers, shifting onto his side to face her. "Only when you're here, Merce. You make me quite wits to let." He gave her a mocking leer. "And your knee is still sticking into me . . . only it's not against my back any longer."

Mercy gasped and quickly drew away from him. But only a tiny bit away. She'd never been this intimate with him except in her dreams, and she was finding the reality infinitely more satisfying.

"That's better," Roc pronounced, even as his body strained toward her of its own volition. "I dislike it when a woman crowds a man in bed. You ought to warn any prospective husbands of this unfortunate tendency."

She leaned over him, up on one elbow. "Rockleigh . . . could you please stop being loathsome for two minutes? Something wonderful has happened."

"I know," he said dreamily as he gazed up at her, his bantering mood all fled away. There was now something so ardent in his lean face that she nearly forgot to breathe. His dark hair formed a shallow fan on the creamy pillowcase, and his cheeks were lightly flushed from sleep. But all she saw was the expression of rapt awe in his gilded, azure eyes.

"I know," he said again in the softest voice possible.

It seemed the most natural thing, at that moment, for her to lower her mouth to his. His arm slid slowly around her back and settled there, a relaxed, easy weight. His mouth opened slightly beneath hers, and she marveled at how well they fit together. His skin was warm against her stroking fingers and as sleek as satin. Until he arched under her, and she felt the steely muscles flex beneath that smooth surface.

He was dappling her face with light touches now, the fingers of one hand seeking out every plane and angle to caress, and still his kiss was soft and sweet. This sweetness, she decided, was almost better than his heat. She melted down onto his chest, onto the wide expanse of naked skin and firm muscle. He groaned into her mouth and arched upward again.

"You belong in my bed, Mercy Tatlock," he murmured as he traced his lips over the tiny dimple high on her cheek. "Damn it, you belong in my life."

She was far past arguing at this point, overwhelmed by the feelings that were spreading inside her like the warm, honeyed rays of the summer sun. It wasn't passion this time, she knew, but something far richer.

"Roc," she sighed, feeling herself near tears. There was gaiety and lightness inside her now, in fullest measure. Enough that they needed to spill over, enough to share with him and the whole world. "Oh, Rockleigh, I . . . I . . ."

He cradled her head between his hands and looked deeply into her eyes. "Say it, Merce. I need to hear you say it. Curse me, but I can't get my tongue around it."

"That's not what I've observed," she answered with a sly grin. "Very well, I'll say it. But if you don't say it back, I will—"

"Rock-lee?"

Two pairs of startled eyes shifted instantly to the doorway. Gupta was standing there, embarrassment ruddying his cheeks. Mercy quickly scrambled away from Rockleigh and sat up, wishing she could hold a pillow over her own burning face.

"I don't wish to intrude, but—"

"I'm sorry, Mr. Bannerjee," she said breathlessly as she slid off the bed. "I still haven't told him. Though I think it would be much better coming from you." She held out her hand. "Come along, Bulbul. We need to leave the gentlemen alone."

Rockleigh watched in bewilderment as the baboon skittered across the floor and clambered up into Mercy's arms. Mercy shot him a smug, mischievous grin, and then carried her charge from the room.

"I thought Bulbul had frightened her out of her wits," he muttered. "That's, ah, how she ended up on my bed."

"Oh, no," Gupta said. "They are great friends now. Miss Tatlock spent half the night holding Bulbul, keeping her away from Sally."

"Sally? What's wrong with Sally?"

"Nothing now. She's resting." He leaned forward and whispered gleefully, "We have a son, Rock-lee."

Roc sat bolt upright. "The devil you do!"

"I hope he does not turn out to be a devil. Maybe we should not have named him after you. No, I think he will stay Conniston Bannerjee. Miss Tatlock said it is a lucky name with all those 'n's, though I am not sure what she meant."

Rockleigh chuckled. "It doesn't matter. All that matters is that Sally is well and that the baby is healthy. He didn't come too early?"

"Mmm, he's a tiny baby, but then so was I, and look how well I grew."

"Oh, Gupta, this is all that is wonderful. I will get up and dress and find us an army to guard the place so that Sally will have no worries."

Gupta turned back to him at the door. "I am sorry about not knocking just now . . . it was perhaps not a good time for an interruption."

Roc waved away his apology. "The lady might thank you for sparing her virtue."

Not that she'll require it much longer, he added to himself.

Gupta lingered another moment. "She is . . . a very good person, this Miss Tatlock. She stayed at my wife's side last night, and you never saw anyone fight as she did, holding on to Sally and scolding her, telling her to be strong and to concentrate. Bossed that baby right into the world, Sir Ryan said."

"That's my Mercy," Roc sighed.

It was nearly nine o'clock before Rockleigh had a chance to get away from Crowdenscroft.

First, he'd seen off Sir Ryan, who assured him that Toby was well on the road to recovery. The man lost some of his habitual sangfroid when Rockleigh presented him with a substantial bank draft. "For Toby *and* Sally," Roc said. "I wager you never expected to play midwife when I dragged you down here."

Sir Ryan drew in one cheek as he climbed into the coach. "It's been . . . stimulating."

Next, Rockleigh had to view the new addition to the household. Sally looked drawn but very happy. The new baby, set in the cradle his father had made for him months earlier, was pink-faced and bore a tassel of auburn fuzz on his round head. "Pathans sometimes have red hair," Gupta explained when he noticed Rockleigh's puzzled expression as he hovered over the sleeping infant.

"So do Yorkshire silversmiths," Sally interjected with a twinkle. "Like my father."

And then, of course, Rockleigh had to look in on Toby. The boy was still pale but seemed to have recovered some of his animation. Rockleigh distracted him with Mercy's role in the birth of Conniston Bannerjee, pointing out wryly that Mother Hubbard had turned out to have a surprising knack for dealing with babies.

When Roc rose to go, Toby said grimly, "Jack's not here, is he? You never speak of him, and Mercy just blushes and looks uncomfortable when I mention his name."

Roc shook his head regretfully. "He never reappeared after you were shot. But that doesn't mean he's been taken by Doncaster. You did say it was his gun going off accidentally that started the other men shooting. If he saw you go down, he might just be off somewhere feeling wretched and guilty."

Roc was riding out of the stable yard when he caught sight of Mercy walking hand in hand with Bulbul along the edge of the overgrown lawn. He was compelled to stop and acknowledge her. Only once he'd pulled up his horse, he just sat there looking down at her and couldn't think of one thing to say. Not that it was an uncomfortable silence. She had raised her eyes to his, and they were alive and warm and very welcoming. A winsome half smile played over her mouth.

After fully thirty seconds of this silent, relaxed communion, Bulbul put her head back and gave several mocking hoots. Roc grinned ruefully, touched the brim of his hat to both females and rode off.

Later, Mercy, he promised silently as Finney let him through the gate. *Once I've completed my business, we'll sort everything out.*

The ride to Tiptree took barely twenty minutes. It was a pleasant town, larger than Crowden, boasting a manicured green encircled by shops. The establishment Roc sought lay on the north side of the green, a double-fronted brick-and-stucco building wedged between a bakery and a chemist. The bow window to the right of the doorway had the words *The Tiptree Trumpet* stenciled across it in gold script.

He dismounted and tied his horse to a nearby stanchion. And felt panic wash over him as he stood there outside the office. As much as he disliked interviews with his father, this was far worse. For one thing, his fond mama was not there to intercede for him. He doubted Mercy's mother could be called upon to fill that role. She was more likely to hold him down while Avery Tatlock thrashed him with a horsewhip.

There was also another problem—even though Mercy worshiped her father, the man had always sounded to Roc like a prosy old stick. He'd come a long way from the arrogant, dismissive fellow he'd once been, but Roc feared he still had little tolerance for stiff-necked, sanctimonious idealists.

He finally steeled himself to walk through the door. The sunlit interior was divided into two sections, an open work space behind a low partition, and a private office in the rear. The two desks that sat behind the counter were covered with papers and a scattering of quill pens and ink pots. The door to the rear office was open.

Rockleigh gave a loud cough.

"In a minute," a man's deep voice called out.

It was more like five minutes, but Roc occupied himself by gazing out the window at a magnificent oak in the center of the green. A rustic bench encircled its massive trunk, where a young couple were enjoying the shade. Roc grinned as the man leaned over and stole a swift kiss. If one were in the mood for alfresco wooing, he couldn't think of a pleasanter spot. Though perhaps a more private one might be desirable.

He turned back to the office, idly scanning the framed etchings that decorated the buff walls. From next door there came a steady, regular vibration; no doubt the pressmen running off the latest edition.

Avery Tatlock emerged from his office with a smile of apology. The younger man beside him had the look of a clerk; he settled at one of the two desks as Tatlock came forward to the waist-high counter.

"Sorry," he said. "I had something urgent to straighten out— we discovered we'd put an ad for a horse feed next to one for the local knacker's yard." He gave Roc a wry grin. It was Mercy's grin to the life. The eyes bright and puckish, the mouth curled up on one side.

"Now, then, how can I be of service?"

Rockleigh wasn't sure how to begin. The man was nothing like he'd expected. In addition to owning a winning smile, Tatlock was a handsome, vibrant man. He was tall and lean, with the face of a Renaissance courtier, aesthetic and canny at the same time. His hair was a silvery shade of white and worn in the style of a decade ago.

"There are several things I need to discuss with you," Roc said. "Perhaps if we could be private."

"Of course." Tatlock swung back the half door in the partition, and Rockleigh went through it and followed him to his office. Papers, stacks of books, and copies of *The Trumpet* littered every surface. Tatlock quickly cleared one of the two chairs that faced his desk, and Rockleigh seated himself.

Tatlock leaned against his desk and crossed his legs, a man at ease in his own territory.

"I think you'd better sit down," Roc said, rubbing at a tense spot that was twitching in his cheek. "Some of what I have to tell you is unpleasant." He looked up. "I'm Lord Rockleigh Conniston."

Tatlock had the same fair complexion as Mercy and her brother, but Roc saw now that he'd gone even paler. "Excuse me a moment," he said gruffly. "Just one more thing I need to take care of, and then you will have my full attention."

He went outside and spoke in an undertone to his clerk. Roc heard the man's chair scrape back, and then there was the sound of the front door closing.

"You haven't sent him for the watch," Roc asked with a cautious grin as Tatlock came back into his office and shut the door.

"No, no." He gave Roc a reassuring look. "There's something I needed him to fetch for me."

Rockleigh waited until he was seated behind the desk before he spoke. "First off, I need to tell you that your son, Toby, is alive and well."

Tatlock's face narrowed. "And—?"

"The thing is, he was shot outside Crowdenscroft three nights ago. I brought Sir Ryan Digby from London to attend him . . . he's had the best care and looks to make a full recovery."

Tatlock's fingers had tensed on his blotter, but his voice barely shook as he spoke. "What was my son doing in Crowden?"

"Trying to prove my innocence, I believe. Your daughter is also in my house."

"You are holding her there?"

Roc drew back in affront. "Of course not. She wanted to be with her brother. Oh, look, she'll skin me alive for telling you this, but she and Toby were not in Brighton at their aunt's. They came to London instead, because she was convinced she could talk me into dropping that pestilential lawsuit. They were staying with a printer in Chelsea."

Tatlock leaned his face on his hands and groaned softly. When he looked up at last, his face was a study in angry frustration. "So you've got both of them now, eh? And you've come here to threaten me. Tell me what you want, sir, and be quick about it."

Rockleigh rose swiftly from his chair and thrust himself over the desk. "What in blazes are you talking about?"

"I know all about you, Lord Rockleigh. Much more now than when I wrote that editorial."

"Mercy wrote it," he bit out. "She admitted to me that she did. So you don't have to bear the blame any longer."

"I wish I *had* written it," he exclaimed as he pushed up from his chair, his eyes full of heat. "I wish I had blasted you and your foul doings right out of this county. Or right out of existence, if there's any justice in the world. But no, my daughter was the one who saw the truth this time and wouldn't rest until it was spoken."

"Oh, confound it!" Roc cried. "Are you going to start up again with this nonsense? There are no foul doings at my estate. Just some boys being trained to—"

"Yes, Conniston," said a voice from behind him. "Do tell us what those boys are being trained for."

Roc pivoted around. Doncaster was standing in the doorway. Tatlock, wearing a relieved smile, moved quickly from his desk and went to stand beside the man.

Rockleigh felt his vision begin to blur. He couldn't comprehend what such a thing meant. If Tatlock the saint was allied with Doncaster the devil, then Roc's whole notion of reality had just taken a punishing blow.

Maybe he was dreaming, still in his bed in Crowdenscroft. But it was no dream when Doncaster took him by the arm and hustled him out of the office. Five men were ranged around the outer room, each one larger than the next. With a nod from Doncaster, they closed in on Rockleigh, gripping his arms. Their faces were grim, unforgiving.

"Tatlock!" Roc called out. "Mercy says you are a fair man— hear me out. It's Doncaster who's been dealing in children. Ask him!" His voice rose in anger. "Go ahead, ask him about Dover, about Mr. Coyle at the workhouse. Or Isabelle at the brothel on Front Street. For God's sake, ask him!"

"Ah," Doncaster purred as he parted his men and came toward Rockleigh. "You've just damned yourself out of your own mouth. How could you know of those people if you hadn't had dealings with them yourself."

"I was looking for evidence against you, insect." Rockleigh's gaze swung to Tatlock. "You mustn't believe him, sir. He has been cast out of respectable society. He sells opium in London and Lord knows what else."

Avery Tatlock gave a disparaging grunt. "And your credentials are so sterling, Lord Rockleigh? Profligate, gamester, drunkard."

There was nothing, he realized, he could say in his defense. Everything Tatlock had accused him of was true. *Had* been true. But there was no way to convince him that those things were now in his past.

He put his chin up. "It appears you have two bad choices, Tatlock. Do you believe a profligate like me, or a bloody pandering liar like Doncaster?"

"I'm no panderer," Doncaster snarled.

"The hell you're not!" Roc would have launched himself at Doncaster, but his men grappled with him and held him back. He twisted in their grip and threw them off.

Doncaster was tugging a pistol from his coat pocket, when Tatlock cried, "Enough!"

Rockleigh was amazed at the command in the man's voice.

"This is not getting us anywhere," Tatlock said curtly. "Two of my children are in that house in Crowden. And apparently one of them's been shot."

"By *his* men," Roc muttered, eyes flaring. "They've been skulking around the place for days now. Toby and his friend Jack walked right into them."

The white-haired man turned to his confederate. "Is this true? I agreed to help you. No one wanted you to rescue those boys from Conniston more than I did. But you told me that my daughter and son were safe in London, and now I find that is not the case. What else haven't you told me, Mr. Doncaster?"

"Let me explain, sir." Doncaster drew in a breath. "We were watching the place on Tuesday night, from up on the wooded ridge that faces the property. Someone outside the walls fired on us. Just one shot. Two of my men fired back before I could stop them. We rode off right afterward . . . I didn't know that anyone had been hit."

"Not only did his men shoot Toby; Jack Skillens has since disappeared."

"I don't know anything about that," Doncaster muttered, then gripped Tatlock's arm with one beefy hand. "You know I'd not hurt your lad on purpose."

"He's lying!" Roc nearly shouted. "He fed me poison in London, and then left me in a storeroom to die."

"That is true," Doncaster said evenly. "I did drug him. Only it wasn't to kill him—it was to make him talk. It was my last chance—the opium I'd been feeding him never took him under enough for me to risk questioning him."

Rockleigh fisted his hands against his head to stop it spinning. "This is madness," he cried. His gaze pierced Doncaster.

"Are you saying you've been trying to find out about the boys since March, when you first offered me the damned drug?"

He nodded. "Months ago, my contacts along the route from Dover to London told me that boys were being conscripted from orphanages and workhouses in that area, all destined for Crowden. I knew you had a property there; I even drove down to take a look at it. I never saw so much as one boy, but the armed guards raised my suspicions a mite. So I enticed you, Conniston, and waited for your opium habit to take hold, because I needed to question you about the house. Then I read that news clipping in Flemish's parlor. Mr. Tatlock had obviously come to the same conclusion as I had, but in publishing that piece, I feared he had alerted you. I knew I had to act quickly, before you got the wind up and moved the boys to a place where my men couldn't find them."

"See," Rockleigh said, shifting to Tatlock, "he admits it himself. He has contacts from Dover to London. What sort of contacts do you think they are, sir?"

Tatlock's eyes narrowed into slits. "I don't think, Lord Rockleigh, I know. They are working for the government. For Sir Robert Poole, to be exact. He's decided it's long past time to end this wretched practice of selling children into vice. And Mr. Doncaster here is his chief agent. He came to me several days ago, after he read that editorial, and asked for my assistance. He and his men have been staying in my home, which is situated not two minutes from here."

Rockleigh felt all the air whoosh out of him, as if someone had landed a hard blow to his belly. He sagged against the man nearest him, in shock and disbelief. If this was true, then Doncaster was no longer any threat. But he could hardly credit it. His mind spun furiously with a thousand questions.

"Why didn't you just come right out and ask me about Crowdenscroft?"

Doncaster frowned severely. "Not a chance. You'd merely have lied to me and then moved the boys."

"Then why not just break down the gate and storm the house, if you had the law on your side?"

"We are not exactly working inside the law here. A man's home is still inviolate when one is only acting on suspicions. I needed proof, and that is why we've been watching the house. And to make sure your men didn't scarper with the boys."

"Shall we take him outside now?" one of Doncaster's men asked. "He looks like all the fight's gone out of him."

Rockleigh forced himself to rally. He stood upright and reached out his hand to Avery Tatlock. "Come with me to Crowdenscroft. All of you, come and see the truth."

"That's exactly where I am going," Tatlock said with a determined scowl. "To bring my children home."

"You won't get inside the gates without me," Rockleigh declared. "My groundskeepers have orders not to let anyone inside."

"You'd think they were guarding the bloody Crown Jewels," Doncaster muttered.

"They were guarding the boys . . . and the people who look after them. From men like you. Or at least from the ones who *do* steal children." He frowned as another pertinent question occurred to him. "Tell me this, Doncaster. If you are working for Poole, why haven't I heard of it? Clipper Donegan is a close friend, and he's practically in Sir Robert's pocket."

"Donegan knows nothing about this. He's far too involved in overseeing the intelligence officers in France. This is a domestic issue. Sir Robert enlisted me because I'd, ah, fallen out of favor with the *ton*. He figured I could use something to keep me busy."

"How did you fall out of favor? No one seems to know the particulars."

Doncaster crossed his arms over his broad chest. "I was a bit too hasty with my fists on a young aristo who was abusing a whore. She was all of twelve. The cub's family had enough influence to turn the *ton* against me. But Sir Robert learned of the true story and knew he'd found the right man for the job." He leaned toward Rockleigh. "I'm not a saint, Conniston, but there are limits to what I will tolerate. Some things I will fight for."

Roc met his eyes. "Then we are not so different, Donnie, you and I."

Tatlock moved to the front of the office and took his hat down from the wall. "Bring him along. I'm not waiting another minute to fetch my children home."

Rockleigh allowed himself to be led from the office. Doncaster and two of his men went off to fetch their horses, while Rockleigh and his captors waited on the pavement. There was no point in fighting off three burly fellows, Roc reckoned, not when he knew he'd be exonerated the instant they set foot in Gupta's workroom. Only it was tiresome, being a spectacle again, even in this little hamlet. The shoppers and strollers around the green were openly staring at them.

"It's a bit ironic," Rockleigh remarked softly to Tatlock. "I was coming here to ask for your help. To raise some volunteers to protect my home from Doncaster."

Tatlock craned around. "You wanted me to help you protect that house of infamy?"

Roc sighed in frustration. "Just think on this, sir. Why would I come to you, of all people, if I had something to hide? You'd ferret it out soon enough; I see you and your daughter share that trait. Nosy parkers, the both of you. Though usually wide of the mark."

Tatlock blanched suddenly. "What of my daughter? I hadn't thought of this till now. Please tell me you haven't . . . haven't . . ."

"Dallied is the word I believe you are seeking," Roc said smoothly, and then added in his best bored-aristocrat voice, "Really, Tatlock, you can't send a young woman into the world wearing such a disgusting bonnet, and then expect men will want to dally with her." To Tatlock's amazement, Rockleigh winked at him. "Got her a new bonnet, though. Pretty as Jack's cat."

"What are you implying, you young scoundrel?"

"You're the newspaperman, Avery. You figure it out."

Chapter Thirteen

Mercy was sequestered in the library, surrounded by books on India, writing down anything of interest—she definitely felt a story coming on—when she heard the commotion in the front hall. She came out of the room at a run, her pen still clutched in her hand.

It was hard to say which shocked her more, the sight of her father or the fact that he was standing beside the wicked Mr. Doncaster. No, it was seeing Rockleigh being held captive between two rough men.

"What in heaven's name is going on here?" she cried, sweeping toward them like a juggernaut in petticoats.

"Mercy! Thank God!" Her father held out his arms to her.

She sailed right past him to confront Doncaster. "You won't get away with this," she said hotly. "Lord Rockleigh's boys are staying right where they are—unless you intend to shoot us all, like you shot my brother, you despicable worm."

Rockleigh was beginning to enjoy things now. Mercy could flay the skin off a pachyderm with her words when she chose to.

Tatlock set a hand on her shoulder to still her, but she spun away from him.

"How can you condone this, Father?" she cried raggedly. "Is this not England, where a man should be safe inside his own home?"

"Mercy, stop this," her father growled. "Has that scoundrel bewitched you, that you can take his side?"

"Let her rant," Doncaster said. "She's nothing more than a gadfly."

"Oh, gadfly am I? Then watch out for my sting, Mr. Doncaster." She took him sharply by the ear, like any experienced older sister, and twisted his head down. "Now," she said, holding the pointed tip of the pen against the fleshy part of his jaw, "you tell your men to let him go."

"It's all right, Merce," Roc interjected softly. "Truly it is."

He knew Doncaster could have easily broken away from her, could have hurt her badly if he'd wanted to, but Roc had recently arrived at the notion that old Donnie had something akin to a soft heart.

Pigs would definitely fly.

She stepped back but did not lower her weapon. Doncaster instantly plucked it from her hand and broke the tip off.

Before she could object, Roc called out, "No more dragons, Mercy. Just lead the way to the workshop. In the south wing and up one flight. These gentlemen are most anxious to meet my boys."

"Boots?"

"Boots!"

Tatlock and Doncaster stood at the threshold of the large work area, which had once been the ballroom, and gaped at the sight of fifteen boys bent intently over their individual tables. Behind the men, Rockleigh lounged against the doorframe with Mercy at his shoulder. He shot her a sideways glance and whispered, "Boots, Miss Tatlock."

She gave him an airy look. "I already knew—Sally told me."

"Nothing but boots," Doncaster repeated. There was a jot of disappointment in his tone.

"Yes, gentlemen," Rockleigh said. "Boots for Wellington's army. I got the idea from Clipper Donegan. He was forever complaining that the soldiers on the Peninsula were marching about with rags tied around their feet. Seven months ago, I discovered that an old friend was looking for work in that exact line." Roc sketched a wave toward Gupta. "I thought it providential, so I set him up here."

"He's a bleedin' wog," one of Doncaster's men muttered.

Mercy gasped. Rockleigh and Avery Tatlock simultaneously turned to glare at the man. Then their eyes met, and they both acknowledged that something critical had passed between them.

"Gupta Bannerjee was a bootmaker in India," Roc then continued. "Made the best dashed boots on the whole subcontinent. British officers from Srinigar to the Punjab swore by him."

As Rockleigh spoke, he drifted one hand behind him and stroked his thumb once along Mercy's arm. It made his vindication that much sweeter, having her there beside him.

"It was Mr. Bannerjee's idea to find homeless boys who needed to learn a trade. Boys with clever hands, that's what Gupta needs." He shot Doncaster a meaningful look. "We have several former soldiers who scour the area for likely apprentices. Once the boys are trained, off they go to a boot manufactory, most usually to a shop I've recently set up in Norwich." He reached forward and laid his hand on Tatlock's sleeve. "They have some chance of a future then. And it's all Mr. Bannerjee's doing."

"No, Lord Rockleigh," Tatlock responded soberly, "it is you who made it happen. I have seriously misjudged you. You might just be a man of vision, after all."

Rockleigh waved away the notion. "No, I am an idler with too much money and a great deal of time on my hands. This has been my only contribution to . . . well, to the general good."

Tatlock smiled sagely. "Sometimes it starts with a trickle. But it's not long before the floodgates are opened and—"

"Heaven help me," Roc interjected softly with a swift grin to Mercy. "He *does* sound just like you."

Roc entered the infirmary first, insisting that Tatlock remain in the hall—it occurred to him that there'd been enough surprises already today.

A solitary candle was lit beside the boy's bed; the rest of the room was in shadow. Toby was awake, though, and he raised his head as Roc came toward him.

"Toby, your father's here," he said, offering him a look of commiseration. "Just thought you might like a bit of warning."

Toby nodded, and then muttered, "Hello, Father," as Roc ushered Tatlock and Mercy through the door. Tatlock perched on the edge of the bed and took up one of his hands. "You're doing well? No complications?"

"Better all the time. Got a parcel of people looking after me."

Avery studied his son intently, then set the pale hand again on the spread. "You'll do, lad," he said gently, and then added in a brisker voice, "This might be a good time for some explanations, now I've got both of you here with me." He put his head up and observed Mercy for a short space of time. Rockleigh was impressed that she did not wither under that scrutiny; he wondered how she'd fare under the eyes of the duke.

"One thing," Tatlock said. "Just one thing I must know. We've had letters nearly every other day from Brighton. How did you manage that if you were in London?"

Mercy gnawed her lip. "Bitsy was aiding us. I'd left dated letters for her in my cottage. She was to pretend they came in the post and read them to you and Mama in sequence."

"Very clever. And whose idea was it," he said with a nod toward Rockleigh, "to take on this formidable gentleman in London?"

"Mine," Toby exclaimed, trying to sit up. "I made her go. In fact, I insisted."

Mercy scoffed. "Oh, stop being noble. He isn't going to thrash me, after all. You know it was my idea from the start. You only came along as my . . . my minion." She flicked a glance at Rockleigh and saw him trying to hide his smile. "Father, please don't blame Toby. I instigated everything."

"She's rather good at that," Roc murmured.

Tatlock did not look pleased. "I've never known either of you to deceive me. I'm saddened to think you trust me so little that you had to lie."

Both Mercy and Toby hung their heads.

Now here was an interesting notion, Roc mused, that a father could evoke such remorse in his children without even raising his voice.

"They thought you had enough worries on your plate, sir," said a concerned voice from the bed beside Toby's. "They were only trying to help."

Rockleigh peered into the shadows. He'd been so focused on the Tatlocks that he hadn't realized Jack was stretched out there, sitting up against the iron railing of the headboard. He was fully dressed, but there was a narrow white bandage across his brow.

So, the surprises weren't over after all.

"Mr. Bannerjee brought him up here not one hour ago," Toby explained.

"Where did you get yourself off to, Young Skillens?" Roc asked. "And what have you done to your head?"

Jack rubbed at his bandage and his eyes lit up. "I was abducted."

Toby propped himself on one elbow. "When Doncaster's men started shooting, he ran back toward the gig and tumbled into a ditch. Knocked himself clean out on a rock."

"Some Gypsies came by and started to unhitch the horse," Jack continued with relish. "They heard me moaning in the ditch and, since they couldn't risk bringing me to a doctor—they'd just pinched my horse, after all—one of them took me up in his wagon."

"You were stolen by Gypsies?" Roc uttered in amazement.

Jack grinned. "It was capital. Once I got over the dizzy spells, I learned how to put a chicken in a trance and how to catch fish without a line. Only then I decided I'd better ask them to bring me back here. I'd no idea Toby had been shot or I'd have made them turn around immediately."

"He had a ripping adventure," Toby complained, "and all I got is a pain in my backside."

Avery Tatlock gave a weary sigh. "Why do I get the feeling there's going to be no lack of adventuring in your future?"

"Gad, I hope so," Toby muttered.

Roc left the Tatlocks to their reunion and went in search of Doncaster, whom he'd left in Gupta's good hands. He still couldn't credit that he and Donnie were on the same side. For twenty-odd years he'd never even *had* a side, never stirred himself to stand up for anything. One small lawsuit later, and his whole life had gone topsy-turvy. He had sides and causes and a skittery feeling in his stomach over a headstrong woman with amethyst eyes.

That was what a man got for having anything to do with lawyers.

"I've been talking to the boys," Doncaster said as Roc met

up with him outside the workroom. "Your Mr. Bannerjee's been doing a splendid job. Admirable, quite admirable. I need to get myself back to London so I can tell Sir Robert about your setup here. He's going to be quite intrigued. I have a notion he might coax a few other gentlemen to sponsor apprentice workshops like yours."

"Yes, well, Sir Robert's always been a persuasive old fellow. Now, if you've got a minute, I'd like a word before you go. I still need to clear up a few details that are nagging me, specifically why your name was so familiar to the flesh peddlers in Dover."

"Can't figure it out, eh, Conniston? I thought you were cleverer than that."

Roc's expression soured. "You'll have to excuse me. My brain's not been working the same since you slipped me that foul poison. What in blazes was it?"

Doncaster wagged one finger. "Ah, no. It's something I obtained in London when I realized that the opium wasn't working. It wouldn't have killed you, I promise. But it is guaranteed to make you sick as a dog."

"My father's cure did that, as well." Roc grimaced at the memory. "But I still can't credit that you intentionally sought me out and plied me with opium, on the off chance I was trafficking in children."

"Why does that surprise you, a man with such a reputation for depravity? I didn't think you'd scruple to draw the line at anything, however low." Doncaster offered him a slight bow. "You have my apologies—next time I won't be fooled into judging a man based on Town tattle."

Rockleigh returned the salute. "I fear I was also guilty of that in your case."

"However, you weren't my only target, Conniston. You'd be shocked at how many supposed gentlemen are involved in that wicked business. But we expose most of them eventually." He sniffed and put his head back. "Not every Society suicide you read about in *The Times* is over gaming debts."

Rockleigh drummed his fingers against his waistcoat. "You still haven't told me about your Dover connections."

"It's very simple. When you want to prevent children from being sold to brothels, you make yourself a potential buyer. Keeps them out of the hands of the real villains and gives you access to the very people you want to shut down. And speaking of that, both Mr. Coyle and the viperish Isabelle won't be in business much longer. But others will take their place, I'm afraid." He looked at Rockleigh keenly. "You wouldn't by any chance be interested in joining me? Put some of that free time you complained about to good use."

Rockleigh had seen that one coming. One part of him wanted to enlist; another part, the cautious Conniston part, was uncertain. He was still rattled by what he'd brushed up against in Dover. It clung to him, like a noxious, sticky spiderweb.

"No, thank you," he said at last. "I have a notion I can put myself to better use elsewhere."

Mercy sat across from Sally in a slipper chair, holding Bulbul in her lap. It had been obvious last night that the baboon had appointed herself guardian aunt to the new baby—lingering near his cradle and gazing up worriedly if he cried—but she now seemed content to observe him from a distance.

Sally leaned from her bed to brush her fingers over her sleeping son's brow, her face beaming with awed wonderment. Gupta, who had left them only minutes earlier, had also worn a serene, slightly giddy expression.

Mercy was just beginning to comprehend the completion a child could bring to a marriage. She had been impressed by Gupta's tender, affectionate manner with his wife; she doubted he'd ever raised his voice to Sally over anything. It started her thinking about another man, one in her own life, who often treated her with harsh, angry words. The more she dwelled on those differences, the more she got a sinking feeling in the pit of her stomach.

This is my lot, she observed to herself. *Some women get the husband and the child. I get the baboon in a little coat.*

Bulbul gave a low growl, as though she'd intuited Mercy's thoughts.

"I know you are anxious to take your brother home," Sally said as she settled against her pillows. "But I hope you will come back and visit. I think after last night I can count you my friend."

Mercy smiled. "Of course I'll be back. I've a mind to come here with a herd of sheep and do something about that front lawn."

"I'm sure Lord Rockleigh will see to that once we are gone."

"Gone?"

"Didn't you know? We won't be taking any more boys after this group. In two months or so, once they're all placed, we'll be sailing to Barbados. Lord Rockleigh has a friend who's staying there. Mr. Bryce will make sure Gupta has work."

"There are people from all over the world in the Caribbean," Mercy observed softly.

"Exactly. I don't think we will stand out so much there. And the climate is warm; Bulbul can give up her coat. Then Lord Rockleigh shall have his house back. I have a hunch he might wish to remain in the neighborhood."

She looked at Mercy expectantly. Mercy looked down at the carpet.

"He's falling in love with you, you know." Sally's tone was gentle, but quite firm.

Mercy's eyes flashed up. "I don't know whether to believe that or not."

Sally went on as if she had not spoken. "I will be very happy if that is the case. For all his wealth and standing, I don't believe Lord Rockleigh's ever had what my husband and I share."

Mercy rubbed the side of her face. "I thought those feelings were there. But things keep changing so quickly."

Sally's brightness faded. "Who has changed? Surely not Lord Rockleigh."

"Perhaps I'm the one," Mercy admitted. "I . . . I don't know what I feel for him from minute to minute."

When had these uncertainties started? she wondered. Surely not that morning—it had been utterly lovely to share sweet kisses in Rockleigh's bed. Since then nothing had occurred between them to make her doubt him. Well, he had gone off to seek her father without telling her; she knew she could have spared him a needlessly upsetting episode if he'd asked her to come along. But he had gone his own way, and she couldn't find it in her heart to criticize him for it. It was one of her own chief failings.

Still, something was making her as edgy as a cat. All her logical thought processes had fled, leaving her floundering in a swamp of confusion, one instant full of whirling elation, the next overcome by misgiving and apprehension. If only she could get Rockleigh alone for the space of five minutes, she was sure he would put all her doubts to rest.

Except that with her father here in the house—a most tangible reminder of the old Mercy—she felt herself being almost rudely tugged back to her former life. She still had responsibilities and obligations, to her family and to *The Trumpet*. That was where her security and sense of satisfaction had always lain. Rockleigh had somehow taken those things from her—and given her she knew not what in return.

Sally interrupted her revery with a tiny cough. "By the look of things," she noted with a wry expression, "you're in as deeply as he is. It's called mooning about, by the way, that ability to just stop whatever you're in the middle of and go off into a long, silent meander."

Mercy felt as though she was about to cry. "I never behave this way. Never."

Sally's eyes danced. "I wager Lord Rockleigh says those exact words into his shaving mirror each morning."

"Then tell me this. If we are both experiencing the same thing, why aren't we in more accord with each other? Because we are not. He said last night that we are neither of us easy with what's happened between us. That's hardly reassuring."

"At least he's being frank about his feelings."

"He's also been quite frank with me about all his appetites for women and cards and brandy. He's an almanac of bad habits, for all that the *ton* sees only a gentleman of fashion. But I was raised to mistrust everything he represents. Our lives, our values, draw us in opposite directions."

Sally said gently, "Then you need to find something that draws you together."

"I don't know if that's even possible. He . . . he's so different from anyone I've ever known."

She recalled that she was speaking to a woman who could have written volumes on that subject.

"Sorry. My obstacles are fairly minor compared to the ones you and your husband have faced."

"Nonsense. Gupta and I have a similar background in trade—he's a bootmaker; my father was a silversmith." Sally sighed. "Not that it was always easy for us. But it's the hard parts that make the good parts better, Mercy. Trust me on that."

"Trial by fire, hmm?"

"If the fire's there, then you've made a decent start."

Mercy acknowledged this with a swift grin. "Rockleigh did tell me once that I was like a fever in his blood. What if I am only a passing fancy, though, something he desires now, but may not desire next week or next year?"

Sally looked thoughtful for a moment. "There is something you should know. He's been down here twice before, after Gupta and I got things running. Both times he barely noticed our charges, even drew away from them, as if he found them distasteful. Yesterday I came upon him in the front hall surrounded by boys. He looked very much at ease." She smiled. "Something's changed him, Mercy. He has the look of a man who's come home at last. Such a man is not going to walk away from the woman who brought him to that place." When Mercy made no response, she added, "Has it occurred to you that he loves you precisely because you are different from anyone *he's* ever encountered?"

"I called *him* a novelty once." Mercy's nose crinkled. "I see now it's not very flattering having that term leveled at you."

"I meant it as a compliment. But nothing I say will convince you, not if Rockleigh himself hasn't been able to effect that."

Mercy set her chin on her hand and sighed. "I wish you would tell me that these are nothing more than maidenly nerves I am feeling."

"I wish I could, but I never had such doubts with Gupta, in spite of the difficulties we faced. We faced them together, you see."

Mercy nodded. "It felt that way while we were driving down here. By the end of the journey we were leaning on each other. It was . . . very comforting. But within minutes of arriving here, we were spitting at each other again."

Sally blew out a breath. "Mmm . . . perhaps you will let me offer you a piece of advice."

Mercy looked at her intently.

"Give yourself some time. You and Lord Rockleigh have been thrown together in less-than-ideal circumstances. First battling over his lawsuit, then rushing down here to look after your brother. It certainly hasn't allowed for a leisurely courtship. You're overtired and overwrought, not in any condition to be making decisions that will affect your future."

"I expect you're in the same state after last night," Mercy pointed out.

"Oh, no. My head is as clear as a bell. It's amazing how clear, now that the difficult part is over. Which is exactly my point. You let things quiet down a bit, and you'll know what course to follow with Lord Rockleigh."

"It's a moot point right now," Mercy said as she lifted Bulbul down and got to her feet. "He hasn't asked me anything yet. Well," she added, "he did ask me to be his mistress back in London. But then he said that would sully the things he admired in me."

Sally barely stifled her laughter. "*He* said that? Good gracious!"

"Yes," Mercy agreed with a rueful grin. "Rather like the hero in a very bad theatrical production."

"Or," Sally said knowingly, "a man who's so heart over heels he doesn't care how foolish he sounds."

Rockleigh saw off Doncaster and his men in the stable yard and then walked around to the front of the house. He eyed the overgrown drive with distaste. Something had to be done with the place, and quickly, if it was going to serve as his rustic love nest—although he could picture himself pursuing Mercy across the tangle of lawn and could almost hear her laughter as he caught up with her under that distant stand of lilacs and tumbled her to the ground.

It occurred to him, as he went through the front door, that neither of them had laughed enough in their lifetimes. But he was going to remedy that. They would laugh and they would lo—

Avery Tatlock was standing near the doorway, conferring with Finney. He immediately turned to Rockleigh. "Your man is going to rig up a litter so that I can transport Toby back to Boxwood. All I ask is the loan of a carriage. I believe the Tatlocks have intruded on your hospitality long enough."

Roc bit back his sharp disappointment. He still had unfinished business with Mercy, and something inside him misliked the notion of her returning home before he'd completed it. "I haven't minded at all. But might it not be best if he stays here until he's on his feet again?"

"No, his mama won't like it that he's recuperating out of her sight. She excels in the sickroom. But you're certainly welcome to visit him." He paused. "You're welcome in my home at any time."

There was a light footfall on the stairs above them.

"Ah, Mercy, there you are," Tatlock said, looking up. "All set?"

She was watching Rockleigh as she came down the stairs, but she wore that give-away-nothing expression again. "I'm ready anytime, Father. Not that there was much to pack." She held up her small valise.

Rockleigh moved at once to take it from her, noting how drained she looked. She didn't appear exactly overjoyed to be leaving. He knew he could put the bloom back in her cheeks, but first he'd have to get her alone. He was racking his brain for some way to separate her from her father, when Tatlock himself •
said, "I'd like a private word with you, Lord Rocklcigh, before we go."

Roc set the valise by the door, cursing the man to his back as he followed him into the library.

"I meant what I said just now," Tatlock began as soon as the door was closed. "About your being welcome in our home. You are not, however, welcome to my daughter."

Roc's breathing hitched for an instant. "I . . . That is . . ."

"She is, as you must have noticed, a very industrious young woman. And for all that I misjudged you in one arena, you are still an idle town beau. I've no wish to see her wedded to such. I am assuming here"—he gave Roc a taunting look that would have speared right through a lesser man—"that *marriage* was your ultimate intention. However, you are exactly the wrong sort of man for my daughter. I must forbid you to court her."

Rockleigh shook off his overwhelming shock at being spoken to as though he were a stable hand, and fell back on his natural air of superiority. "I cannot comprehend why you are telling me this, sir. Have I done or said anything to make you believe I've formed an attachment—"

"Oh, horse twaddle. D'you think I'm blind? You're clearly besotted with each other."

"You've a vivid imagination, I give you that, to have surmised so much after seeing your daughter and me together for—what was it?—fifteen minutes all told."

"One minute would have sufficed. And it's your fault I caught on. She knows how to be a little discreet, like any good newspaperman. Although that scene in the hall with Doncaster was something of a giveaway. You, on the other hand, are not discreet. You gaze at her like a hungry urchin in front of a bake-shop window."

Rockleigh's temper started to bubble up. "Well, it's about time some man looked at her that way. You've kept her shut up in that newspaper office like a nun in a cloister."

Tatlock's head snapped back. "I never have!"

"Toby says she didn't have a normal upbringing, not the way your other children did. How could you do that to her, make her so different, make her practically an outcast from society? I know you're not wealthy, Tatlock, but you are a gentleman. She could have had a come-out on some small scale. Made some friends, met some young men. But no, you kept her to heel, like—like a favorite pet—"

Rockleigh stopped abruptly. He'd just stumbled onto the answer to the question that had been nagging at him for days. He understood now why he and Mercy had been so drawn to each other, nearly from the start. She was her father's pet, his chosen successor. As he was his mother's pet, her indulged youngest child.

So there it was—they had both been firmly placed on a narrow path of parental expectation. Mercy was required to do much, and she excelled at it. He was required to do nothing, and he also excelled at it. Each parent, for all their apparent affection, had stunted something in their children, and, furthermore, had made them feel set apart from their siblings. Mercy had become, as she'd admitted to him, rigid and righteous, while he'd turned out amoral and heartless.

But all that was changing. Somehow, they'd each enabled the other to break away from those narrow paths. She'd made him aware of those around him, spurred him on to seek something worthwhile in his life. He'd shaken her out of her starchy, sterile world and given her a first taste of passion. And in the end, they'd both gained a badly needed dose of humility.

"Lord Rockleigh?"

"Sorry," Roc said in a more controlled voice. "It occurs to me that my mother treats me that same way, like a cherished pet. So even though your daughter is industrious and I am idle, we do have that in common." His eyes met Tatlock's. "You made Mercy believe she was her own woman, sir. Filled her head with all the ideals of liberty and equality. But it was a sham. She is quite bound to you. To the point that she had to tell you a lie in order to go to London and defend you, mainly so she could live up to those lofty ideals."

"That's a complicated logic," Avery said with a frown. "However, I think I understand. She wanted to aid me, but she knew I wouldn't let her go."

Rockleigh leaned across the table, palms flat on the shining surface, and said intently, "You still won't."

The man opposite him said nothing, just stood there with a thoughtful, almost mournful, expression on his scholar's face.

"I'll see to arranging a coach for you," Roc muttered. He bowed stiffly, inadvertently mimicking his own father, and walked to the door.

The man called out to him, "I'm sorry."

Rockleigh turned, his voice icy. "No, you're not, Tatlock. You've struck your blow against the idle town beau after all. Much better than a puny quill pen, don't you think?"

Roc managed to corner Mercy in the hallway near the infirmary. "Whose idea was this abrupt departure?"

She put her chin up. "Abrupt how? Toby's well enough to be moved now, and my father has a great need for me at home."

"And what about what I need from you, Mercy?"

Her eyes narrowed. "You don't mince words, do you?"

He caught hold of her shoulders. "Answer me, damn you. If what you feel for me does not match my feelings for you, then I wish you'd come right out and tell me."

She shook him off with a low growl. "How in blazes do I know what your feelings are, you great pinhead, when you've never once told me? And no, I am not going to say it first. I was willing to this morning, but that's changed."

"What's changed?" His azure eyes had darkened to a stormy gray-green. "The only thing that's different is that I discovered

Doncaster and I are allies. What does that have to do with you and me?"

"*I've* changed, Rockleigh." Her mouth tightened for an instant; then her expression softened. "You see, I spent the night watching Sally giving birth. I sat with her and the baby while you were off having your adventure in Tiptree, and then again just now, to say my farewells. It was impossible not to notice that whenever Gupta is with her, there is a tenderness between them, a concern, that you and I don't seem to have for each other. Look at us now, spatting and spitting. It's all we ever do."

"Not all," he whispered as he cupped her chin and stroked his thumb over her mouth. "There is this."

She pulled back with a soft curse. "I have to be more to you than a combination mistress and sparring partner. And you have to be more to me than a beguiling, dazzling drug." She gave a tiny cough. "I think you know how that feels."

He lowered his head. "Is that all I am to you? Just something that intoxicates you?"

"I need to be nourished, Rockleigh."

"Oh," he drawled, "the honey buns again. Tasty, but not very good for you."

"See, now I've made you turn sarcastic. I didn't mean to. I don't know how to explain my reservations—"

"Fears, Miss Tatlock. Call them what they are. And for your information, I am at times nearly overcome by my own fears. You frighten the daylights out of me."

Her eyes widened. "How could I possibly do that?"

He pushed her back against the wall and lowered his mouth until it was within whisper distance. "Because," he said raggedly, "I know how much you can hurt me."

He thrust away from her, leaving her standing there, breast rising in agitation.

Dear Lord, she moaned to herself. What kind of torture was this now, to be responsible for hurting someone else? Especially someone she cared about, a man who had never before let his guard down until she came into his life. The guilt tore at her and would not let up.

"Rockleigh," she called out softly, even though she knew he was beyond the sound of her voice. *"Oh, Roc."*

*   *   *

He saw them off from the front steps. Finney and Gupta carried Toby's litter—a sling made of canvas—through the door and settled him in the estate's aged coach. Jack climbed in after him. As Tatlock came through the front door, a challenging look passed between him and Rockleigh.

Roc then held out one hand to Mercy, who was lagging back in the doorway. "Coming?"

She took it, then leaned up and whispered, "Please wait. I need some time to deal with my . . . my fears."

He looked down at her, wanting her with every iota of his being and furious with her for leaving him. "I'm not good at waiting, Merce."

She fought back a frown and drawled, "Oh, is that your new motto then, 'He waits not'?"

One cheek drew in. "'He burns' would be more apt." He tugged on her hand. "How long then?"

"One week, two weeks . . . I don't know." She added under her breath, "I can't believe we are having this conversation on your front steps."

"Then stay." At her shocked expression he added quickly, "Stay for supper, I meant. I'll drive you home tonight."

"It's no good, Roc. I'm too wrung out to deal with this. I might say the wrong thing, make the wrong choice—"

"You already have," he said under his breath.

"Mercy?" Her father was motioning impatiently from the coach's window. "We need to get your brother home."

"I can't stay," she cried softly to Rockleigh. "Oh, don't you see?"

"No, I don't." He leaned in closer. "But I will tell you one thing. For all that your father considers me a heartless profligate, my feelings for you will not alter. But take care, Mercy— if I am forced to await your pleasure, then you just might find yourself awaiting mine."

"I don't understand—"

"Mercy, please!" Her father's voice now held a hint of anger.

Rockleigh released her hand and stepped back. "Off you go," he said in a bright, artificial voice. He turned away from her then and disappeared through the open doorway.

Chapter Fourteen

One week went by, and there was no word from Rockleigh. This did not concern Mercy too greatly. She was sure he was indulging in a monumental snit.

Of course, since he had chosen to remain in the neighborhood, she heard his name a dozen times a day. There was endless conjecturing about him from the denizens of Tiptree; a few facts even slipped into the mix. He was finally doing something with the exterior of the house, Mrs. Hatcher told her mother. This Mercy knew to be true. Jack had driven past Crowdenscroft while on an errand for the newspaper and reported back the progress on the old place. The local carter mentioned to her father that Lord Rockleigh had hired him to haul furnishings down from several exclusive shops in London.

"I vow Crowdenscroft will be a showplace again," her mother pronounced. She said it so often that Ralph took to mouthing it behind her back as she spoke.

Bitsy, on the other hand, was barely speaking to anyone. Her punishment for her role as conspirator in the London deception was two months of tending the chickens. She found this extremely demeaning, especially if the handsome boy across the lane happened to catch her at it. She complained bitterly to her father and then demanded to know what Mercy and Toby's punishment had been, as the principal players, so to speak.

He had gazed across the dinner table to his eldest daughter, whose expression, Mercy was well aware, was the conspicuously bland exterior of someone whose feelings were only barely kept in check, and then to his son, who was just now beginning to walk with the aid of a crutch, and said he believed they'd both been punished enough.

Four more days went by with no word, and Mercy grew a bit alarmed. When she'd told Rockleigh to wait, she had no idea he would sever their connection so completely. She had foolishly assumed he would come to Boxwood—to pay a sick call on Toby, perhaps, or to make himself known to her family in general. Surely ardor would overcome anger.

But as the days passed with no sign of him, she knew she had committed a serious error—expecting him to second-guess her. He had taken her request quite literally, leaving her alone to sort out her feelings.

However, her feelings for him had come clear even as their coach was driving away from his estate. She'd felt as though she were leaving behind something vital to life, as necessary as the air she breathed.

It occurred to her now that Roc had never seriously wooed anyone—conquest was more his metier—and so the rules of courtship were probably as confounding to him as this whole being in love business was to her. Perhaps he needed a nudge.

So near the end of the second week, she began a letter to him.

Her first epistolary effort ended up in a crumpled ball on the floor. Four more attempts were, likewise, discarded. It seemed a simple enough thing, writing to the man she loved, asking him to come to her. But the instant her pen touched paper, she lost all her powers of persuasion. The first letter sounded arch, the second too robustly jolly, the third and fourth were mewling supplications, and the fifth was so riddled with literary allusions that she might as well have been writing to Mr. Gribbings.

How did one set one's heart down on paper? She seemed able to do it for everyone's cause but her own.

"I'm good at waiting," she told herself once she'd decided to forgo the letter. "I have plenty to occupy me each day. And he will come soon. I know he will."

To reassure herself, she would remember the mischief in his eyes when he teased her or the soft, throaty way he spoke her name just before he kissed her. Most of all she recalled what he'd told her—that she had the power to hurt him. He'd laid aside all his defenses for her, and she couldn't think of a better measure of a man's regard.

No, she was the one who'd had her defenses up that last day. Cautious, guarded, maybe even a little heartless. She could have blamed her reaction on a dozen things, but that didn't alter the fact that she had behaved like a nodcock. It probably served her right that he was paying her back in her own coin.

There was some distraction in her newspaper work, though it had lost much of its appeal. She frequently caught herself daydreaming of Rockleigh, when she ought to have been working. Her stories about London, especially those about the theater, had inspired a flurry of positive letters from their readership. She was currently working on her third piece for *The Trumpet,* determined to wring the last drop of drama from her encounter with Lovelace Wellesley and Lord Troy. But she knew her enthusiasm for those stories had everything to do with the man who had made them possible. They made her feel connected to him.

Her father, as was fitting, had allowed her to write the retraction to the pernicious editorial. She labored over it for days, and then looked anxiously up from her desk while he read the final draft aloud.

> We have taken it as our duty to cast a harsh light on the ills that beset society and have often been gratified to witness the steps taken by those in power to rectify them. In this manner we have served to better our town and our county. However, there are times when judgment is faulty, when inference replaces fact-finding, and at these times, blameless men may be targeted in error.
>
> Such was the case with our recent editorial regarding the estate in Crowden. The gentleman in question was the victim of our misplaced and overly zealous criticism. There is nothing to support our allegations against him, and indeed a great deal of evidence to counter them. Suffice to say, this newspaper and those behind it are most grievously sorry. We regret any harm done to the reputation of this gentleman or any pain we have caused the members of his family. In future, we will be scrupulous in our investigations and vigilant in our search for the

truth. The pen is indeed mightier than the sword—unwisely wielded, it can smite the innocent as surely as the guilty.

He handed the sheet back to Mercy. "Well done. I believe the word 'grovel' comes to mind."

"He'll like that," she said. "I'll send it next door for setting; it should make tomorrow's paper."

He laid his hand on her shoulder. "You haven't heard from him, then?"

"No." She shrugged lightly. "He's no doubt busy with his house."

He perched on the edge of her desk and said in a weary voice, "I fear I bungled things for you, Merce. I told Lord Rockleigh he couldn't have you."

She made a tiny, hitching noise in her throat.

Tatlock sighed. "It was such a confusing day, one minute thinking he was a scoundrel and then discovering he was actually a decent chap. But I couldn't imagine you'd be happy with a man who had such an unsavory past. I still can't. The upshot of it was, I came right out and forbade him to court you."

Her head was reeling from this unexpected revelation. She'd had no idea Rockleigh and her father had discussed her. She had a swift, painful insight that her father's interference had accounted for Rockleigh's brusque behavior when he'd accosted her in the hall. And, fool that she was, she'd unwittingly sided with her father when Rockleigh baited her.

She tried to muster an even tone. "Don't blame yourself overmuch, Father. Lord Rockleigh's not the sort of man who would let mere words keep him away from something, not if he really wanted it."

"He appears to have done so this time. I only wonder whether it's out of indifference or deference. A significant distinction, you must admit." He chuckled softly. "I might actually approve of a man who heeds a father's wishes."

She gnawed at her lip. "Did it ever occur to you to ask me what *my* wishes were?"

There was a marked silence in the small office. She saw an expression of guilt and dismay cloud his face. "No," she said in a low voice, "you didn't think to do that. For all your radical views on matters political, you're still mired in tradition when it comes to being a parent. How could I know my own mind? I'm only a foolish female."

His expression darkened. "I never thought that, Mercy. Not for an instant. Not that you were foolish, only that you were unschooled and naive. You had no armor against the wiles of a practiced rake."

"You do yourself and me an injustice, Father." Her voice had gone flinty. "I had the armor you gave me—the wisdom to know right from wrong. You also taught me to judge a man by his actions, not his reputation. I came to see that Lord Rockleigh was capable of decency, loyalty and even kindness." She hesitated a moment and then added, "I wasn't going to tell you this, since it's not my secret to reveal. But Mr. Bannerjee's wife, Sally, is an Englishwoman, a governess he met in India."

Tatlock's brows rose. "And Lord Rockleigh condoned this unusual marriage?"

"Sally told me he aided them to wed. When they came to England three years ago, Gupta refused his offer to help them yet again. It wasn't until this past autumn, when Sally was increasing, that Gupta asked for Lord Rockleigh's assistance. They had met with prejudice everywhere they'd lived—you of all people can understand that—so they needed to find a safe haven until the baby was born." She paused for a breath. "Father, you and I profess such high, noble principles, but Lord Rockleigh Conniston, profligate and idler though he was, actually acted on those principles. He took a stand . . . he made a difference."

Her father digested this with a sober expression, then took up her hand. "Shall I write to him, Merce? Tell him I've no objection to his suit?"

She shook her head, set the curls at her crown to dancing. "No, that isn't the only reason he's staying away. I made him angry the day we left Crowdenscroft. I told him I was confused and that he had to wait a bit. His response was to tell me that I might end up waiting myself."

"He likes a stalemate, then, your Lord Rockleigh?"

She gave a brittle laugh. "Good heavens, Father, all we ever do when we're together is try to get the better of each other . . . in tiny, infuriating increments." She gazed up at him in bewilderment. "Can that possibly be love?"

"It's one variety. The sort that occurs between two strong-willed people. Your mama and I have an easier time of it. She favors melodrama, and I have always enjoyed being her audience."

"You make marriage sound like a theatrical production."

"All the world's a stage, Merce," he said with a wink. "Or a chess game, in your case."

"Well, it's very perplexing. Maybe I am a foolish female, after all, to have expected things to go smoothly."

He toyed with a letter opener for a time, then said, "You could write to him, you know. Let him know the home fires are still burning, so to speak." He gave her a crooked grin. "And you do have a persuasive turn of phrase."

She again shook her head. "I can't coerce him into anything. I know that much about the man. Still, it's wretched to sit here and do nothing."

"Write to him," he repeated. "One of you has to break this ridiculous stalemate. And it's been my experience that females are usually the better peacemakers."

She realized then that she'd wanted Rockleigh to take that role. However unfairly, she had placed the entire onus on him. Because he had never once sought her out in London, except at her instigation, she needed him to come to her now without inducements. It would be the final proof of his steadfastness, one that she required absolutely.

And who are you to make such demands? she immediately asked herself. He was not a rook on a chessboard that she could manipulate at will. If he ever allowed that, it would sully everything she felt about *him*.

"Very well," she said. "But I believe I'll wait another week, in case he is planning to come to me."

He nodded slowly. "Do what you think is best, Merce. I've just retired from playing the interfering parent. In the meantime, you might want to think about visiting your aunt Clarissa. The Regent is in Brighton, and I imagine there are all sorts of entertainments going on down there. My sister could take you about, dress you up . . . I assume she knows about bonnets and such."

Mercy wasn't remotely tempted. "And who would help you here? I need to finish my story on the cowpox outbreak, and Mr. Gribbings just sent me the final draft of the Hannibal Horror. Only it's not so horrible any longer." She rubbed his sleeve comfortingly and smiled up at him. She was aware that it never reached her eyes. "I'm fine, Father. Truly I am."

He went back into his office then, looking only slightly relieved. The instant the door closed, Mercy put her head down on her desk and groaned. It was the second time in her life she'd lied to her father. She wasn't fine. Something fearful was starting to grow inside her—doubt.

The man's estate was less than twenty minutes away. Distance was not an excuse for avoiding her. Still, she reminded herself, they'd been apart for only two weeks. Exactly the amount of time she'd requested. It would be just like Rockleigh to make her wait an extra week, if only to gain his point.

It was all a matter of blind faith, Rockleigh decided. He'd set the matter in the hands of fate, as much as it rankled him to relinquish control over his life. Things would follow their own course and he'd win or he'd lose. However, he mainly focused on winning—he was a man who rarely courted loss, and this one might prove the most painful of all.

It wasn't as though he didn't have things to occupy him. The house demanded much of his time and energy. Walter had come down from London to help oversee the redecorating of the interior. The man had proven himself the possessor of a superior eye in the case of Mercy's bonnet, and Rockleigh trusted there would be no pastel Persian carpets in Crowdenscroft.

There were also all those letters he had to write, to politically inclined friends and influential relations. His mother would have approved of the piles of correspondence that were carried from Crowdenscroft each morning. It seemed his Benning side was coming to the fore with a vengeance.

It was only at night, after falling into bed at the end of each exhausting day, that Roc allowed himself to think of Mercy. It was inconceivable that she might turn him away. His pride reminded him that he'd been sought after by every eligible lady in the *ton*. A bit of humility would creep in and also remind him that Mercy Tatlock was no simpering miss to be impressed by practiced smiles and facile charm. No, what she required was a man of action. He had every intention of becoming such a paragon.

At the end of two weeks, the house was finished. A liberal

application of gold coins had inspired the workmen to great speed. Most of Gupta's boys were gone by then, and the polished, gleaming interior seemed full of empty spaces. The Bannerjees suggested he invite some friends to stay, pointing out it was time the house was opened to visitors. Roc knew they were thinking of him, believing he needed a distraction.

Guests *would* distract him, he knew, from his worry over Mercy and the fear that she might not be swayed by his sacrifice. Perhaps sacrifice wasn't the right word. It was an atonement. Or, better yet, an affirmation. Whatever he called it, he realized he was actually starting to enjoy the challenges of his new role. However it played out—and he had already met with some setbacks—he knew he could never return to his aimless, fruitless way of life. This risky endeavor had begun to compel him, and he suspected it would continue to do so, with or without Mercy's approbation.

Dover had changed him inalterably, he knew. It had completed the metamorphosis that Mercy had begun back in London. He imagined that men returning from war carried that same need—to exorcise their demons and create something fine and lasting in a dark, ephemeral world.

He still dreamed of her every night. Waking up was the worst part of the day, knowing that she might only ever be part of his dreams. But he would not force himself on her, as much as his nature inclined him in that direction. He'd relinquished his control, cast aside his cautious and assessing nature and set his future happiness in a pair of slim, capable hands. He waited . . . as instructed.

But oh, how he burned. Living each day in a state of longing and fretfulness—aching to be with her, worrying that she would not ultimately choose in his favor. And afraid, so afraid, that she had helped him to discover his heart only to end up breaking it.

She drew up the pony trap beside the stone wall that enclosed Crowdenscroft and tethered the fat piebald to a bush. It was a glorious June morning, far too pleasant to sit stewing in the newspaper office. She'd told her father she needed some fresh air and had gone at once to ask Ralph to harness the pony.

She just wanted to see the place, she told herself. Maybe,

once she'd done so, she might gain the courage to walk up the drive and knock on the front door. Maybe.

Her first indication of change was the gate, which now lay wide open. The railings had been painted a shiny black, the spear tips golden and gleaming. She peeped around the tall column that supported the gate and her eyes widened. The weedy drive was now covered with fresh gravel. Crisp white stones marched in two columns along either side, bordering a shorn lawn that was even now sprouting fresh green grass. Her gaze moved to the house. The windows and the porch had been painted a deep forest green, echoing the tendrils of ivy that laced their way up the buff stone facade, and the overgrown bushes along the front had been neatly trimmed back, revealing trellised flower boxes full of summer blossoms.

It was a lovely house, she realized, emerged from its cocoon of neglect like a glorious butterfly. All it had needed was a tasteful hand to make it shine. The same sure hand that had disposed of a dreadful brown bonnet and replaced it with a delicious confection of straw and feathers.

He made me shine, she thought wistfully. *He made me laugh . . . he made me feel pretty and desirable.*

She recalled how when she'd returned home from Crowdenscroft, she'd startled her mother by requesting several new gowns and—truly shocking—hair ribbons. So what if Rockleigh had turned her a little frivolous? He had also made her very happy.

That thought drove away all her fears. She would march right up to the house and—

The front door opened, and a half-dozen people spilled out onto the drive. They were dressed for an outing, the gentlemen wearing driving coats, and the lone woman, a petite, dark-haired lady, clad in a stylish cerise carriage gown. Mercy caught sight of Lord Rockleigh almost instantly—taller than the other men, he wore a biscuit-colored coat and topboots. He was standing beside the brunette, his head lowered to speak to her. When she responded, Mercy heard the carrying sound of male laughter.

Three carriages had appeared from around the corner of the house, each led by a groom. She watched him hand the young lady into his curricle—the one *they'd* ridden in from London—and then she had to turn away.

Pain clenched her insides. Leaning back against the wall, she took several gasping breaths until the spasm diminished into a small, hard knot.

He belongs with these people. Had she really expected him to give them up, to languish alone in his tumbledown estate, thinking only of her? She'd vowed that she would not turn into a Juliet over Rockleigh, but perhaps she'd expected *him* to turn into Romeo, wandering his grounds by night like some lovesick wraith.

She acknowledged that, somehow, her presence in his life had enabled him to become a better man. But it was unfair to ask even a better man to forsake everything that was familiar to him. She had no right to do that and would have bristled in outrage if he'd asked her to relinquish her family or her work for *The Trumpet.*

As for the petite lady in the delightful gown, Mercy was not going to jump to any conclusions. She'd been wrong about the boys, so wrong about Sally Banner. Just because Rockleigh was taking a young lady driving did not necessarily mean he had abandoned *her.* It was small-minded and narrow to think it.

But that, she knew, was the problem. Seeing him with his elegant friends, with the stylish young lady, had given her a terrifying insight. Her life *was* narrow and provincial. She had no place in Rockleigh's elevated sphere. A few paltry new gowns and a scattering of hair ribbons did not make her acceptable there. She wasn't sure she even wanted to be—a month ago she had been quite content in her own world.

A mere month ago. And now she was caught somewhere between two worlds, unsure if she would ever fit in either of them. Her own life felt increasingly empty, yet she feared that a life of idle pleasure with Rockleigh would soon lose its luster.

Find something that draws you together. Sally's words had been well meant, but they were hardly practical. What endeavor was there, Mercy wondered, that could simultaneously engage a man of fashion and a woman of principle?

She was puzzling out this problem when she realized with a jolt that the carriages would be coming down the drive at any moment. Running back to the trap, she untied the pony and clambered into the seat. She urged the piebald into a reluctant trot and only breathed a sigh of relief when she was off the main road, where the carriages would not overtake her.

She drew the pony up beneath the obscuring fronds of a drooping willow and returned to the problem at hand. There had to be something Rockleigh could undertake that would involve them both. She could, perhaps, interest him in writing essays, a most gentlemanly pursuit. He might seek to be made magistrate for the district, another occupation that was perfectly acceptable in the eyes of Society. Or he could use his wealth to set up and administer charities and benevolent societies, a minor eccentricity that would surely not place him beyond the pale.

Stop trying to order his life, she admonished herself. *Or at least wait until he's back in your life to sort this out.* It occurred to her that he might be quite content merely playing the part of husband and father, an endeavor that would be guaranteed to draw them together. Yet, as stirring as it was to envision a lifetime at his side, as much as she ached to hold a child of Rockleigh's within her arms, she suspected they both required a larger canvas—a greater contribution to the general good, to use his words—to be truly happy.

Three days later, a parcel arrived for her. It contained a pair of fine quill pens and a note that read:

> *To replace the two you lost, one burned to revive a fainting man, one broken by Doncaster. You paid your debt to me—that retraction must have cost you dear—so I am repaying mine to you. Yr. obed., C.*

At first she'd been elated—he'd made contact with her at last. But after she'd reread the note a dozen times, she still could find nothing of the pining lover or the hopeful suitor in his words. They were brisk and businesslike. He'd merely repaid this piddling debt and closed the book on her.

So that was that, she thought numbly. He wasn't coming. Over, finished, done.

She purposefully thrust the two pens in the deepest drawer of her desk and buried the note under a pile of books on the shelf beside her. She recalled, in the midst of her pain, that the pen Doncaster had ruined had in fact belonged to Rockleigh.

She had a thought to send it back to him, but that might smack of trying to start up a correspondence. No, she would keep the pen and hope that mice eventually gnawed it to a stub.

Sally Bannerjee arrived at Boxwood the following Sunday afternoon in a pony trap, her new son beside her in a bulrush basket.

"Just like Moses," Mercy pronounced as Sally lifted him from his blanket.

"It's a pity you've been too busy to visit," she said to Mercy as they strolled toward the orchard. "You wouldn't recognize the house. It's been painted and polished on the outside, and there are new furnishings in all the rooms. I believe Lord Rockleigh intends to live there. He and Mr. Flemish have been entertaining their London friends in the house this past week."

Mercy settled under a tree and held up her arms to take Conniston. "How pleasant for them," she said as she cupped the baby's head against her shoulder. She wasn't going to mention that she'd seen those friends for herself.

Sally eased herself down beside Mercy and then gazed up at the fluttering greenery above them. "Sir Robert Poole is one of the guests, and I find him a most delightful old gentleman." She added wryly, "For a politician."

Mercy turned her head slowly. "Sir Robert Poole is staying in Crowdenscroft?"

"Didn't you just hear me say it? He seems quite taken with Gupta. Sir Robert served his military time in India, and you should hear the two of them reminiscing about the place."

Picking idly at a stray thread on the baby's lawn gown, Mercy couldn't prevent herself from asking, "And who else is at this house party?"

"Besides Sir Robert, there's a Mr. Vincent, very elegant and amusing, and a gentleman named Clipper Donegan, who has the look of an absolute rogue." Sally's eyes danced wickedly. "Oh, and there is one young lady come down to stay from London. Very petite and dark, she is. All the gentlemen find her pleasing, but one in particular finds her bewitching. She's there with her mama, of course. And *three* lady's maids!"

This wasn't exactly what Mercy had wanted to hear. Served her right for prying. Until now she had been able to pretend that the petite lady had merely been someone's sister or perhaps the wife of one of the guests.

She wondered how Sally could blithely tell her that Rockleigh was bewitched by another woman. *Maybe he's not the gentleman she means,* she told herself.

But then Sally added, "I overheard Lord Rockleigh telling Mr. Flemish that he'd rarely seen a young lady make such a difference in a man's life."

Mercy tucked her face into Conn's chubby neck and inhaled his sweet scent, trying to force the baby's namesake out of her thoughts. "When are you leaving for Barbados?" she asked at last, by way of distracting Sally from the house party.

"We're not." Her eyes lit up. "That's the best part. You see, Sir Robert has decided that Gupta shall continue to teach bootmaking in London. Even if the war ends, he believes there will be returning soldiers who will require boots. And there are always plenty of homeless boys who need work. With Sir Robert sponsoring us, I think Gupta and I might meet with a bit more tolerance."

"I'm very pleased for you," Mercy said as she climbed to her feet with an audible groan. Goodness, Conniston was starting to weigh nearly as much as Bulbul.

They were at the gate, where Sally's pony trap was tethered, when she tapped Mercy on the arm. "You haven't asked me anything about Lord Rockleigh," she said in a low, concerned voice. "I kept waiting for you to bring him up. Don't you want to know how he goes on?"

Mercy sighed and shook her head. "I hear enough from the town gossips. It's Lord Rockleigh this and Lord Rockleigh that. Now that he's finally opened the doors of his home, I doubt he can keep any secrets from the people of Tiptree."

Sally gave her a cryptic smile just before she climbed into the trap. "Oh, I wouldn't say that, exactly."

After she'd gone, Mercy wandered back to the orchard and lounged in the shadow of her favorite tree. She could hear Bitsy out by the chicken coop, grumbling louder than August thunder as she scattered feed for the hens. Ralph was sketching down by the stream—she could see just the top of his tow head over the grassy bank. Toby was practicing archery with Jack behind the house; their mother had decided it would help to strengthen his back. From the results Mercy had seen yesterday—arrows sticking out of everything *except* the straw target—she realized her brother was lucky not to have faced Rockleigh over pistols. He had no aim whatsoever!

Her mother was in the kitchen concocting some exotic recipe involving red wine and rutabagas, while Father and his conservative crony were playing chess in the parlor.

They were all here, all together, just as she'd pictured it that day in the infirmary. But somehow, instead of feeling blessed, she felt bereft. Oh, if one were trying to recover from a broken heart, there were worse places to do it than a comfortable country house like Boxwood. But the bucolic surroundings only made her long for the bustle of London and the man she'd met there.

Maybe she should go to Brighton after all, find some dashing soldier to take her mind off that scoundrel in Crowden. She closed her eyes and tried to picture this military paragon in her head. But all she could see was a shimmering haze, a flash of white teeth and the glint of aquamarine eyes. All she could hear was that whispery, ragged voice saying, *Mercy, Mercy*—

"Mercy?"

She sat up with a gasp of alarm and rubbed at her face. It was only Bitsy.

"There's someone here to see Papa," her sister said portentously. "Someone very elegant and imposing. They're speaking in the parlor this very minute. Do you think we should go and investigate?"

Investigate, to Bitsy, meant eavesdrop. This time, however, Mercy was of a like mind. She could think of only one elegant, imposing man who would have reason to call on her father.

The sisters tiptoed through the rose garden—Bitsy complaining when the thorns snagged her gown—and got as close to the parlor window as they dared. Mercy's heart was pounding so loudly, she wondered her sister didn't comment on it.

But her anxiety was for naught. The gentleman in the parlor, who was seated facing away from them, had a head of thick white hair and the shoulders of a street brawler under the fine fabric of his coat.

Bitsy crept right under the sill and crouched down. She whispered over her shoulder, "The gentleman is saying . . . since he

was in Tiptree, he decided to stop by and speak to
Papa . . . something . . . something . . . must be kept secret until
next week." She turned to Mercy and hissed gleefully, "Ooh,
that has possibilities. Now Papa is saying . . . that he will be
pleased to write an endorsement for . . . somebody. I can't make
out the name." Her face fell. "Oh, it's just boring old newspaper
business. I vow, nothing exciting ever happens in this family."

They snaked their way back to the bricked path. Bitsy
primped at her fair curls. "Now that I've finished with the chickens, I think I'll take a walk along the lane. Care to join me?"

Mercy declined. Bitsy's walks along the lane had only one
object—to capture the notice of the young man who lived there.
As she watched her sister saunter off, she suffered a moment of
overwhelming regret. If only she'd been as tenacious with
Rockleigh as her sister was with their hapless neighbor. She
should have called on him during those first weeks or lingered
in Crowden on market day, hoping to run into him.

She should have written that blasted letter.

Instead she'd found herself stricken, for the first time in her
life, with indecision and an inability to take action. She had
barricaded herself behind the door of the newspaper office,
waiting and fretting. Now it was too late; there was another
woman in his home, someone of his own class who mixed easily with his friends. Someone with three lady's maids, while
Mercy hadn't even one to boast of.

She'd hesitated and she'd lost, all because she had let a moment of indecision sway her heart.

You swayed him as well, Mercy, her annoying inner voice
pointed out. *Doesn't that tell you how much the two of you had
progressed? He listened to you and heeded your wishes.*

So maybe it wasn't too late. Rockleigh had pledged his de-
votion to her a mere four weeks ago, a speck of time in the general scheme of things. Tomorrow morning she would write to
him. She'd throw off this strange paralysis that had beset her
and take action at last.

Chapter Fifteen

Rockleigh mustered all his reserves as he approached the *Trumpet*'s office. He was done with waiting; for all his rare patience, he'd gotten nothing in return. Even his package, meant to tease Mercy into a response, had gone unacknowledged. So now he would, perforce, get her attention in person.

He vowed he would not spar with her or bait her, but would be all tenderness and concern. Still, he reflected a bit peevishly as he went through the door, how long did she think a man could fan the flames of affection by himself before they died down to mere ashes?

Mercy was sitting at one of the front desks, scribbling on a sheet of stationery.

"I'll be with you in a minute," she said without raising her head.

He leaned his elbows on the counter and let his eyes savor her. Under her lace-trimmed pinafore, she wore a celestial blue gown. Cream-colored ribbons were woven through the capped sleeves and along the edge of the bodice. Utterly charming, he thought. Her hair had been pulled up into a loose knot at her crown; stray tendrils formed a haze of tawny gold all around her face. To add spice to this pristine picture, she bore the usual ink smudge on her finger, and there was a long quill pen sticking out of one pinafore pocket.

Armed to the teeth, he thought. Armed with beauty and with her own inimitable style.

When a minute passed and she still did not look up, he went to the wall rack and took down her bonnet. Hiking himself half onto the counter, he reached out and skimmed it neatly onto the letter she was writing.

"What?"

Ah, she looked at him then. And went quite wide-eyed. He crossed his arms on the counter and gave her his most dazzling smile. In the past, countless women had swooned over that smile. He only wanted one to swoon now.

"Oh, it's you." She sat unmoving, still staring at him with that startled expression.

"I have some business with you," he said smoothly.

Her voice was bright and brittle when she spoke. "Do you need to place an advertisement? I imagine you're going to require extra servants, considering all the changes you've made to your house."

He leaned his chin on one hand. "Mmm. I'm definitely here to make inquiries of a domestic nature."

"I've got the forms here somewhere," she said over her shoulder as she began to rummage around in her desk drawer.

Focus, Mercy, she told herself, forcing her hands not to tremble.

How wretched of Rockleigh to appear at this moment, when she'd been only halfway through her letter to him, dredging her mind desperately for just the right words to tell him how she felt. If only she'd been able to come up with those words, she could speak them now.

She shot him a sideways glance, then quickly lowered her head. He didn't appear to be in the throes of a romantic decline. Rather, he looked fit and tanned, achingly handsome and totally intimidating. No, she couldn't just come right out and bare her heart. She still had such a fear that he had gotten over her, that he was only here because some scrap of honor made it necessary for him to confess his defection.

She gave a little grunt of victory as she located the form, then pushed her chair back and approached the counter. "Fill this in, just here." She tapped her forefinger on the top few lines.

His hand flashed out and covered hers, pressing it down against the sheet.

"Don't," she said in a stricken voice. "Please."

"I think you know why I've come here."

She nodded once. "It wasn't necessary."

His fingers wrapped around her hand and squeezed it firmly. "What if I disagree?"

"Not here," she said abruptly. "I can't do this here."

"Then come walking with me."

"I'm far too busy. It's deadline tomorrow and we're running behind."

Rockleigh moved to one side, set his fingertips on the edge of the partition and called out, "I say, Tatlock. Can you spare your daughter for the space of ten minutes?"

Her father stuck his head out of his office. "Oh, hello, Lord Rockleigh."

"Well, can you? Spare her?"

Mercy turned to her father and with great emphasis mouthed the word "no."

Tatlock observed them both for a moment or two, and then smiled. "I don't see why not."

Muttering under her breath, Mercy snatched up her bonnet from the desk. Rockleigh tsked at her as she drew the ribbons into a tangled knot.

"Come here," he said, holding out his hands as she came through the half-door. "You still haven't learned to do it properly."

She sidestepped him neatly. "My ribbons are just fine," she said. "And you get ten minutes and not one second more."

He walked beside her across the green and motioned to the bench that encircled the trunk of the massive oak. She perched on the edge of the wooden seat, facing the street, her hands clasped on her knees. He settled back against the trunk and willed her to look at him. Her head never budged an inch.

Still didn't work worth a damn.

After a long stretch of silence, she said in a low voice, "This is very awkward."

"Awkward how?"

"It's clear we have nothing to say to each other."

He chuckled softly. "I have a great deal to say to you, Miss Tatlock. But right now I am occupied with looking at you. That is a delightful gown, by the way."

"That is hardly what you rode into Tiptree to tell me, now is it, Lord Rockleigh? And it's not necessary, whatever you have to say. I believe I understand the situation."

He shifted forward. "Perhaps you would have the courtesy, then, to explain it to me."

She shot him a look of impatience. "Is it not obvious? There was no word . . . no message sent. I should think the conclusion a person drew from that would be foregone."

He tried not to grind his teeth. "A *person* was told to wait. You could at least have had the courtesy to tell me to stop waiting if I was wasting my time."

Her brow furled. "I was speaking of myself, Lord Rockleigh. *I* was the one who was waiting."

He slid toward her. "Are you doing this on purpose, Mercy? Making my brain spin?"

She set her chin and looked away from him.

"Just humor me a minute," he said with a touch of annoyance. "Did you or did you not ask me to give you some time?"

"Yes, of course I did. But when weeks passed without a word from you . . ." She turned to him and gave a small, careless shrug.

Rockleigh was often torn between the urge to kiss her and to throttle her; right now the throttling instinct was far in the lead. He drew a deep breath to steady himself. "And did it occur to you, Miss Tatlock, that it was up to you to communicate with me?"

"I don't recollect that we ever discussed the protocol."

"Sweet God in heaven!" he exclaimed. "Of course we didn't discuss it. We were standing on my front steps with your father's gimlet eye upon us."

She reared back and said intently, "I remember something else about that day. You said you would make *me* wait, by way of turnabout. So I hope you will excuse me if I was expecting to hear from *you*."

Rockleigh dragged one hand through his hair. "Isn't it just like you to lay the blame at my—" He pulled himself up abruptly, recalling his vow, and then said tamely, "I'm here now, Merce."

"And just as full of heat and bad temper as ever," she observed.

Even if by some miracle he still cared for her, Mercy saw

that nothing else had changed. They couldn't even conduct a lovers' reunion without bristling like two cats in an alley.

She sat purposely looking away from him, trying to feel some glimmering of joy that he had come to her at last. Mainly she wanted to box his ears in irritation. And then kiss him into a frenzy. He still had that power over her.

"How is Toby faring?" he asked in a matter-of-fact voice, breaking the strained silence.

"Much better. We've all been working double time to keep him from getting bored. And things have been lively at the paper. Two local farmers are engaged in a heated lawsuit over a piece of pastureland. We've had a rash of burnt hay ricks and damaged fences. No poisoned ponds yet, fortunately."

"I can sympathize," he remarked under his breath. And then his voice deepened. "So I gather you've been too busy to spare much thought to our . . . situation."

"It's been an eventful month." She met his gaze head-on. "For both of us, from what I understand."

"What do you mean?" he asked cautiously. "What have you heard?"

"Only that you're finally doing something with Crowden-scroft."

He hitched one shoulder. "Oh, that. It was long past time the old place was fixed up." He coughed softly. "I thought you might be referring to something else I've been involved in recently."

He waited, but she refused to take the bait. Not that he'd intended to use it as bait. His decision had certainly been made with Mercy in mind, but he did not want it to influence her. He needed her to accept him with all the tattered remnants of his past misdeeds trailing behind him. Something in his pride demanded that.

Mercy continued to stare straight ahead. Roc wondered what was so fascinating about a jumble of brick-and-stucco shops. He drifted his arm across the back of the bench until it was directly behind her. A few strands of her hair tickled the skin of his wrist, sending an electric thrill up his arm.

She shifted away from him with a tiny sigh of annoyance.

He felt the cold clutch of fear then for the first time. He'd never had any trouble getting Mercy to engage him in the past.

Even when they'd been at odds—and when were they ever not?—she had always responded to him. Her silence now and her severe, rigid posture unnerved him.

He canted his head toward her and said in a low voice, "Tell me the truth, Mercy, and let there be an end to this. Have you truly moved away from that place we once shared?"

She looked down at her hands, clenched tight in her lap. "I suspect one of us has. Though no promises were made between us . . . you don't need to feel obligated to me. I'm . . . I'm truly sorry that circumstance or misunderstanding caused us to lose our way." She offered him a tiny, wistful smile. "I suppose it wasn't very real, if it could be lost so easily."

He opened his mouth to object, but she was already getting to her feet.

"Now that we've sorted things out, I'd better go. Father will be looking for me."

Roc's eyes hooded over. "I see you've placed yourself back under his thumb."

"You make it sound like indentured servitude," she protested. "Anyway, you might be interested to learn that I'm going to Brighton next week." If he'd looked closely, he'd have seen her faint blush. "My aunt will be taking me around to all the summer parties."

His expression, he knew, gave nothing away, but there was a slight tic in the corner of his cheek he couldn't control. He reached out and grasped her arm as she turned to go. "You said ten minutes. It's barely been five. And I won't give up a second of it. Not after you made me wait four long weeks—"

She tried to pull back from him; instead he tugged her toward him, down onto the bench.

"Stop this!" she hissed.

"What am I supposed to do then?" he cried, not caring that there was open entreaty in his voice. "Just walk away as if there was never anything between us?"

"You have other amusements now."

"The devil I do!"

"Houseguests, friends come to stay. Young ladies come to stay." She instantly set her hand over her mouth. "Oh blast! I shouldn't have said that. It's none of my concern who you spend your time with."

He released her and crossed his arms over his chest. "Who told you about that?"

"I saw her myself." Before he could ask when or where, she added, "Sally Bannerjee told me all about her when she was here yesterday. She said you found her bewitching." She put her chin up. "You see, I did my research properly this time."

He was shaking his head. "That interfering little busybody. I should have her hide, coming to you with such tales." His cheeks narrowed. "Though maybe I should thank her. It made you jealous, didn't it? That's why you're being so frosty with me. You've got your petticoats in a bunch over my having a young lady down to stay."

"Jealous?" She scrambled to her feet and spun to him. "I am no such thing. I barely give you a thought from one week to the next."

"Liar!"

"Scoundrel!"

"Bluestocking!"

"Coxcomb!"

He opened his mouth to fling another insult at her. Instead he snatched up her hand and set his mouth hard against the palm. He felt her tremble, as though the ground beneath her slippers quaked.

"Oh, Mercy," he crooned against her skin. "I've missed you so much."

She stood staring at him, as white-faced as she'd been that first day when he'd laid hands on her in anger. Now, however, the expression in her eyes was one of fierce longing.

"We have to face it, Merce," he said, smiling up from over her curled fingers, "We will never stop being at odds with each other."

"I don't see how this can work," she said weakly. "Not where there is no respect or tenderness."

"I respect you enormously, baggage. And as for tenderness—" He coaxed her down onto the seat and took up both her hands. "It's there, Mercy, in every breath I take. Because I love you." He raised one sardonic brow. "Will that do?"

"Oh," she rasped softly, "you said it first."

"Well, somebody had to." His grin faded as he laid his hand on her cheek. "But that doesn't mean I won't fight with you or

vex you. It's not my nature to give in easily. Nor is it yours."
He held her with his unwavering azure gaze. "It won't be a
level road for us, sweetheart, but I vow it will be the same
road."

She sighed and closed her eyes as she leaned into his touch.
"That is all I ever wanted, Roc. To share that with you." The
corner of her mouth twisted up. "A very wise person once told
me that the hard parts make the good parts better."

"Who said that? They might just be right."

"An interfering little busybody."

"Ah. Well, *she* ought to know." He cocked his head. "And I
do believe we've just gotten past one of those hard parts. It's
been hellish."

"I know. Worse that hellish. I was an idiot, Rockleigh. Hoping you would come to me, in spite of what I said. I didn't mean
to test you like that. It was a daft notion to begin with. I . . . I
seem to be having a lot of those this year."

"I bless the one that brought you to London, Mercy. Brought
you to a soulless scoundrel." He slipped the long quill pen from
her pocket and traced it teasingly over her cheek. "You've
goaded me, ridiculed me, and generally worn me to a frazzle."
He looked at her through his brows and grinned. "I've never
been happier."

He shifted her around then and drew her back against his
chest. The mingled scents of vanilla and printer's ink drifted
over him. The leaves above them rustled; the breeze stirred the
grass. Time seemed suspended as they reclined there against
the wide oak. If people stopped in their errands to stare at them,
neither of them cared.

Mercy occasionally leaned her head back and nuzzled the
side of his neck with her chin, each time evoking a long, deep
sigh of contentment. This was what she had wanted from him
all along, she realized. Their volatility was certainly stimulating, but this relaxed, easy way of being with someone, of
touching and being touched—in affection, not passion—was
nearly perfect. Not that she minded the passion, but this was
more intimate somehow. It wrapped around her like a comfortable shawl. *He* wrapped around her—a friend for her soul and
a lover for her heart.

When he shifted away from her, she couldn't contain her disappointment. "Rockleigh?"

"It's been ten minutes," he said, looking down to adjust his cuff.

"The devil it has!"

His eyes danced. "This is delicious. I never got to tease anyone, being the youngest of the Connistons. I am looking forward to a lifetime of your irritation, Mercy. I do believe it is what binds us together."

She set her fingers over his mouth. "There is also this, as you once pointed out to me."

"There is, indeed. I don't suppose you'd like to explore some of those . . . possibilities?" She shivered as he turned her hand over and ran his teeth lightly along her knuckles. "Like this, for instance."

She drew in a deep, badly needed, breath. "W-wait . . . just one question. What did you mean before, when you said there was something else you'd been up to recently?"

His mouth formed an unspoken "oh." So he hadn't gotten that one past her.

He leaned forward and whispered up against her ear, "I'm running for a seat in Parliament."

This resulted in a gratifying gasp of surprise and approval. "Rockleigh, you rogue! And how long has this been going on?"

He shrugged. "Since the day you drove away from Crowdenscroft. I had to come here with something to lay at your feet besides my profligate past."

She set her hands on his shoulders and tipped her head until their brows touched. "Your heart would have sufficed, Roc. It always will." Then she chuckled softly. "But how I fretted that we would never find any course to draw us together. Thank you, my dear, dearest Rockleigh, for finding the perfect solution." She shook him in delight. "I could kiss you!"

"I wish you would." He drew back, his eyes challenging her wickedly. "I want to see how Mercy Tatlock kisses a man who loves her."

Now here was grist for her mill—she'd never yet refused a challenge from him. She leaned into him and set a tiny kiss on one corner of his mouth.

"Paltry," he grumbled.

She poked him in the ribs. "Hush. This requires a deal of concentration."

Her next foray was a bit more successful—she slid her lips along his, back and forth, until his mouth curled up in response to her teasing and she heard a soft groan rumble up from his chest. Her hands clutched his shoulders then, fingers pressing into the hard muscle. Another groan, and his mouth was open beneath hers, his own hands urgent at her waist, shifting her across his lap.

Her senses reeled as she explored the heated recess of his mouth, shyly at first and then with increasing confidence. Their tongues met, she arched into him, and the next instant he had propelled her back against the trunk, cushioning her with one arm, as he took her mouth from above.

Mercy moaned his name as his arms tightened around her, implacable steel bands that refused to allow any separation between them. His body bore down on hers, masterful, relentless, urgent. She was powerless to stop him and would have murdered anyone who tried.

But no, she was not powerless. She knew, somewhere in her dazzled brain, that it would take only the tiniest whisper from her and he would stand away.

This then was *her* power, that she had only begun to comprehend in his London parlor. He would do her bidding at any cost to himself. Lord Rockleigh Conniston, the infamous care-for-none, had given that rare gift, that privilege, to her alone.

"Roc," she murmured, needing to tell him that she understood at last.

But he was too intent on kissing her. She shuddered as his mouth tore away from hers and left a trail of fire along her jaw and down the column of her throat. As he sucked gently on her skin, she felt his tongue press against her, moist and tantalizingly bold. And then his teeth, raking over the rise of her breast.

She cried out. His caresses turned demanding, nearly harsh, and though her body ached where he touched her, it ached even more where he didn't. She had him by the shirt now, her fingers locked on the soft linen inside his coat, tugging him closer, urging him onward.

Rockleigh was gasping when he wasn't kissing her, snatching oxygen from the air. He groaned as her fingers twisted in his hair, forcing their lips closer together—as if he'd ever needed coaxing to touch her.

The taste of her was the most potent drug he'd ever encountered—rich and lush and utterly intoxicating. The feel of her under his hands was driving his body into a thrumming state of desire. She destroyed all his control, until he feared to overwhelm her with his need.

No more dark delights, he thought, only delights taken in darkness, taken with Mercy. He had only one appetite now, and it consumed him even as it replenished him.

"Marry me . . ." he panted hoarsely against her breast. "Stanley's uncle . . . bishop in Hastings . . . special license . . . *God . . . oh, God.*"

"Yes," was all she managed to gasp out before they were again entwined.

Eventually they subsided into a less ardent communion; the need for discretion had filtered into their respective brains at about the same time. It occurred to Mercy that she lived here and had to face her neighbors. Rockleigh, on the other hand, had determined that it was not good *ton* for his firstborn to be conceived on a park bench.

"Well met," he murmured raggedly against her brow, holding her head between his hands, his fingers twined deep in her hair. Her bonnet was now half down her back, the ribbons a hopeless tangle of lavender satin.

"I have great plans for us, Merce," he said, then added slyly, "Between your persistence and my endurance, I expect we will be invincible."

"Don't say that," she said with a tiny, mock frown. "Just remember Hannibal."

"Hannibal?"

"*He* thought he was invincible and look what happened when he tried to attack Rome. First of all, there was a large mountain range—"

"The Alps?"

"And a certain Roman general—"

"Scipio Africanus?" He chuckled. "Don't look so shocked, sweetheart. I did attend Cambridge, after all."

She touched him on the nose. "Who is telling this story, sir?"

He bowed from the waist. "My apologies, I defer. But I warn you, I'm going to kiss you again after you get to the elephants."

He would defer, he knew, for the rest of his life. Defer to her zeal and her curiosity, to her great heart and her sometimes wrong-headed righteousness. There was only one place he would not defer, and that was in the choosing of her bonnets. A gentleman of the *ton* had to draw the line somewhere.

The duke's open carriage was approaching the green at a sedate pace. He and the duchess had made an unannounced visit to Crowdenscroft to view the refurbishment. To their dismay, Rockleigh had not been at home. However, Walter, his estimable man of all work, had told them he could likely be found in Tiptree.

Now the four occupants of the carriage—His Grace and Stanley Flemish, who sat facing the duchess and an animated young brunette—craned their heads about, wondering which shop Rockleigh might have gone into.

"Oh, stop the carriage!" the duchess cried when they were halfway along the green. She flung out one beringed hand. "Look, it's Rockleigh and Miss Tatlock."

"And how can you tell?" His Grace drawled, raising his quizzing glass.

"I surely know my own son."

"I meant the girl. You can't see her face—that's for certain."

"I'd know that bonnet anywhere."

All four of them unabashedly observed the couple on the bench, who seemed to be engaged in an Olympian bout of kissing.

The duke finally looked away, his brow creased. "I must say, he is still behaving outrageously. How does the cub expect to achieve a Parliamentary seat with this sort of behavior?"

"Well, it's one way of winning votes," Stanley said. He then grinned at the young lady opposite him, who was giggling behind her fan. Among other things, she thought him a veritable wit.

The duchess sat back with a smug smile. "Ah, Barrisford, didn't I tell you back in May? I saw the way he looked at her in that teahouse." She set one hand upon her throat and sighed.

"It appears we're going to have a marriage celebration after all."

"Two, don't you mean?" her husband said. "Have you forgotten Torrance and Miss Blythedale?"

The duchess began to knead her reticule. "There's something I haven't told you yet. I, ah, received a letter from Torry just as we were setting out for Crowdenscroft. I didn't want to miss seeing the old place, and I knew if I told you, you'd go haring off back to Devon. For what is, in truth, a fait accompli."

"My dear, what are you talking about?"

Stanley reached over and patted her hand encouragingly. "I think you'd better tell him, Your Grace. I'll catch him if he faints."

"Torry has been to Scotland," she pronounced slowly.

"Scotland?" the duke echoed. "What's wrong with that? Our crops are all in order—he was welcome to take a jaunt. Anyway, Scotland's a decent place to visit. Wonderful barley."

She flashed him a look of impatience. "He went to Gretna Green."

The duke assimilated this at once. "Don't tell me he got that Blythedale chit to actually elope with him. Well, good for her. I didn't think she had the pluck."

"It wasn't Jessica Blythedale he took with him," Her Grace said darkly.

The duke's face began to lose its merry humor. "Then who?"

"Do you remember Mary Peters, the head gardener's daughter? She came back from Ireland last month to visit her father." She paused and then blurted out, "Torry ran off with her."

The duke sat in thunderstruck silence for almost thirty seconds. Stanley timed it on his watch.

The duchess sighed sorrowfully, attempting to disguise her jubilation at this turn of events. Mary Peters, for all her common birth, would be a far better match for her firstborn than that stuck-up Blythedale creature. And now Miss Tatlock was kissing her Rocky in such an enthusiastic manner that the duchess just knew the young woman was Benning to the bone.

It was all coming together very nicely. If only Trent could stay out of the sights of the French snipers, life would be nearly perfect.

"How did this happen?" Barrisford said at last. "How did Torrance come to lose all regard for his position and his duty?"

Her Grace shrugged delicately. "Torry did mention that someone had recently written to him and pointed out that he didn't have to marry Jessica Blythedale if he didn't want to. This person advised him that saying no to people was easy once you got the hang of it." She tipped her head. "I wonder who it could have been."

But the duke was already on his feet, leaning out over the carriage door. "Rockleigh!"

Avery Tatlock, unlike the passengers in the carriage, only watched the couple kissing under the tree for a moment or two. Until he was sure his daughter wasn't going to do something rash to Lord Rockleigh—box his ears or strangle him with his neckcloth. After that scene with Doncaster in the hall of Crowdenscroft, he figured Mercy might be capable of anything.

But, no, she seemed quite amenable. Perhaps even eager.

He turned away from the bow window with a smile. There was much to be done. First off, he needed to pen a nice ringing endorsement for a candidate who was running for a soon-to-be-vacated seat in the Commons. Although there was nothing at all common about this particular young man. Anyone who had Sir Robert Poole—one of Tatlock's personal gods—as his sponsor had to have very special qualities.

Still, that hadn't prevented Tatlock from sending a message to Crowdenscroft yesterday informing the gentleman in question that if he wanted *The Trumpet*'s endorsement, then he'd better get himself the hell into Tiptree and square things with the publisher's daughter.

Avery Tatlock considered himself an honorable man, but he wasn't above a little coercion now and again.

He made his way to his office, thinking how neat a trick it was, this shifting from a life of wealthy indolence to a career in politics. It was also the one thing guaranteed to impress his daughter. Well, unless the gentleman in question had purchased *The London Times*. Barring that, a run for Parliament—on a reform ticket, no less—would be better than a diamond bracelet for inspiring Mercy's affection.

Tatlock toyed with the numerous themes he might combine

in his endorsement, wondering how he could possibly set them all down. There was the awakened conscience, the dawning compassion for those in need, the breaking with tradition, the letting go of old habits. And ultimately, the redemptive power of love.

No, he thought as he dipped his quill in the ink pot, he'd keep it simple. He would write from the newly formed convictions in his own heart.

There are distinct choices that men of passionate nature face—to use their power and their persuasion as a force for evil or as a force for good. When they choose the latter course, then no matter how imprudent or intemperate the deeds of their early life, having once taken the higher road, they can never be drawn down again.

Signet Regency Romances from

ELISABETH FAIRCHILD
"An outstanding talent." —*Romantic Times*

BREACH OF PROMISE
0-451-20005-5/$4.99

The village of Chipping Campden is abuzz with gossip when the local honey merchant, Miss Susan Fairford, leases her old home to a mysterious young gentleman who calls himself Philip Stone. Time will tell whether bachelor and beekeeper can overcome their fears in order to discover just how much they have in common.

CAPTAIN CUPID CALLS THE SHOTS
0-451-20198-1/$4.99

Captain Alexander Shelbourne was known as Cupid to his friends for his uncanny marksmanship in battle. But upon meeting Miss Penny Foster, he soon knew how it felt to be struck by his namesake's arrow....

THE HOLLY AND THE IVY
0-451-19841-7/$4.99

Mary Rivers's Gran has predicted a wonderful Christmas in London. And when their usually prickly neighbor, Lord Balfour, is increasingly attentive, Gran's prediction may come true—if the merry Mary and the thorny Lord can weather a scandalous misunderstanding and a chaotic Christmas Eve ball!

To order call: 1-800-788-6262